Purity

(Cursed #3)

CLAIRE FARRELL

Purity
Cursed Series, Book 3
Copyright © 2013 Claire Farrell
Edited by Red Adept Editing
Formatting by JT Formatting
Cover Images supplied by:
Nejron @ Dreamstime.com
Sbelov @ Dreamstime.com
Y0jik @ Dreamstime.com

ISBN-13: 978-1482363128
ISBN-10: 1482363127

Find out more about the author and upcoming books online at **http://clairefarrellauthor.com/blog/** or friend her on Facebook at **https://www.facebook.com/clairefarrell27**

Prologue

Goodbyes
June

Perdita left her house, keys in hand, steeling herself for another trip to the hospital. Her father didn't want to see her, so she would sit in the hallway again. At least he'd know she was there, and not with anyone else. Not choosing anyone over her family.

Not this time.

She turned a corner and felt a strange creeping sensation that caused the hairs on the back of her neck to stand on end. She turned slowly, half-expecting a werewolf attack. It would be exactly like her nightmares.

But it was him, standing there, looking at her as though nothing had changed.

Everything had changed: her life, the magic, even her family. Nothing would ever be the same, and now she was forced to go through it alone.

He was still the same boy she once dreamed about, the same boy who made her insides feel as though she had just ridden on a roller coaster when he looked at her. Except these days, the stress was permanently present in his expression. The bags under his eyes matched her own. The biggest difference was that he had become part of her nightmares.

She should have turned back, kept going, but her foot took one step toward him, and his to her.

His eyes locked on hers, and she fought the desire to run. She wanted to hear his voice one more time, to feel close to him just once more. Even though the curse that tied them together had broken, freeing them both, she still fought the need to be near him, next to him, a part of his life. She couldn't imagine waking up and not wanting to be with him. She didn't remember what that felt like.

But she promised her father. A sincere promise, for a change.

"I came to say goodbye." The words burst from his mouth as if he had been waiting to say them for days. He glanced away, closed his eyes for a second, and began again.

"I mean ... I came to tell you what's going on." His cheeks flushed with colour, and she realised he pitied her, that this was embarrassing to him.

The last lingering hope had already curled up and died inside her. "You don't owe me anything," she said as coldly as she could manage, hurt scrambling its way out of her mouth before she could stop it. Pride wouldn't allow her to take back the words or soften the harsh edges of her tone. She had to protect herself.

He retreated as if she had struck him, putting a clear distance between them. He gazed at her until she twitched, reminded of the times he'd drunk in her features as if committing them to memory. A reminder of everything she'd been trying to forget.

Those days were gone, she told herself, and she turned to leave, but his voice caught her in its hold again, stopping her in her tracks.

"How's your dad?"

The wrong words. Anger burned in her throat and bristled in her chest at her pain and frustration with everything in her life. It wasn't his fault that her father lay in a hospital bed, but she couldn't keep the anger from her eyes, nor the chill from her words.

"Worse. We had a fight before I went to take care of Amelia. Before... while I was gone, he relapsed from the stress. He begged me to stay, but I didn't, so..." She lowered her chin, unable to bear the sympathy in his eyes. She longed to reach out and touch him, to find the comfort she needed, the comfort that had once been hers to take, but the memory of how it had been cut out of her life was still too fresh to make that kind of a mistake.

"I'm so sorry." His voice sounded tight. "We're dealing with it. I promise you. We're going after them. We won't stop until we fix this. I'll make sure they never hurt you again, Perdita."

She forgot to avoid his eyes. "What on earth do you mean, you won't stop?"

His eyes narrowed. "I'm going to make them pay. I'm doing this for you."

"Doing what exactly?"

"Making you safe." His pupils dilated into black shells that reminded her of his grandfather. His *mad* grandfather. "We're going after him. Vin, I mean. We're going to find him and end this once and for all."

She was interested in spite of herself. "You know where he is?"

"Not exactly, but Willow's leading the way. We're not giving up this time. We're going to make all of them pay, hunt down every last one of his pack."

"So you're going to keep fighting? Keep chasing shadows, hoping for a war?"

"You don't understand. We're protecting you. All of you. You might not be... not be mine anymore, but I'm never letting them hurt you again. Hurt anyone I... hurt *anyone*. I won't allow it." The last sentence was a growl that triggered the memories she wished she could forget.

"So more people have to suffer? More people have to die? Don't you think you've done enough already?"

Her voice rose as the pressure and turmoil collided together in her brain. His expression changed, but she couldn't pull back,

3

couldn't stop her emotions from flooding his.

"Why is there only ever violence with you people? Why can't you even try to break the cycle? Someone innocent always gets hurt when werewolves get violent."

"Are you talking about Amelia's behaviour after she shifted for the first time? She didn't mean for that to happen. None of us did."

She stared at him in disbelief, at how much of a non-occurrence his sister's violent attack had been to him. She had nightmares about his family, while he glossed over what happened.

"Besides," he continued, apparently oblivious, "this is for you as much as anyone else."

"No, thanks. I don't want any more blood on my hands."

"Don't," he said softly, reaching out a hand. "Ryan said—"

She backed away from him. "I don't care what Ryan said!"

"You're the one who told me to trust him."

"I know I did, and I know what you're doing. But it's… you're becoming one of *them*. Don't you see it?"

"They killed my parents," he said, his voice more of a growl than ever. "Am I supposed to let that go?"

She looked away, full of regret at his obvious pain. She wanted to comfort him, to make it all okay, but those days were over. Ryan told *her*, too.

"I'm sorry about your parents, but I can't believe they would want this life for you. For any of you. I know Lia didn't want it. There's a difference between protecting your family and looking for trouble."

"There's no other way, Perdita. The only way I can protect *anyone* is to get rid of the threat. This time for good."

She couldn't stop her body from trembling. He wasn't her Nathan anymore.

"You saw how hard it was for me, and yet you still treat death so lightly? You're not even trying to change the way things are. The only solution is violence, each and every time, and it's always the ones who don't want it who get hurt." Her lower lip quivered, and a lump in her throat threatened to break through her skin. "Sometimes … sometimes I wish I'd never laid eyes on you, Nathan."

She turned away before she begged him to stay.

***

Nathan watched her walk away, leaving broken pieces of his heart in her wake. He didn't know what to say, what to do. All he wanted was what they had before.

She hated him, was truly disgusted with him, and now that the curse had been torn apart, there was nothing keeping her at his side. Her words cut deep, searing into his soul as he saw the truth of them. He saw what he would become, but all he could do for her now was to keep her alive.

He preferred her alive to hate him than face the alternative, and he wasn't so sure the wolves would ever leave her alone. Ryan's word wasn't enough of a guarantee.

He followed her at a distance, slightly ashamed of himself, but unable to walk away for good until the very last second. That last glimpse of her would always be etched in his brain. He would have to keep it buried to get through whatever came at him next.

He knew ending the curse was the right thing. He knew that was the way the world was supposed to work, but it had unbalanced every experience they had ever shared. He didn't know if he could win her back, but he had to try. His wolf still recognised his mate, and that would never change for him.

First, he had things to do: keeping her safe and getting rid of the hate that lived inside his chest. His wolf didn't make it any easier, but at least his animal side would do anything to protect her, even if it meant doing the very things that would make her turn on him.

But as the wolf mourned, the human had to stay in control, at least until faced with enemies.

Then he could say goodbye to his humanity for a while. Then he could be the animal he was born to be. It was all he had left.

And maybe one day, when the danger was gone, he could work at being normal.

***

Ryan
July

Ryan stalked her through long grass, hidden in the shadows of overhanging trees. She pranced through the grass as if she hadn't a care in the world. She was small but deceptively fast, so he upped his pace when hers increased slightly.

Her scent filled his nostrils, and he couldn't have walked away if he tried. He had to teach her a sorely needed lesson.

A twig snapped to the right, and her head jerked around, sunlight turning what was brown into gold. Smothering a growl, he crept forward, preparing to pounce.

She was gone in a flash, running on four legs into the distance before his hind legs could bend into a leap.

Foolish girl. She couldn't hide.

The wolf to his right leaped through the undergrowth and onto the flat green area she had run to, but he would never catch her. She was too fast, already widening the distance between them.

Ryan stood a chance. He had managed to catch up to her every other time. She hadn't quite built up her stamina yet, but she was getting faster, smarter, and more attuned to her wolf side. He couldn't let her win. Not yet.

He didn't hold back, and he was on her tail soon enough. She spun and twisted, turning and swerving to avoid his fangs. She feinted left, ducked right, and twirled around back the way she came. She faced the slower wolf then, her tongue hanging out in a wolfish grin as she easily dodged out of his way. Teasing him.

She trotted daintily to her left and led them both on another merry chase, using everything he had taught her to keep out of their grasp. When she finally tired, Ryan was too weak himself to make much of an effort. She sat abruptly, watching him approach with what he knew was the wolf equivalent of a self-satisfied smirk.

He snapped half-heartedly at her jaw before lying next to her, breathing heavily and enjoying how peaceful she made him feel. When she relaxed, they all did. She batted him with a paw, a distinctly human expression on her face, and relaxed, sinking to the ground on her belly.

She had won. For the first time, she had beaten them both. Usually, one manoeuvred her into the other who then managed to take her down with ease. Not this time. She was almost ready.

Byron was the last to join them, panting hard from the exertion. He licked his niece's muzzle affectionately. Ryan looked away, seized by painful memories of his own stolen daughters.

He had to admit to being proud of this baby werewolf. More than that, he was awestruck at being around a wolf he suspected of being an omega, a rarity amongst them. It didn't seem possible that the wolves he had once fought against would have the only omega in existence, but he couldn't deny how at ease he was around her.

Ever since the first time he had changed forms, he had been consumed with a rage deep in his blood, the madness that buried itself deep inside each and every werewolf. The constant simmering of anger had never been fully appeased until this child had come into his life. Though a waif of a girl, she was turning out to be one of the most important things that had ever happened to him.

He enjoyed helping her learn. His own change had been abrupt and dramatic, full of fear and loneliness and anger. It had taken him a long time to control his urges. The little she-wolf was surrounded by those who could lead her on the right path and teach her self-control and discipline.

She had managed to control herself quickly once shown the way, despite her unexpectedly violent change. He envied her agility and the sharp intelligence of her wolf. The instinct was deeply bred in her, and she welcomed it with open arms.

She had something he had never seen before: Becoming a wolf wasn't a part of her, something to be discarded as soon as she was back on two legs. She *was* wolf, true wolf on two legs or four, and he knew she could be a great ally when the time came to fight. If he was right about the omega power, she could be the key to helping him bring his daughters home. She could be the balance the werewolves badly needed. All parts of the plan were fitting into place perfectly.

Almost all.

If only the boy would come home.

Chapter One

Perdita
Dublin

A knock at my bedroom door startled me enough to run a line right through Nathan's eyes. "Hold on," I called out, covering the drawing.

Gran glanced down at the lock as I opened the door. "I was wondering if you wanted to come downstairs for lunch. You've been working hard all morning."

"I don't know if—"

"I could use the company," she added, knotting her fingers together as if in prayer.

I wasn't hungry. Eating had become something on a list of things to do everyday, but I knew I had been neglecting her. "Fine. I'll be down in a sec."

She hesitated before jerking her chin into a nod and scurrying down the stairs. I tore up the last picture I had drawn, stuffed the scraps of paper into an overloaded bin, and followed her downstairs.

She flitted about the kitchen like a nervous bird, and I wanted to tell her to relax, but my throat kept drying up.

"Any news?" she asked with a plastered-on smile.

I shrugged. I spent most of my time either at the hospital or at home. I didn't have much to talk about.

"How's the drawing going?"

Pushing food around my plate, I tried to cover a sigh. "Okay."

"Phone calls," she blurted after a couple of moments of tense silence, and I realised she had been making a serious effort to draw me out. "Phone calls. I knew there was something I meant to… Joey called to remind you about your work experience interview this afternoon. And Tammie called a number of times." She cleared her throat. "Again."

"Thanks."

"Maybe you should talk to Tammie. She's called so many times now that—"

"She doesn't really deserve it."

"I know, but she's tried to be there for you since, well, since—"

I held up a hand to silence her. "I get it. I'll talk to her next time she calls, okay?"

She smiled gratefully, and the ache in my chest eased slightly.

"But if Joey calls again, tell him I'm not a child, and he's not my father."

Her smile grew warm. "I think he's excited that you're getting back to yourself. They've missed seeing you lately."

"I'm grounded, remember?"

Her face fell. "I know that, but—"

"But nothing. Grounded means grounded. I only agreed to the work experience because Dad seemed to like the idea."

My school had sent letters describing in great detail what would happen if any of my group of friends experienced any more suspicious absences in the next school term. When Dad said I was grounded until I moved out, I totally believed him. Work experience at the local public library would be my only opportunity to go outside alone once he came home from the hospital.

"Well, I'm sure he'll calm down eventually," Gran said

brightly, ever the optimist. "Once he gets home, everything will start getting back to normal. He'll soon see he's overreacting about Nathan and Amelia."

I stood abruptly. "Nathan's gone, so it doesn't even matter what Dad's rules are anymore. I don't care about that anyway. I have to get back to work."

"It's your summer holidays, Perdy."

"Yeah, well, I need to work on my portfolio. Pad it so I've something to show at the end of the school year. I need the practice anyway. I've a lot of catching up to do."

She got to her feet. "You'll be happier once your dad's home." She sounded as if she were trying to convince herself.

Dad wasn't any better, still freakishly weak from a werewolf bite that everyone thought had come from a wild dog. All I got from him lately was anger, and when he came home, there would be nowhere to hide from the tension and awkwardness that had swallowed our lives.

As if she knew what I was thinking, Gran patted my arm. "You're not still blaming yourself, are you, love?"

I shook my head. "Of course not. I just have stuff to do."

I ignored the lost expression on her face and returned to my room. I sketched for a little while, doing my best not to think too much about the subject matter. It was strange how blocked I had been under the influence of the curse. Once that had been broken, the emotion flooded out of me through the media of pencil and paint. I drew and painted, and my wrists ached every day, but I still kept going.

I couldn't stop.

The paintings were so dark that they sometimes scared me, but they were my best work ever. It had taken heartbreak and pain to draw out what I had always fully intended to express in every shadow. It was exhilarating.

Except for the reminders. *He* was in every painting, one way or another. Whether a shadow or a figure, a wolf or a pair of eyes, his presence was unmistakable.

Scrunching up a page, I decided to drop the drawing and get ready for my interview. My cousin Joey had been the one to come up with the idea in the first place, and he had put my name down without asking me. Dad's reaction had sealed the deal. I didn't have much interest in the library, but seeing as my presence seemed to depress my father, and he appeared momentarily happy at the idea of me doing work experience there, I figured it would help if I stayed out of his way as much as possible.

I practiced smiling in the mirror. Joey had made a point of telling me I looked so miserable that it made him physically sick, and I had decided that wasn't the Perdy I wanted to be anymore. If I didn't think about Nathan, I would be fine.

Perfect.

I strolled to the library after listening to my grandmother's overly enthusiastic wishes of good luck. We all already knew that I'd be getting the work experience slot. Nobody else wanted it.

The breeze was cool enough to lift goose bumps on my skin, but the day was nice enough. Still, I found myself constantly looking over my shoulder. Nathan might have been gone and the werewolves fighting their battles elsewhere, but I never felt safe anymore. Not for a second. Breaking the curse didn't change how I saw the world. It didn't make me forget the dangers out there.

No. No thinking. Perfect smiling happy face only.

As soon as I stepped into the musty library, I realised why nobody wanted to work there. The place was pretty disgusting, all dust and weird damp old book smells. Every surface looked as though it needed a good scrub.

A sudden hacking cough tore through the silence and made me stumble. I frantically glanced around to see who was there and almost died with terror when an ancient old lady appeared to rise up from behind the counter like a decrepit bride of Dracula. Her face was a perfect example of crankiness, and my heart sank. I automatically gave her my best smile, but maybe I was a little too eager because she looked slightly repulsed.

"Um, I-I'm here to interview for the work experience p-placement," I stuttered.

She looked away and coughed into a handkerchief. "You're late."

"Um, I don't think—"

"You'll arrive at eight forty-five every single morning. No excuses. You will stay until six and lock up. During the day, you will clean and organise. You will not eat in the library. You will not use a mobile phone in the library. You will have one hour for lunch. Not a minute more." She peered at me. "You may call me Mrs. Reed, and you *will* work hard."

"I… okay. That's… I mean, that's fine. Okay."

She made a huffing sound. "Monday morning. Eight forty-five. Bring a packed lunch." She turned and began sorting through a pile of books on the counter, completely dismissing me.

"I… see you then." I walked out feeling as though I'd just been in a dream, or maybe a nightmare. Mrs. Reed wasn't quite what I had been expecting.

I called Joey. "So, Mrs. Reed… she's weird, right?" I said before he could say hello.

There was a pause, and then he laughed. "You'll get used to her. She's just set in her ways."

"I feel like you've gotten me into something here."

"Oh, come on. What else do you have to do? Mope around missing your boyfriend?"

"Joey!" I couldn't believe he would say something like that.

"Perdy. Are we supposed to pretend this year hasn't happened at all?"

I stopped walking and stared at the phone. What was with him lately? "No," I said after a moment. "I don't expect anyone to forget, but that doesn't mean we have to discuss it in detail."

"Or at all, eh? Look, I'm not asking for details, but it'd be nice to get back to normal."

I made a sound of frustration. "Everyone keeps saying that. What's normal, anyway?"

"Normal is you being a part of the real world again."

I could hear the irritation in his voice, and I swallowed hard before saying, "I *am* a part of the real world. Now more than ever. You all got what you wanted, remember?"

"You say that, but you're the one who acts as though you want to pretend Nathan doesn't exist anymore. I've never wanted that."

"It's hard, okay? Besides, he's not here. He might as well not exist. I want to move on because nothing's ever going to go back to the way it was."

"See, this is what I don't understand. The two of you have been like… Romeo and Juliet level of obsession. It was weird, but whatever. It worked for you two, apparently. And then it's over. Just like that. No fallout. No fight. No reason. And then he just disappears? It makes no sense to me."

I opened and closed my mouth a couple of times as a dozen different sentences I couldn't say sprang to mind. "I have to go."

I hung up on him before he could dig any deeper. I could see what was freaking him out. I knew there weren't enough answers for him. He would always be curious. That was the way Joey lived his life: constant nosiness and an inability to leave anything alone once there was some question he couldn't immediately answer.

I kept other people's secrets, and the truth wasn't logical enough for my cousin. Sometimes I wished I could tell him, wished I had somebody, anyone at all, to talk to about it, but everyone had an opinion on Nathan. Everyone wanted to know more.

In those kinds of moments, I wished I still had Amelia, but she hadn't come to see me or even called.

Gran greeted me at the front door, twisting a ring around her finger. "Now, don't be angry with me."

My heart threatened to stop. "Why? What did you do?"

"Tammie called again, so I asked her to drop over. Don't look at me like that, Perdy. I'm your grandmother. I know what's best for you… most of the time. Maybe I shouldn't interfere, but you need someone. You won't talk to me, and you have to get whatever it is on your mind off your chest. Please. *Please*, stop isolating yourself." Tears glittered in her eyes.

Out of surprise and guilt, I nodded. "Fine. I'll see her. I'm not trying to… I'm not ready for the other stuff, okay? There are things I just can't talk about right now. I'm sorry, Gran."

She hugged me, her grip unrelentingly tight. "Well, then talk about other things. Unimportant things. If it doesn't make you feel better, don't do it twice, but at least try. For me."

I gave an exaggerated eye roll. "Blackmailer."

"That's my girl." She threw her arm around me and led me inside.

Tammie stood when I entered the room, seemingly unsure of where to look. I had a sudden pang as I realised everyone acted around me the way we all reacted to Dad. That wasn't a good sign.

"I'll be upstairs," Gran said. "You girls have a nice chat."

Tammie grinned at me as Gran left the room, an old familiarity returning. "Some things never change, eh?"

"I don't know about that." I sat down, and she sank into the chair again.

"I've been trying to get in touch with you." She avoided my eyes. "Ever since I heard…"

"I know. Didn't think we had much to talk about. Not after everything."

"I've apologised a million times."

"Doesn't mean so much to me anymore. You told me not to bother you," I said coldly. "And you said it because you knew I'd take it."

"I just… I miss you, okay? When I heard it was over, I wanted to make sure you were okay. But more than that, I want to be friends again." She gave a nervous laugh. "Turns out I need you more than you need me."

"You have Joey."

"And who do you have? Look at me."

I did, but I saw something in her eyes I hadn't noticed before. "What's wrong?"

"Nothing new," she said with a wry smile. "But I'm not here to talk about me. I'm here for you. How are you doing?"

I huffed out a sound of disgust. "What do you care? You hated him."

She cocked her head. "I didn't hate him. Not really. I just wasn't comfortable around him. Besides, he and his sister stole my best friend away. Can you blame me for being a little peeved?" She smiled, but the expression didn't reach her eyes. "No matter what happened between us, I still care about you, Perdy. That doesn't disappear overnight."

I gazed at her, again seeing pain flit across her expression. "Seriously, what's going on with you?"

"Stop avoiding the subject." She laughed, covering her mouth. "I hear you're grounded for all eternity. Old Man Rivers is still way harsh, I see."

"I deserve it this time. I messed up... messed up everything, really." I shrugged. "Besides, I'm only grounded until I move out."

"So until next summer?"

I scraped some paint from my fingers with my thumbnail. My repetitive drawings wouldn't get me into any college. "Maybe. Maybe not."

"You're still going to college, right? I mean, art college," she said urgently.

"I've a lot of thinking to do. Maybe Dad's been right all along. I can't keep dreaming forever."

"What?" She stared at me in amazement. "Are you actually serious? Perdy, what's the point in living if you don't have dreams? Why on earth would you do anything other than the one thing you've wanted your entire life?"

I leaned back at the ferocity of her tone. "Um, wow. Chill a little, Tams."

"I can't *believe* you're giving up. Wait a minute. Is this over Nathan? Are you actually giving up over a *boy*?"

"I'm not giving up anything. And not over a *boy*, but thanks for the judgement. I'm just saying I have options, and maybe what I think would be fun isn't actually for the best."

"I'm so having a word with your dad over this," she muttered. "That's like… it would be like when one of those old celebrity couples who have been together forever split up. Your entire life changes because even *they* couldn't make it work."

"What? I mean… what? How is—"

"Don't act like you don't understand! If you give up on the one thing that'll make you happy, then what chance do I have?"

I rolled my eyes. "Really, Tammie? Thought we were on about me here. And by the way, when it looked like Nathan was making me happy, you absolutely hated it, so don't give me that crap."

Her face paled. "It was never meant to be like that. I didn't mean to come across that way, but I thought—"

"I'm tired." I sighed wearily, not even faking it. "Like, really tired. Can we not do this right now?"

"Uh, yeah, okay. Sorry. Can we talk again? I mean, like we used to? Just hang out or whatever?"

"Grounded," I reminded, ushering her out of my house before she could persuade me otherwise.

Gran came up behind me immediately, and I knew she had been listening. She got in my way when I tried to make it back up the stairs. "Perdy, you can't give up on what you've always wanted to do. Your father's not himself right now, that's all. It'll change. He won't honestly expect you to give up. You've worked so hard. Even now, you're still working hard."

Thoughts blazed through my head about how filling my portfolio was less the truth than the fact that I was trying to paint away my feelings for Nathan. I was trying to get him out of my head. "Maybe I'm the one who's changed my mind, Gran. Everything's changed. Everything. I can't be the same person anymore, so maybe everyone should give me the space to make up my own mind."

I brushed past her and ran up to my room. I could barely keep my eyes open. The nightmares probably disturbed my sleep too often, but as soon as I lay on my bed and closed my eyes, *he* popped into my head. No way could I sleep after that.

All I was left with was thinking about how my plans might change. I wasn't trying to please Dad, or at least not only that. Everything I knew in my life had been turned upside down. I had murdered somebody, but I couldn't tell a soul. I couldn't even prove what I had done. Maybe I didn't deserve to live my dreams.

I wasn't the same person anymore. Art was a release, but I couldn't do anything for a living with the same few pictures that kept flowing from my fingers. My mind had gone one-track, and that wasn't conducive to creativity. My plans had to change.

Maybe art would always be a hobby for me, but so what? I'd just have to look at something more sensible for a career. Maybe I had to be more like Dad.

What bothered me was the way everyone forced their opinions on me. Sometimes I wanted a neutral point of view from someone who wasn't invested in my decisions, from someone who didn't have a motive regarding Nathan and his family.

My mother, Meredith, had gone home a couple of days after the curse had been broken by Amelia, unable to deal with a shell-shocked daughter. She hadn't run away in the night at least. She had discussed it with me, explained her reasons, and only left when I nodded my acceptance. It had hurt Gran, but I was perfectly fine with it.

Until now.

I needed somebody I didn't have, somebody I never really knew I needed. It was kind of a strange turnaround for me, but as I kept telling people, everything had changed.

Her voice wasn't familiar, and her habits were unknown to me, but when my mother answered her phone, I felt an odd sense of relief, as though maybe she was somebody I could talk to about unimportant stuff, just as Gran wanted.

"How are you doing?" she asked, sounding a lot more relaxed than the last time we spoke.

"Okay." I hesitated. "Well, not really. Dad's coming home this week."

"Ah. If it gets too much, you could visit me, you know. If you wanted."

It surprised me that she actually sounded sincere. "I think I should be here for him."

"Anything else going on? Any changes on the boyfriend front?"

"He's still gone. I don't know if he's ever coming back." I was proud of how steady my voice was as I said the words out loud. Maybe I was getting used to it. Maybe I would be okay soon.

"It might be good for you both to have a break from each other anyway. It'll give you a chance to really think about what it is you want. If he's worth it, he'll wait. You're young. You'll have lots of time once your dad gets better."

If he ever got better. The werewolf bite hadn't exactly done him any favours.

"I think it wasn't my choice anyway."

"Then don't waste your time on him," she said sharply. "Sorry. Wow. Protective streak finally made an appearance."

I laughed with her, feeling slightly better. "I'm starting work experience on Monday. In a library."

"A library? I didn't take you for a librarian."

"Funny. It was Joey's idea, Dad seemed interested, and it's the only way I'm getting out of the house for the summer, so I figured, why not?"

"I could always talk to Stephen about it. He's acting way too much like your grandfather did, and we all know how well that turned out."

I chuckled. "I'm not eloping. Don't worry."

"But you *will* run away whenever you get the chance. You might wait for something legitimate, like college, but that's what you'll end up having to do if he keeps acting this way."

I had thought the exact same thing, many times. But life had changed, and I knew my conscience would fight me to the bitter end if I tried to run away from Dad. After all, he was ill because of me. The only way I would run was if he made it clear he didn't want me to stay, and although I had been getting that vibe from him of late, I couldn't believe that was what he really wanted.

"We'll be okay," I said. "He'll get over it. He always does."

At least, I hoped he would.

Chapter Two

Nathan
Near Balme

I pulled my scarf tighter across my chin, shivering uncontrollably. Stupid mountains. Stupid summer snow. Why anyone would want to stay in a hut there, of all places, was a mystery to me. Shuffling my feet to make sure I didn't lose any toes, I watched the same story repeat itself. More suspicion, more aggression, more rejection.

Willow had been taking us from place to place around Europe for weeks, each more secluded than the last. I couldn't help suspecting the entire idea was a way to lead us straight into a trap.

We were looking for werewolves, loners, exiles, or small families managing to live unmolested by the main pack. We wanted help. We needed it. Vin would keep sending his werewolves after my family if we didn't stop him. Even aided by Ryan and Willow, the wolves who had deserted him, we were still outnumbered. We needed to be certain of victory when we went after Vin.

All Opa wanted was Vin. All Jeremy wanted was power. All Willow wanted was to get back to Ryan. And all I wanted was to forget.

Byron and Opa had fought hard over our leaving. Opa had conceded, but after we left, he insisted to Jeremy and me that we could combine our efforts and simultaneously find werewolves to join us while we figured out where Vin was hiding.

The old man shook his head again, vehemently this time. He had greeted us a half-mile away from the hut his family were staying in, a place often frequented by travelling werewolves, or so Willow said. Much lower on the mountain was some kind of tourist accommodation, which was where we had ditched the truck we hired, but this particular place had been built by werewolves, designed to keep them out of sight and out of mind.

The man wasn't as well covered as we were, but he seemed better able to stand the skin-whipping wind, although I didn't see how a human could survive in the middle of nowhere. At least werewolves could hunt.

The elderly man before us wasn't a werewolf, but his grandson was, according to Willow. Numbers had dwindled significantly. I could barely understand the man's dialect, but my grandfather was capable of having an entire conversation with him in French. Mémère's language. The man swore once, and even I could understand that. Opa kept speaking rapidly, insistently, crowding the old man.

I glanced at Jeremy, who shrugged. Opa was in charge. We would wait until he said we could leave. Willow sidled up to the old man, and my wolf went on high alert. She could easily switch sides again, no matter how much Jeremy helped her addled brain.

Snow began to fall, swirling tufts of delicate fluff that managed to keep a white curtain over that part of the mountainous range. The scenery was beautiful, but the hate gnawing at my chest made me eager to leave it behind forever.

"Shouldn't he be speaking Italian?" I whispered to Jeremy.

"Maybe he's not Italian. We're close enough to the border, so who knows where he's from? Willow reckons they move around frequently. Wherever Vin isn't, they'll be."

The old man stomped away.

"Wait!" Opa called out, sounding desperate.

A snarl from behind us had Jeremy and me stripping and swearing about the ridiculous cold.

A light brown wolf stood on a stone ledge, baring its fangs at us.

Willow shook her head. "Don't bother. He won't attack. It's a warning." She added under her breath, "Idiots." When Jeremy glared in her direction, she cleared her throat. "But there could be others, and they know the snow better than you all, so let's get out of here."

"But—" Opa began.

"It's a no," she said firmly, keeping her eyes on the wolf. She headed back down the trail.

The snowfall rapidly turned heavier. We ended up stripping nonetheless, all of us turning wolf to make it easier on us on the way back to the car. Running on four legs in thick snow was almost as difficult as hiking on two, but we eventually ended up on easier ground again. We found the spare clothes we had left and dressed quickly, shivering even when we got into the vehicle.

"No more snow," I muttered.

"Where next?" Opa demanded.

Willow shook her head, but she answered anyway. "I know of one in France. He hides in a city about four or five hours drive away. We might as well go to him, but he's not what you're looking for."

"They're all male," I said, curious at the realization.

She glared at me. "Females are special, pup. Rare."

I thought of my own little sister, already a werewolf by birth, and my grandmother, who had been turned into a werewolf by my grandfather. Were they really such a rarity, or was that something to do with the curse again?

"Why did he say no?" Jeremy asked.

I groaned. Who even cared anymore?

"He said we had bad blood, black magic blood, and he wouldn't touch us in case we infected him," Opa said.

So it was still fear, but one of a different kind. Most of the wolves were too terrified of their alpha, Vin, to join with us. Jeremy kept insisting we should make them too terrified of us to say no, but so far, we had managed to keep calm in the face of so many refusals.

Besides, Willow was right. We couldn't fight in their territory. We had been skiing and hiking around the Alps dozens of times, but that wasn't the same as living or fighting there.

The truck rattled down the trail, then finally onto a decent road. The hike had been exhausting, but the chill was what sent me to sleep as soon as we made it back to the tiny hotel on the outskirts of a small town. We had been to so many that they all blended into one.

***

I awoke in yet another ugly, sparsely furnished room, shivering as though I would never burn the cold from my bones. Every day, I opened my eyes to the same thought.

I wish I had stayed at home.

We had stale toast and tepid coffee for breakfast. A familiar gnawing in my stomach warned that my wolf desired something more substantial. We would both have to wait.

"We'll keep moving," Opa said after a few moments of silence. "Keep moving, and we'll find someone who will help us."

Jeremy and I exchanged glances. We were running out of people to ask. Willow began humming again, an eerie little song that we had learned would lead to an episode even Jeremy couldn't drag her out of. We took her to the room Jeremy and I shared so we could keep a close eye on her while Opa talked about his plans some more.

"She said she would take us to a city next," he said. "There's more chance of us bargaining with a civilised werewolf. I have a good feeling about this."

"We could go home," I couldn't help suggesting. "The others are alone. What if something happens while we're chasing rainbows out here?"

He glared at me. "Are you a coward, Nathan?"

I rolled my eyes. "Here we go."

"Opa, maybe he's right. Nobody wants to stand with us, but at least we have Ryan and Willow. Maybe that'll be enough." Jeremy sounded as fed up as I felt.

"And what do we do when we go home?" Opa asked in a harsh voice. "Wait for them to come after us again? We haven't found him, and that's because he's running scared. Don't you see it? He doesn't want to face us, and that's why we have to keep chasing *him*."

Jeremy looked away, and Opa turned to me. "What would you rather do, Nathan? Chase him or let him come back to the family, to Perdita?"

I stood to leave. "You don't get to talk about her. Not after everything. You definitely don't get to use her against me. We should be home. The entire family needs to be together. Byron was right. This is pointless."

He shouted after me, but I couldn't listen anymore. I understood his hate, but it felt like such a waste of time to dart from one place to another with nothing to show for our efforts. I stood outside in the cold, staring at the bright blue sky that belied the chill of the wind. I had left with Opa, only too happy to get away from Amelia and Perdita. I hated that Amelia had broken the curse... except I didn't... not really. But I needed to blame someone, and I had chosen her because it was easy. The curse had to end—I knew that—but the way it had ended had wrecked everything.

Opa was drifting further into the darkness in his head. Every day, I felt as though maybe I could join him there, but a niggling chill in my chest reminded me that Perdita wouldn't approve. That was the worst feeling of all.

"Hey," Jeremy said, stepping outside. "Cheer up. The cold is getting to you."

"That's not what's getting to me."

"So it's the girl then. Still? You didn't have her for long."

I frowned. He didn't get it.

"Drop the sulky face," he snapped. "You think you have it bad? At least you found your mate. You're the one who dropped her as soon as things got tough. I didn't even get a chance to find mine."

"I didn't—"

"Enough. I'm getting really sick of you moping around. *You* wanted to come with *us*. Don't forget that. You jumped at the chance. Yeah, it gets tough, but you can't keep running away from your problems."

"What are you talking about?"

"You've done it your entire life, Nathan. Don't mistake it for something noble. You tried to avoid every part of what you are, and you're still doing it, one way or another. Either snap out of it or decide what it is you really want to do because nobody deserves to put up with you like this." He stormed back inside, leaving me open-mouthed with shock.

Was I really that bad? I followed him after a while, humbled by his reaction. He stood in the hallway, his face tight with tension.

He sighed when he saw me. "Forget about it, kid. We're all struggling right now. We haven't hunted properly. I'm sorry I let rip at you before."

"Is that what you really think? That I'm running away?"

His eyes narrowed. "Aren't you? I'm not telling you what to do, but if it's making you this unhappy, then maybe it's time to reconsider it, you know?"

I shoved my hands in my pockets, feeling like a child.

He stepped toward the door. "Come on. We're going for a real run. Get all of this stress off our backs. Willow will be back to normal soon enough, and we won't get the chance."

"What? Now? Here?"

He grinned. "Don't chicken out on me now, man."

I shrugged. "I suppose I could carve out some time in my busy schedule."

He shoved me and walked ahead, chuckling. "You're a weird kid all the same. I've got the keys to the truck, so we can drive out and find somewhere decent to run. No snow, I promise."

In the truck, he blared heavy dance music on the radio as he started the engine. "Want me to teach you how to drive or something?"

"Okay, what's the deal with you today?"

He laughed. "I have a lot of energy to burn up." He pressed on the accelerator. "So what's it been like, living with my dad all these years?"

"Didn't see him a whole lot until recently," I admitted.

"Yeah, he wasn't around much for me either."

"He's been different lately, though. Maybe you should give him another chance." The tension between father and son hadn't gone unnoticed by me.

He pulled off the road sharply. "Couldn't give a crap about that sort of thing, to be honest. Gonna go off-road for a while. Have a real adventure."

Excitement and unease fought to win a war in my gut. Jeremy was different than I remembered.

"How are you really doing since the shit hit the fan?" he asked after a few minutes.

"Mind the ditch." I pointed to the side. "Fine. Keeping on. All that good stuff."

"Why the hell did you leave home if it was going to make you so miserable?"

"I just… I had to do something. Ryan reckons she's safe away from me, but how could he possibly know that? They got away with murdering my parents. How am I supposed to sit at home and wait around?" I exhaled loudly. "But this feels as much of a waste of time as that. At least at home…"

He nodded. "You can look out for her. Think Amelia's getting on okay now? The way she went for your chick was nasty. Vicious little thing. Even I wasn't that bad the first time."

"Byron would let us know if he needed help with her. She seemed fine afterward, as if nothing even happened."

His laughter startled me. "She was on her best behaviour because you looked as though you wanted to kill her yourself. Oh, man, how did everything get so messed up with the family?"

"Secrets and lies," I muttered.

"He wants to leave Dublin," he said, giving me a wary glance. "When whatever he wants is done. Reckons there's nothing there for us anymore but bad memories. What do you think about that?"

I ignored the way my heart began to thud in triple-time. "Not a lot. Who knows when this will end? Maybe it would be for the best." I wasn't sure I could walk around our neighbourhood, knowing she was nearby but not being able to talk to her. "Perdita's dad hates me now, so that's one good reason to get out of there."

He gave a low whistle. "That was some introduction to the family. Him getting bitten at our house, of all places. I knew I had made a mistake coming home right in that second."

"Opa reckons he might be able to help Perdita's dad get better."

"Then why hasn't he? Pulling your strings, I'd say. Watch yourself, Nathan. We're not in the loop. Don't forget that."

"We should be."

"Yeah, well, certain things are out of our hands right now. Won't always be that way, though." He grinned. "So you still think the girl's perfect?"

"Perdita? Nobody's perfect. But she was perfect for me. She was always herself, never trying to show off or be anyone else. You get what you see, and with our life, that's a great thing."

"The curse hit you too young. If it had just waited a while, you could have avoided this whole mess."

"Yeah," I murmured, but I didn't agree. Not at all.

"This looks like a good place." He slowed down and came to a stop. "Time to eat." He was out of the vehicle and sprinting toward the nearest copse of trees before I could open the door.

Shaking my head, I soon followed, desperate to be wolf. I

stripped and changed into my wolf as quickly as possible. Wolf was reluctant, which was strange, considering the hunger. I ignored that fact as my entire body shifted into its animal form, cracking and twisting into the beast that was always inside me. I let out an inhuman sound and followed Jeremy further away from the truck, relishing the freedom paws gave me. I was only a tiny bit miffed that Jeremy had lied about the snow. We left a trail of prints in the patches of snow behind us, but there was mostly sodden grass ahead, so I couldn't complain too much.

I felt better and worse as wolf. The need for the mate we had lost was overwhelming, but it was easier to soothe the wolf with the hunt and the simplicity of running free. I could forget for a little while and that was likely the real reason Jeremy had brought me out. To forget.

So I did.

At first, we ran for ages, ignoring the rest of the wildlife. I soon realised I was catching familiar scents as the snow grew deeper under our paws again. Jeremy was leading me back to the place we had been the day before.

He glanced back at me, his eyes wild with excitement, and I hurried to match his pace. He yelped a little and ducked under a low hanging branch. We weren't hunting for food anymore, and every sense in my body thrilled with the adrenalin rush.

I couldn't have said how much time passed, but we ended up close to the werewolf's hut before sunset. I didn't feel the cold anymore. I just felt anger, pain, and a desire to make somebody pay. I knew that Jeremy wanted the wolves to fear us, to decide we were the greater adversary, and for once, I didn't care.

We approached the hut with care, but Jeremy howled a challenge. Less than five minutes later, a wolf ran from the back of the hut to greet us. He was the same wolf as before, light brown, no bigger than I was. He was no match for the both of us, but he came at us as if he had an entire pack behind him.

Jeremy lay down and jerked his head at me as if to say, "Go

ahead. Take it all out on him."

My heart jumping out of my chest, I approached the wolf. He circled me, snarling and baring his fangs. I wasn't afraid, not at all. In fact, I was eager to fight, eager to tear his flesh apart with my teeth. The rage was all-consuming, fed by every slight, every event that had ever caused me anger. I imagined the young wolf to have killed my parents, to have attacked Perdita, her father, and my family. I saw Vin in him, and my sight turned red with anger.

I ran, barrelling into him until we were both rolling across the ground. He snapped aggressively, desperate to reach my throat, but I outmatched him with my anger. I heard shouting in the distance, and before I could react, the wolf was out from under me, racing back to the hut. I followed, confused, until I saw Jeremy racing toward humans.

Fire! The old man waved some kind of lit torch, and a young woman stood in Jeremy's path. I realised the wolf had run to protect his own, his family, his *mate*.

Full of shame and disgust, I charged at Jeremy, even as the other wolf flung himself in front of his loved ones. I caught Jeremy's flank as he launched, forcing him to slow. He was too wild. He whirled around to face me, eyes black with anger.

I let out a warning snarl, and he backed away a step, but he had wound up too close to the others, and the werewolf snapped at Jeremy. Surrounded by two of us, Jeremy thought twice and raced away from the hut.

Panting, I glanced at the three of them, werewolf and humans, more sorry than I could ever say. I bowed my head a little, hoping I looked apologetic, but the werewolf was understandably wary and angry. He bared his fangs until I moved off.

Perdita was right. I had become the exact kind of monster I was chasing. I ran, following Jeremy and hoping he didn't drive off without me in his anger. I found him tearing into a large ibex, despite a stomach injury from the ibex's long, curved horns. He snarled at me, livid with anger, so I left him there and headed back to the truck.

I couldn't hunt after that. I sat in the truck and waited for him. When he finally returned, he was dressed and clean with no outward sign of injury, but he didn't get into the truck straight away. He leaned against the door, gagging, before joining me.

"I don't want to hear it," he snapped.

I didn't say a word, but I knew I would never follow Jeremy. He could never lead me. I didn't want to be that kind of werewolf, that kind of man. I was finally seeing clearly.

The drive back seemed to take forever, but that was partly because of the deathly silence in the truck. No music, no talking, and we both made a point of turning away from each other. Byron had been right about us. There would always be competition and tension between us because I knew I would never let Jeremy above me in the pack, and I could guarantee he thought the exact same thing.

We got back to the hotel to find a furious Opa struggling with Willow.

"Where have you been?" he demanded. "She's been throwing herself against the wall for the last hour."

Blood matted her hair, making it stick to her temples. Her skin was incredibly pale, but the blankness in her eyes was what stood out.

"I'll deal with her," Jeremy said.

"Sure that's a good idea?" I couldn't help asking.

Opa looked at us both with a great deal of curiosity.

"Think *you'd* be able for it?" Jeremy retorted.

"No more leaving without my permission," Opa said. "This journey isn't over, and I won't have you wasting your energy. We could be attacked at any time."

I stared at Jeremy in disgust. "Yeah. That's the worst that could happen."

I stayed in the room I shared with Jeremy for the rest of the evening, going to bed early to avoid seeing him.

My family wasn't as perfect as Amelia once liked to make out.

Opa and Jeremy were one and the same, capable of doing terrible things. I wasn't that far from becoming exactly like them. Where did it end? Perdita's words echoed in my head all night. I couldn't stay with them for much longer. I needed back in the security of Byron's protection, his roof, his rules. I needed to be around people who thought that violence and murder were last resorts, not first options.

I needed to go home.

Chapter Three

Perdita

A trickle of red ran from my wrist and pooled in the crook of my inner elbow. I brushed the liquid away impatiently, staining most of my forearm in the process.

"Oh, my God!" Gran exclaimed from the doorway.

I rolled my eyes at her exaggerated excitement. "Yes?"

"That looks *amazing*. He's going to be pleased, so pleased, when he sees it."

That was the welcome home banner Gran was making me paint, but I was so nervous about Dad's return that I kept making a mess.

"Oh, I can't wait to hang it up. I can only imagine how happy he'll be when he comes home."

I couldn't take any more. "Gran, he's dreading coming home. He hates everyone in the world right now, and we're going to bear the brunt of it. A stupid homemade banner isn't going to change that."

Her face fell.

"We'll be okay eventually, but I can't pretend he likes me very much right now. He's never been this pissed at me before."

She walked behind my chair and rested her hands on my shoulders. "I know, but he's not himself at the moment. That's all. We'll get through this together." She released her grip with a breathy gasp.

I looked around to see her holding a sheet in her hand: a picture I hadn't torn up yet.

"Perdy," she said, her voice trembling, "This is just *wonderful*."

"What?" That hadn't been the reaction I was expecting.

She put down the page and flicked through a sketchpad, then her gaze fell upon the bin full of scrunched up pages. She glanced at me. "You didn't." She grabbed a handful of pages and made an attempt to straighten them out.

"Gran, that's private."

"Private?" Her face cleared of confusion. "Oh, because it's Nathan. But they're so beautiful." She held one out, but I refused to look at the image. "How can you draw this and think you have any place in the world other than as an artist of some kind?"

"Stop it." I hurried to the bathroom where I scrubbed at my hands. The red paint swirled around the basin, invoking bad memories, and I washed those away, too. Nathan was away fighting violent werewolves, while I stayed home to paint banners and hide sketches.

"Perdy," Gran said from the doorway. "Why are you upset with me?"

"I'm not upset with you. I'm just... I can't stop drawing him. Even when I'm not thinking about him, out he pops from the end of my pencil. It's annoying, that's all."

"You care about him. It's only natural to find it hard to get over your first love."

I choked out a strangled laugh. "Haven't you heard Dad? Teenagers don't *love*."

"Oh, don't give me that. *He* did when he was a teen. That's what his problem is."

"Gran..."

"It's nothing to be ashamed about. You tell me he's a good boy, and I believe you. You say he hasn't done anything wrong, and I believe you. But when you tell me you don't care, when you tell me you're over it, those are the things I can't believe. Not because there's something wrong with you, but because you're perfectly normal."

"I miss him," I whispered. "I miss... everything."

"You could always talk to him."

"I can't. I don't want to. I need to forget about this year, do whatever Dad wants, and when the time comes, go where I need to be."

She hesitated. "I want you to be happy."

I tried to smile. "I know, Gran. And I *am* happy. I'm just stressed about Dad right now." I brushed past her, but I knew she didn't buy it.

Dad was coming home the following afternoon, and I wished I knew how to fix the badness between us. I would do anything to make him better again.

Gran and I cleaned up the entire house, bought all of Dad's favourite things to eat, and consulted with a tired-looking Erin on what we could do with him for the rest of the summer holidays to stop him from losing his mind completely. Of course, we didn't vocalise it so bluntly, but I could totally tell we were all thinking the same thing.

"He'll probably want a lot of rest," Erin said doubtfully as she peered at Gran's list of activities. "I mean, he's still very weak."

"Yeah, but sitting around doing nothing makes him grouchy." I frowned, concerned by Erin's wan complexion. "Are *you* getting enough rest?"

Dots of pink appeared on her cheekbones. "I'm fine."

We spoke some more about the logistics of bringing Dad and his newly acquired mountain of hospital stuff home. He had pills to take, exercise routines to follow, all kinds of things designed to get him back to himself.

"Is he ever going to be the same again?" I asked.

"Of course," Gran said.

But Erin wasn't sure at all. "It'll take time," she said at last.

The guilt from that truth had been shadowing me for a while. The uncertainty and fear were derived from my actions. I had killed a werewolf, so his vengeful daughter had attacked my father. Although Jakob Evans had hinted that he knew how to fix Dad, the Evans family had kept their distance. No amount of hospital tests and pills could cure whatever was wrong with my father.

The next morning, Gran insisted on hovering around me until her nervousness had me wound just as tight, so I decided the banner was dry enough to hang up. When I finished, I climbed down from the stepladder and eyed the banner carefully. A little crooked, but maybe nobody would notice. I folded the ladder and prepared to go back inside.

"It's a bit off," a voice behind me said.

I dropped the ladder with a clatter that made me wince. I turned, saw who it was, and took an automatic step backward.

"Hey," Amelia said somewhat sheepishly, and then it obviously dawned on her that there was fear on my expression, because she held up her hands. "I'm not going to… I wouldn't hurt you or anything, Perdita. You know that, right?"

I shrugged. "Can't be too careful these days."

"I was afraid you'd be like this." She looked crestfallen, and it annoyed me.

"Kind of hard to have a better reaction, considering the last time I saw you."

Last time had been all fangs and claws. Not the best first wolfy impression. But I took a step toward her, unable to stop myself, unable to keep away for another second. Her family was the light I was desperate to touch, despite knowing it would eventually burn me to ash. They were the only people who knew what I had done and didn't judge me for it. I couldn't find peace elsewhere.

I stared at her, trying to swallow the emotions rushing around my body. "I like your hair."

She rubbed the back of her shorn head. "I needed a change." Although the back of her hair was cut tight, the front reached her chin and was dyed a teal blue.

"A lot's changed."

She inched forward as if unsure of herself. "I've wanted to come see you. To apologise. But I was kind of under house arrest until they were sure, well, until they were sure I wouldn't hurt anyone." She held up her chin, a strange mixture of pride and uncertainty fleeting across her face. "I can control it now. I'm so sorry, Perdita."

I inched closer to her, remembering the fangs and single-minded determination to tear out my throat. I flexed my fingers. "It's okay."

"It was the shock. And the hunger. All of that time I was sick, it was really the wolf starving, so when the time came, I couldn't get control. The wolf took over, and I saw what was happening, but I couldn't do anything to stop it. I was trapped in there, watching myself…" She shook her head.

"Ryan helped me," I said, remembering how Nathan hadn't.

She nodded enthusiastically. "He's helping me now, too."

"He didn't leave?"

Her face fell. "No, that was just Opa, Jeremy, and Willow." She cleared her throat. "And Nathan."

I shrugged. "He told me he was leaving."

"Did he?" She looked away. "That's good, I suppose."

"If you say so."

"He *hates* me now. That's why he left. To get away from me."

Frowning, I saw she really believed her words. "I doubt that, Amelia."

"It's true! He's blaming me for everything. He couldn't wait to get away from me. I didn't know he would be like this."

I knew it was me he was running from, but I didn't think I could convince her of that. "Um, how's Cú?" I held my breath. I had been afraid to ask about Nathan's dog. Amelia had hurt him in her attempt to get to me, and I had basically lived in terror ever since in case he had died trying to protect me.

Her cheeks flushed. "He's okay. His injuries weren't as bad as they looked, but…"

"But what?"

She shook her head jerkily. "He's missing you. Like, really bad. He had that bond with you, and well, he's pining for you now."

"I miss him, too," I said wistfully, not altogether sure who I was talking about.

Amelia's jean pocket thrummed loudly. She automatically reached for it and paused, her fingers hovering briefly.

"It's okay," I said. "Answer it."

She grinned, and she was a new person. All of the time I had known her, I had thought of her as happy, but there was her real smile. Everything had changed.

"It's probably just Connor," she said before faltering. "I, um—"

"I'm not that bad," I said. "I do actually want other people to be happy, you know."

She squeezed her eyes shut. "Of course you do. I don't know what it feels like for you. Did everything just stop?"

I swallowed hard. "The curse stopped." I watched as her eyes widened with realisation. "I thought you didn't like Connor that much," I added to interrupt her train of thought.

"I do." Her face lit up. "I really do. We've been texting a lot. I lied and told him I was away because of a death in the family. The way I felt before was all Kali's fault."

"Kali?" I squinted. How much had I missed?

"Oh! I forgot you don't know the full story yet. I have so much to tell you."

I shoved my hands in my pockets. "I don't really have time for that. Dad's on his way home, and I'm kind of barred from, well, everything, but especially your family."

"I understand that. But it's important we talk soon."

"I'm serious, Amelia. I can't see you anymore. Dad's not been himself. The only time I'm going to be allowed out of the house is when I start work experience next week."

"Work experience? Where?"

I sighed. "At the library. But I still can't see you. I promised."

She hesitated, appearing a little disappointed, but I waved her on and went back inside. I was serious about making an effort to stick with Dad's rules, especially since seeing Amelia had hurt more than not seeing her.

Dad and Erin arrived within the hour, distracting me from thoughts of Amelia. Gran and I hurried outside to greet them, but Dad's expression was one great big thundercloud. Erin attempted to help him out of the car, but he brushed her away impatiently, struggling to exit the vehicle by himself. His eyebrows knit tightly together, and Erin's lips pressed into a thin line. They had obviously been arguing again. It was as if he thought being sick was a good enough excuse to be awful to absolutely everyone around him.

"Can I help?" I asked, taking a step toward him, but his glare had me backing away.

"I can get out of the car and into the house myself," he snapped, but for one agonising second, he appeared to fall until he managed to balance with his walking stick and pull himself upright.

He didn't look at the banner. He didn't look at me. He strode into the house slowly and carefully, keeping his head high. I knew his pride was wounded, but he was being ridiculous.

Gran darted around us nervously with offerings of tea, lunch, and anything else she could think of to appease him. He remained in a rotten mood, refusing everything. My own frustration grew along with the darkness of his disposition.

"I was thinking we could go out to dinner tomorrow," Erin said pleasantly. "All of us."

"No, thanks," Dad said. "I don't want the entire neighbourhood staring at me."

"Dad," I said, "they aren't going to stare. People have been worried about you."

His gaze fell on me for the first time. "Do you really think you should be drawing attention to yourself? After everything you've done?"

I rolled my eyes, but I didn't say anything. He was right. I had let him down in ways he didn't even know about, and I was sorry for it. The punishment seemed to be eternal, but nothing was worse than the one Nathan had doled out.

Chapter Four

Nathan
Lyon

We had been driving for hours, but at least the snow had stopped falling. The sky was still a pure blue, and the biting cold wind had vanished a half-hour ago. We were back into nice, boring, thankfully warm sun. I was glad to get out of the mountains.

I opened the window all the way, relishing the warmer breeze against my skin. Jeremy was still ignoring me. He could sit in the back with Willow and act like a statue for all I cared. I grew more and more eager to go back to Ireland with every minute that passed.

We checked in at a hotel in the city, but we had barely taken a breather when we left on foot to follow another of Willow's leads. She had given us all kinds of crap about moving further into Vin's territories, but we had come up with nothing useful. I got the feeling she was scraping the bottom of the barrel.

We walked along cobblestone streets between tall, crowded buildings. A lot of different noises and scents distracted me, and my wolf grew antsy.

To my surprise, Willow led us to a crooked building that housed flats above a shop. We needed space to move. How could a were-wolf survive in a tiny flat? Even walking up the dark stairwell made me feel as though I might suffocate. I heard a dog barking behind the first door we passed. Poor little yappy thing must have gone mental stuck in there alone.

Our destination was the lone flat on the top floor. The stench of rival werewolf choked the air. We were definitely in the right place. Jeremy nodded at me; the presence of a potential enemy overrode the tension between us.

A scrawny man in his thirties answered Jeremy's brisk rap on the door. He glared at us until realisation hit. He backed away, avoiding eye contact.

"Malachai," Willow said.

He looked at her sharply, confusion muddying his blue eyes. "You look… different," he said slowly, probably biding his time.

"We're here to talk," Opa said. "We aren't a threat to you right now. Can we come in?"

Malachai hesitated, then reluctantly invited us in to his flat. Lines were gouged into one white wall, as if he had clawed it in a rage, but I pretended not to notice. Willow and Malachai sat on a two-seater sofa, but the rest of us stood until Malachai grew so uncomfortable that he ended up getting to his feet, too.

"What do you want?" he asked, still avoiding our eyes and edging around the room in a way that made me want to pounce. "Did Vin send you? What's going on now?"

Opa and Jeremy exchanged glances. He didn't know us, didn't know we weren't part of his pack. That seemed impossible to me.

"Do you remember Ryan?" Willow said. "The Scot whose daughters you helped kidnap?"

His face paled, and he shook his head. "Not… kidnap. I was… Vin told me to… it's not kidnapping to bring home the pack."

"These are the Evans wolves," she told him, pointing at us. "Do you understand yet?"

"No, Willow. No!" He stared at her in horror, putting as much distance between him and us as possible. "What are you doing? Are you crazy? Why would you bring them here?"

"We're here to help you. All of you," Opa explained, almost gently. "We can end Vin's time as alpha. We can help you free yourself."

Malachai trembled. His weakness provoked my wolf, and I struggled to stay calm. Too many scents, too many emotions in such a small space.

"Get out," Malachai hissed when he found his voice. "Get out before you get me killed. He's alpha. I'm his. That's how it is. If he finds out you were here—"

"We can protect you," Jeremy said, but his tone was dull, as if he had already given up hope. He probably thought Malachai wasn't worth protecting.

"I have a pack. I don't *need* your protection."

"But you're here alone," I pointed out.

Malachai's eyes fell on me with hatred in their midst. "Not for long," he said, managing to colour his words with spite.

Jeremy took one step toward him, but the man flinched so violently that my cousin made a scornful sound. "Let's get out of here. Leave the coward to his own devices."

We left the building and walked back to the hotel in silence. Another failure. At least if Ryan was all we had, there was one decent wolf backing us up. I couldn't call Willow a "good" wolf, but she seemed capable enough as long as someone told her what to do. I just wished we had more fighters on our side. Our pack had increased by one, but I couldn't imagine my weepy, attention-seeking little sister would be much use in a fight.

"Have we done enough yet?" I asked. "Are we going home?"

Opa glanced at me. "We're not going home until we have something to go home with. Willow, there are more, are there not?"

She nodded sullenly, her eyes focused on the ground. I hoped Malachai's words about the pack hadn't gotten into her head.

"Willow?" Jeremy coaxed with a gentle tone.

"There are more, but you saw Malachai. We would be lucky to find anyone worth keeping."

"Numbers are numbers," Opa said briskly. "It's the impression we're looking for. Besides, we still haven't found Vin. That wolf obviously hasn't heard from his alpha in a while, which means Vin really is in hiding."

"Or that he doesn't trust Malachai," Jeremy said.

"Either way. He's not in the loop. Vin has to be holed up somewhere. Have you thought of any more locations yet, Willow?"

"We've already been to most of the ones I know about. You saw how deserted they were."

The sites we had visited had mostly consisted of poorly constructed huts in remote parts of woods and mountains and forests. The pack obviously travelled frequently and lightly, whoever the pack consisted of. Willow hadn't been as forthcoming as I imagined, and I couldn't figure out if she was truly ignorant or merely feigning it.

She went to her room as soon as we reached the hotel, which was pretty normal for her after we had visited a pack member she knew.

"Give her some time alone," Jeremy said when Opa protested. "This is difficult for her."

"The journey's only going to get harder," Opa warned.

They launched into a battle discussion, so I headed to my own room for a bit of peace. I lay on the bed and stared at the cracks in the ceiling. It was the only way I could ignore the way the walls closed in on me, the way everything reminded me of Perdita. I didn't want to see new places without her, didn't want to enjoy what the city had to offer if she hated me. The look on her face the last time I had seen her had tattooed itself onto my brain. I would never forget her words, never forget the coolness in her eyes that made her seem like a stranger.

I jumped off the bed in annoyance. I was supposed to be calming my wolf, not agonising it. I found Jeremy and Opa and tried to take part in their conversation, but it turned so often to anger and violence that I felt guilty for even trying to keep up.

"What now?" I asked as we ate together that evening.

Jeremy stopped eating long enough to wait for the answer.

"We'll see what Willow says," Opa said. "Actually, Jeremy, go knock on her door and remind her she needs to eat. We may be gone in the morning, and she needs the energy as much as we do."

Jeremy rolled his eyes, but he obeyed. He came back a couple of minutes later, his body practically vibrating with tension. "She isn't in her room. The door's wide open. Nobody's there."

Opa stared at his food. "Perhaps she went for a walk."

"And left her door open?" Jeremy snapped.

I found it hard to swallow. We were getting used to Willow's eccentricities, but sometimes, after she had seen pack, she was a little harder to deal with.

"This is Willow we're talking about," Opa said calmly. "Let the girl have her space. In the morning, we'll move out. Get away from this place if it bothers her so much."

Jeremy didn't come back to our room until late that night. I knew he had been looking for Willow, despite what Opa said. He knew her better than Opa or I did.

"Willow back yet?" I asked to break the silence.

"No," he replied through clenched teeth. "Like the man said, maybe in the morning."

He tossed and turned for hours, keeping me awake, but even when he finally slept, his snores kept my eyes open. I couldn't remember how many strange rooms I had slept in lately, couldn't remember the last time a bed had felt restful. Once again, I regretted leaving. I had been so upset that I had wanted to put my focus on anything other than feeling. Stupidly, I realised.

In the morning, when we checked her room again, Willow's bed hadn't been slept in. Her clothes were there, and we spotted no signs of a struggle. She had vanished.

"Did she run, or did someone take her?" Jeremy asked, scowling at Opa as if he had been the one to rip her out of our grasp.

"We need to find her," Opa said at last.

We circled the area around the hotel, but we didn't pick up any scents. We were used to Willow not leaving a proper trail; she backtracked and hid her scent without even being aware of it. But there were no distressed scents, nothing that said whether she had been running or taken.

"Malachai," Jeremy grunted when Opa wanted to give up. "She must have gone back to him. She might still be there. Something might have happened."

"Perhaps she's persuading him to leave his pack," Opa said slowly.

Jeremy exchanged a frustrated glance with me. "Fine. Whatever. Let's just go."

"I'll wait here," Opa said, "in case she comes back. You two may run along."

I could tell by Jeremy's expression that he didn't particularly appreciate being spoken to that way, but again, he didn't openly react. Jeremy and I set off together, both of us hopped up on nervous tension.

"You really think she's there?" I asked.

"No, but I think that twit did something." He let loose a growl that startled a pair of passing young women.

"She was never ours, though."

"She wasn't anyone's. The poor thing isn't aware enough to protect herself. Ryan's going to lose his shit." He let out a sigh. "I'm not gonna be the one to tell him."

"We might find her."

"I have a bad feeling. I knew there was something up with her. You know how she gets. I should have paid more attention, stuck by her side more."

I shook my head. "That gets her more agitated. This could have happened any night while we slept. This whole trip has been one massive waste of time. Willow and Ryan should have been kept together."

He shrugged. "Let's just get this over with."

By the time we got to Malachai's flat, Jeremy was noticeably seething with anger. I couldn't concentrate on anything else while he acted that way, but as soon as we stepped inside the building, we both froze.

Blood. We could scent it as clear as anything. With one look at me, he raced up the stairs. I followed, but the werewolf's flat was empty. The door was open, but unlike Willow's, it hung from the hinges.

What little furniture he had was flung about the place, and *there* was the blood. A streak on the wall, a couple of drops on the floor. The scent was strong because it was relatively fresh, but it was covered by traces of numerous strange werewolves.

"Can you pick up Willow, or is that still from yesterday?" I asked, inching my way around the room and struggling to decipher what had happened.

"I can't… I can't tell. There's not enough space, not enough air. Goddamn it!" He leaned his forehead against the one tiny window and gazed outside. "They were here. I can't believe they came here. Why didn't they come for *us*? Why Willow?"

"They didn't want to face us? They wanted Willow to tell them what we were up to? I don't know. Malachai did boast that he wouldn't be alone for long. I mean, how do we know Willow didn't plan this, didn't walk away herself? How do we know we aren't walking straight into some trap?"

He banged the window with his fists, and one thin crack grew along the centre of the pane. "These wolves drive me crazy. We should get back in case they go after Opa. He's an annoying sod lately, but he's still family."

He strode out of the room. I moved closer to the kitchenette, closing my eyes to try and sort through the scents. Willow's blood. Not much, but it was there, in the sink. Along with a long, curled blond hair. Hers, too. I didn't think she had walked away all by herself.

Ryan was going to kill us.

We headed back to the hotel. Opa was fine, which annoyed me all over again. Why wouldn't they come for us, away from innocent people? Why did they have to attack the ones who couldn't defend themselves?

"She's gone," Jeremy told Opa. "There had been wolves in Malachai's flat. There's blood. But she's gone."

"Did you follow the trails? Track them down?" Opa asked excitedly.

"Eh, no, we came straight back here to make sure they'd hadn't gone after you," I said, irritated by his lack of interest in Willow's disappearance.

He made a frustrated sound. "A wasted opportunity. We could have gotten somewhere today."

Jeremy shook his head in disgust.

"We should go back," Opa said.

"No," I said. "I'm going home. I'm sick of this. Willow's gone from right under our noses, and who knows how many wolves are on their way to Dublin? I'm going back. That's where I belong."

Opa sneered. "Where you belong? We wander. You see the other wolves. We might not live in huts in the middle of nowhere, but that is our life, too. We can't stay in one place for too long."

"It hasn't been too long," I said. "It doesn't matter what house I go to because I know where my family is. I know where I should be."

"He can let Dad know exactly what's been going on," Jeremy said, and I smiled at him, surprised and grateful.

Opa growled. "Fine. Go. Protect the house. We'll stay on Willow's trail to see if we can pick up something. Perhaps Malachai will return."

Jeremy's face had hardened again, but I didn't care.

I was going home.

Perdita

I was early to my first day of work experience, but Mrs. Reed glared at me as though I were an hour late. Still, it was preferable to home. Dad had continued to play the grumpy old man all weekend, and Erin's face had grown more and more pinched, her smiles less easy. Something was definitely brewing. It almost seemed as if Dad were *trying* to cause an argument between them.

Mrs. Reed explained what the numbers on the spines of the books meant, and I began the gargantuan task of stacking and categorising what appeared to be a decade's worth of books. I sneezed more often than not, but once I got used to what I was doing, I had time to think. Too much time.

I wondered what Nathan was doing while I figuratively curled up and died in a library stockroom. I brushed myself off and kept going, feeling productive as one stack lowered slightly.

I did everything Mrs. Reed asked, and on my lunch break, I sat outside on the steps, eating a sandwich. It was a beach day, so there wasn't much chance of anyone voluntarily stepping inside the library. There was no tension, no drama, and life seemed normal.

Nice.

Boring.

I brushed that thought away, too, and got back to work. By the end of the day, I felt absolutely scruffy. Mrs. Reed still treated me as though I were likely to steal her purse, and my back ached from bending, but I felt better. Being somewhere new, somewhere I hadn't already made memories, worked for me.

As soon as I got home, everything went back to our family's new idea of normal. Dad wore the same foul expression, and the rest of us walked on eggshells.

"I was thinking we could all go for a drive tomorrow," Erin said over dinner. "The weather's so nice, and we could bring a picnic, have some fun outside."

Dad glared at her. "If I have to sit around, I might as well do it inside where it's cool."

She frowned. "We could do something indoors."

"Not this week," he said in a weary voice.

"It might be good for Perdy to get outside for some fresh air," she said.

"She gets fresh air on her way to the library." His tone turned dangerously cold. "Isn't that right, Perdita?"

Perdita? I gulped. "Yeah, Dad. Who needs fun when you have the library?" I said it lightly, but his eyes grew stern. His eyebrows might as well have been joined together what with all of the furrowing going on up there.

"We both know why you're grounded."

"I know." But I couldn't help glancing longingly at the window, wishing I could be out there doing anything, anything at all, as long as it wasn't sitting at that dinner table with my grumpy father.

"You aren't going out there."

"I know, Dad."

"And speaking of that, hand over your phone."

I gaped at him. "Seriously? What if I have an accident on the way to the library and need to call an ambulance?"

"Perdita."

"Fine." I reluctantly handed over the phone, but it killed me to let go of my last grasp of freedom.

"And stop with the puppy dog eyes. Right now," he snapped.

"I wasn't even looking at you," I muttered.

"She hasn't done anything wrong, Stephen," Gran said, but her voice shook.

Dad glared at her, and she looked down at her plate. For the first time in my life, Dad was intimidating my grandmother, and it was all down to that stupid werewolf bite.

I laid down my fork. "I'm not very hungry."

"No," Dad said. "No more moping."

I stared at him, incredulous. "Look who's talking!"

"Perdy," he said warningly.

"Sorry," I whispered and went back to pushing food around my plate, because I couldn't swallow past the lump in my throat. If I were obedient, he might soften. If I did what I was told, he might get over whatever stage of depression he was going through.

"You don't have to be so hard on her," Erin said. "She's been through a lot, and if her mother—"

"That's enough!" He slammed his palm on the table, making everything jump and clatter.

Erin leaned forward, gazing at Dad unfalteringly. "Do *not* speak to me in that tone. Her voice was low, but she was impressively rock steady. "You can't take it out on us forever, or you might wake up and find yourself alone some day."

"Maybe that's what I need," he said. "Maybe it's the people I'm surrounded by who—"

Erin stood abruptly. "Ruth, Perdy, enjoy your evening."

She turned and left without another word, leaving Gran and me in stunned silence. Dad cleared his throat and stabbed at his food with his fork.

"Dad," I whispered. "Go after her!"

"For what? She wanted to leave."

"Did you hear the way you've been talking to her? I'm surprised she stuck around this long. If you aren't an idiot, then run after her. Like, yesterday."

"Go to your room," he said without looking at me.

"Gladly. Maybe *you'll* stop feeling sorry for yourself while I'm gone." I ran upstairs, and for the next half hour, I could hear Gran and Dad's argument filter upward. The speed in which everything had gone wrong made me shiver. What I wouldn't give to go back, to change everything for the better.

***

I headed into the library early again the next morning, eager to get away from my own home. As far as I knew, Dad hadn't even called Erin, and I feared he was wasting his chance with her.

Sick of sneezing, I decided it would be more beneficial for me to dust the library as much as possible to make the air slightly cleaner. After moving things around in the stockroom the day before, I uncovered a stench that had made me fear something had died in there, so it was definitely time for a spring clean.

Mrs. Reed sat at the counter all day, blowing her nose with old-fashioned handkerchiefs, eating chocolates, and reading a door-stopper of a book. She watched me every now and then with little interest. As long as I kept moving, she didn't seem to care what I did with my time.

The grime clung to my skin, despite my best efforts to clean. I might as well have had a job in a coal mine for the amount of dust clogging up my lungs.

I had my lunch on the steps again, knowing that was about as far as Dad would allow. Before my lunch break ended, Amelia showed up.

"I know you said you couldn't see me, but this is me seeing you, so you have no choice, so it's okay," she said without taking a breath.

"Um, okay?"

"I can stay?"

I thought of Dad. He wouldn't be happy. "I don't think that's a good idea. Dad—"

"Look, I really need to talk to you. It's about your dad."

I straightened. "What about him?"

"There's a lot you need to know. A lot that's happened. Some of it could help your dad." She squeezed her eyes shut. "Potentially help your dad. I mean, I don't know for sure, and I'll need your help trying to figure it out, but I really think we could do this. Fix it."

I stared at my shoes, thinking of how unhappy Dad was, how he had essentially driven Erin away, how all of those things had happened because of me, and I hadn't done a thing to fix them. If I had a chance, even the tiniest chance, of helping Dad get back to normal, I would grab it with both hands. It was worth the risk, worth the aggro, worth anything to help him. "Fine. Talk."

She exhaled loudly and sat next to me. I fought the desire to move away.

"Where to start?" she said, but she sounded excited. "Remember I told you the story of my family, how the curse began and all of that?"

"Yeah…"

"Well, it was all wrong." She flung out her arms. "Everything! I'm being confusing, sorry. I'll start at the… remember when I started having those dreams?"

I stared at her. "Of course I remember."

"Well, they weren't dreams. They were memories. And when I used the spirit board? We heard from my ancestor, and she was the one who sent me the dreams. The memories, I mean."

"I'm just confused now."

"Okay, there was this gypsy girl called Kali, and her father was a chovihano—that's like a gypsy witch—and she was the seventh daughter of a seventh daughter, so she was a werewolf mother."

I squinted. "Naturally."

"Just bear with me. It'll make sense by the end." She giggled. "Hopefully, anyhow. So he was this money-grabbing creep who did some kind of black magic deals to make sure he had seven daughters, because the seventh would be worth a fortune. He was training her to be the *chovihani*, so she would be a witch *and* have werewolf children to protect her clan. He wanted her to be as valuable as possible so he could sell her at the highest price."

She blew out a breath and spoke faster. "But she hated him, didn't want to be sold to the richest potential husband. She fell in love with a non-gypsy, a gaje, but worse, the guy was married. They ran away, had a baby, her father came looking for her to kill her, and the pair of them cursed each other, which kind of screwed up both curses, and her son was basically my first wolf ancestor."

"I thought you said the wolf thing was a good thing to them. Valuable, I mean. So why would that be the curse?"

"Yeah, that's the point. That's never been the curse. The father of the baby gave the child to his wife to raise before he killed himself." She made a face. "And the wife lied about the curse because she didn't want the boy to know she wasn't his real mother. He wasn't cursed to be a werewolf, just to be basically, um, obsessed with finding his soul mate. When he did, he would fall too hard, and the soul mate was destined to die, and he was supposed to go mad, pretty much. But now I've ended the curse, so…"

I thought about Jakob and Byron and was gripped with the fear that it was too late for Nathan.

"Wait," I said. "What's this got to do with my dad?"

"Oh, I didn't tell you the best bit. So Kali, my ancestor, she was stuck when she died. Like, unable to pass over without passing on her power. She kept trying to communicate with me, and she basically asked me to take it, and I said yeah. That's what ended the curse."

"Again, Dad?"

"I have her power. Somewhere. I mean, I don't know for sure if I can use it or anything, but she wasn't just a witch, she was a healer, and if I could find out about that kind of power, about gypsy magic, or even just some healing spells, then maybe—"

"You could help my dad." I thought it over for about ten seconds. "I'm in."

She grinned. "I knew I could count on you. So we need to research, and well, look where you're working."

"Um, it's not that great in there. Selection-wise, I mean. Lots of old books."

"But old books are probably the best place to find the answers. We could find something about werewolf legends that might help, or gypsy magic, or anything even remotely similar. We just need a clue, some idea of where to start."

"What about the spirit board? You said it was Kali who tried to communicate with you before, so why not now?"

She squirmed. "I would rather not do that again, to be honest. At least, not without a bigger group. It wasn't particularly safe what we did."

"Gee, thanks."

"I'm sorry, but it was Kali! She kept influencing me, making me feel things I shouldn't. Once she left me, I was fine again, but she had gone kind of crazy, and that made me a little off."

"Crazy like your grandfather," I said. "Like Byron sometimes. Like… Nathan?"

"Don't say that," she said miserably. "Byron's doing much better now. He's not as cold as he was. He feels like family now. And Nathan's just mad at me."

"But your grandfather?"

She nodded. "He's not getting any better. He's still so determined to get revenge."

"When I saw Nathan, when he came to say goodbye, he was the same. He made it sound like they were out for the kill, like they weren't coming home without blood on their hands."

She rubbed the back of her head, a newly formed habit. "If he comes back to us, he'll be okay. He shouldn't have left in anger like that. It just made him worse. We can't rely on him or Opa right now. We have to figure this out ourselves, and hopefully, find a way to fix your dad."

"Think it's possible?"

She brightened. "It's definitely possible. If only Opa would talk to me more, then I could probably piece the things he knows together to help me. I feel as though there's something locked inside me, and once I have the key, I can really use it to help us all." She looked away, suddenly sad. "It's at times like this that I wish Mémère were here. Her family was different, too. She came from psychic women, and Mémère was still into that kind of thing before she met Opa." She sighed. "So much was lost with her, Perdita."

I patted her hand. "You'll be okay."

She nodded. "I will, just as soon as I figure everything out. Between what Ryan says about the alpha power and what we could do if we can access gypsy magic, maybe we can avoid the whole fight to the death thing, after all."

"I'm so on board with that. But listen, Dad can't find out I've seen you, okay? He's taken my phone, and he won't be Mr. Chirpy if you turn up at the house. Don't say I didn't warn you."

"No problem. I'll just see you here. Maybe you can help me on your lunch break or something."

"I can try. Don't have a clue where to start, but hey, at least we'll be doing something."

She smiled "It's definitely worth a try."

I thought of Dad. *Anything* was worth a try.

Chapter Six

Nathan

I paid the taxi driver with shaky hands and lifted my bag stuffed full of dirty clothes out after me. I stared at our house, at how strange and unwelcoming it looked, and gave a low whistle, but no dogs came running.

Shrugging, I hauled the bag over my shoulder and strolled down the driveway. I couldn't scent anyone around, and I was kind of glad for it.

I let myself in, dumped my bag in the utility room to deal with later, and headed straight to my room. Ignoring the urge to sleep in a familiar bed, I jumped into the shower, thankful for the hot water. I washed away weeks of travel, strange beds, and frustration under the spray.

The house felt as empty as the hollow part in my chest. I headed into the kitchen to see if I could rummage up anything edible. To my surprise, I found the fridge well-stocked, and I spent a number of minutes pulling out things to make a sandwich. It was nice to eat familiar food again, in my own kitchen, in my own house.

It was just a pity nothing else felt the same anymore.

I was halfway through the sandwich when the front door opened and voices filled the hallway. There was a pause, then someone called my name, and three figures hurried into the kitchen, closely followed by some wolfhounds. Cú was the last to enter, and he crept to my side with a low whine.

"Is he okay?" I asked, my voice rising in panic. "I thought the vet said he was healing nicely?"

"He's healthy," Ryan said. "But he's mourning."

"Mourning?" Then I understood. "Oh." He missed Perdita. He had attached himself to her to protect her, and she was gone from him. I leaned over to pat his belly, trying to ignore the lump in my throat at how miserable he looked, at his puppy-like whimpers when he licked my arm. I should have never left him.

Lifting my head, I realised everyone was staring at me. Byron with an unrecognisable gleam in his eyes, Ryan with that same staid patient look that was now familiar to me, and Amelia… Amelia watched me with a little fear. I hadn't left on the best terms with her, and I had to admit, I still carried some of the anger that had driven me away in the first place.

Byron shocked me by rushing over and hugging me. *Byron.* "Good to see you back where you belong," he said, slapping my back.

"Um, thanks," I said, extracting myself from his iron grip.

"News?" Ryan asked.

My stomach churned, and I pushed away the sandwich. "Nothing good. I'm only home to tell you what happened."

"What's going on?" Byron asked, worry obvious in the clench of his jaw.

"Willow vanished," I said.

Ryan's nostrils flared. "What happened?"

I shrugged. "We don't know. Not for sure. Jeremy went to her room to ask her to come eat with us. Her door was open, and she was gone. We waited until the next day, but she still hadn't turned up."

"Jeremy," Ryan spat.

"He didn't touch her," I said. "He helped her. I swear to you, he never hurt her, and he's as pissed as you that they took her."

"They took her?" Ryan asked incredulously.

I ran my hands over my cheeks, trying to settle my head. "That's what we think might have happened. We went to see some werewolf in Lyon who knew Willow. She was a little off afterward, but she's always off, so it's hard to tell. There were no scents around, no sign that Willow ran or was taken from the hotel, so we decided to go back to that same werewolf in case she was there."

"And?" he asked impatiently.

"The place was empty, but the door had been practically ripped off the hinges. There was some blood, and the flat had been turned over. Who knows what happened?"

Ryan paced the room, clenching his fists. "How could you let her vanish from under your noses?"

"We couldn't be on her twenty-four hours a day, Ryan. We did the best we could. We followed her everywhere, and it was all for nothing."

"No werewolves?" Byron asked in surprise.

"Oh, there were werewolves all right. But not many. Mostly one in each occupied place, surrounded by their families. Nobody was interested in doing anything but getting us away from them as quickly as possible. We're bad news as far as they're concerned. Whether they're scared of Vin or just hate us, nobody's going to help, and now we're another wolf down." I shook my head in disgust.

"Is it possible she went back to Vin?" Byron asked.

"That would be signing her own death warrant," Ryan said. "But if she was distressed, it's possible."

"Maybe the wolf we went to see contacted someone, told them we were around. Maybe Willow went to see him. Wrong place, wrong time." I stared out the window, dying for a run. "All I know is we wasted our time out there. We should have been here all along."

"Where's Opa and Jeremy?" Amelia asked.

"Still looking for Willow. Maybe they'll find her and bring her back." I somehow managed to sound way more confident than I felt. I didn't know if she had gone willingly or not, but whatever happened, I couldn't be sure that Jeremy and Opa were safe. I threw the sandwich in the bin in disgust. "I need a run."

"You can't," Amelia said.

"Try stopping me," I snapped.

Byron gripped my shoulder a little harder than necessary. "No, she means you can't run *here* anymore. There's been a regular police presence since you left. They're watching for wolves, dangerous dogs, anything. They reckon we must run dog fights, and they don't seem to have anything better to do, so we've been driving out to hunt. It's a pain, but we don't have much choice."

"You could move on," Ryan said.

I wondered whose side he was on, then wondered when there had become sides to take within my own family. "That's what Opa wants."

Byron hesitated. "Now's not the time."

"Any signs of the werewolves here?" I asked.

"No," Byron said. "But maybe it's because of the garda cars. Maybe they've given up."

"Or maybe they're waiting until we stop looking over our shoulders," Ryan said. "We still need to discuss how we get my daughters back."

"And we will," Byron said firmly. "But we need the rest of the pack back first. We can't go off on any fool's errand right now."

"You mean like Opa is," I said under my breath.

Byron glanced at me sharply. I realised he had made it sound as though Ryan were part of our pack, but that wasn't possible.

I bent down next to Cú, concerned by the listless way he lay on the floor, his breathing scarily shallow. "Maybe we should bring him to the vet again."

"That won't help him," Byron said. "He's lost."

I scratched behind Cú's ears. "That makes two of us. I need to get some rest," I added, seeing the pity in Byron's eyes. "I'm wiped. Wake me if there's any news."

I ran upstairs with a heavy heart. Nothing felt right. Being home wasn't the way I remembered it, and the desperation to escape rose again.

I paused outside Amelia's door, resting my fingers on the handle as I remembered the last kiss with Perdita—our desperate goodbye before she locked herself in the room, and everything changed. A shudder shook my body, and I moved to my room in a hurry. It didn't do any good to dwell on what had been.

I didn't think I would be able to rest, but I fell into a deep sleep almost straight away. I hadn't even undressed or gotten under the covers.

***

I awoke in the middle of the night with a rumbling stomach and decided to search the kitchen again, but I wasn't alone.

Amelia sat at the table, watching me with calm eyes. "I waited up for you."

I groaned. "I'm not in the mood for talking."

"You need to talk. You need to listen, too."

"I'm tired, and I'm hungry. Talk all you want. I don't care." I pulled open the fridge, hearing her tut behind me.

"There's leftovers on the top shelf."

I pulled out a couple of tubs to check if they were interesting.

"You need to talk to her."

An open tub slipped through my fingers and spilled all over the floor.

"Sorry," she said as I swore. "But it's true. She needs—"

"Amelia! I don't want to hear this." I bent to clean up the spill. Pasta sauce. Nice and messy.

"At least let me explain what happened," she pleaded. "I was trying to help everyone. I didn't know what would happen. I

61

couldn't control anything. I tried, but I didn't know how. I wasn't ready for the wolf. Nobody had warned me. I thought everything would be better. The same, except better. I promise you I would never—"

"I'm not interested," I said coldly. "I don't care what you thought or what you did. I'm not interested in any of it anymore."

"Nathan. Stop this. It's stupid. Look at Cú, for heaven's sake."

I stormed out of the room.

"She was going to *die*," she called after me.

I knew she was right. I knew she had done the right thing. But I couldn't face it yet. I couldn't accept that the curse had taken everything except the things I didn't want. I was still a werewolf. I was still hunted by other werewolves.

And I still had all of these crazy feelings for a girl who was probably terrified of my entire family, including me.

Chapter Seven

Perdita

It had been days since Erin walked out of my house, and Dad's mood had gone from terrible to worse. I was more determined than ever to help Amelia uncover all of the madness related to her ancestors, but a solution might come too late to save Dad and Erin.

I hadn't seen Amelia in a couple of days, and I worried she had changed her mind, or worse, that something werewolfy had happened, and I would never know about it.

To keep my mind off things, and in an attempt to make Dad's life better, I decided to take some time after work to go and see Erin. Dad would probably flip about my interference, freak out that I was late home, and find some new thing to be disappointed in me over, but I had to do something. If I could just persuade Erin to wait it out, that Dad would be back to normal soon, then everything would be okay again.

As soon as Mrs. Reed let me go, I sprinted to the bus stop, hopped on the next bus, and travelled into the city to find Erin's flat. I had never been there before, but she had pointed it out one day as we drove by, so I was pretty sure about where I was going.

I had to press a buzzer and wait to be let in, but Erin greeted me at the main door. She notably didn't invite me inside her home.

"Perdy, I didn't expect to see you here."

I shrugged. Now that I was there, I wasn't quite sure what to do. "You didn't come back," I said, rather stupidly.

"That's between your dad and me. I can only do so much."

"But if you could give him a chance, wait around a bit for him to get better, and—"

She held up her hands. "This wasn't my decision. I'm not staying away over one little fight. Your father has made it clear what he wants, so I have to move on. You understand that, right?"

"Not really. He needs you, and you care about him. I know you do."

"It's not that simple. I can't help him right now, and if he needs to be by himself, then he can go ahead. I'm making things worse for you and your Gran by being around."

I sniffed. "He's miles worse without you."

"I doubt that." But she smiled.

"He's... it's not his fault. He isn't well." The werewolf bite was slowly destroying him.

She sighed, and I thought I saw pity in her eyes. "Lots of people aren't well. They don't usually treat those who love them the way he has. I can't sit there and watch it, Perdy. I just can't, and I don't know how to make it better."

"So you're giving up?"

She seemed sad. "It's not my choice. You should get back before he notices you aren't home."

I turned to leave, but she drew me in for a hug. "If you ever need to talk," she said. "I *will* listen. I'm just... it's awkward right now."

I wished I could tell her what was going on, show her there was a reason Dad couldn't help the way he was acting.

Walking from the bus stop, I became convinced I heard footsteps behind me. I glanced around nervously, still stuck in the past, terrified of what might be coming for me. Nobody was there, and I cursed my paranoia. It hit me at random times, leaving me looking over my shoulder, afraid of shadows and ghosts and things that didn't exist anymore.

Dad was standing in the doorway when I finally made it back home. I rolled my eyes at the expression on his face, unable to stop myself.

"Where were you?"

"Nowhere. I'm home now. Leave it alone, Dad."

He followed me into the house, livid with anger. "Were you with *him*? Were you at that house when I specifically said—"

"Oh, Dad. Not now, please. He's gone. He left, okay? Why isn't that enough to satisfy you? I wasn't anywhere near his house."

"A likely story. Where were you, then?"

"At Erin's! Trying to fix your mess!"

He spluttered for a couple of seconds. I could see in his eyes that my visiting Erin was way worse than the idea of me hanging around at Nathan's house. I hadn't realised there was a higher bar of failure, and I gulped down a sudden regret.

"How dare you? How dare you cross that line? Are you kidding me, Perdy? You know better than that. You're never to go there again. Do you hear me? Never!"

The regret quickly turned to irritation. "Enough! I won't be going back because you've messed up for good. You're an idiot! It's bad enough you're trying to ruin *my* life without spoiling the best thing that's happened to you as well."

He shouted my name, but I ran up the stairs, getting a sadistic pleasure from the fact he would struggle to follow me. We couldn't be in each other's presence anymore without an argument breaking out. What was happening to us?

When I finally stopped hiding in my room, Dad refused to look at me, and Gran kept glancing at me pointedly in an attempt to figure out what had happened.

Dad ignored both of us, and Gran followed me upstairs to catch up on the gossip, but she seemed as horrified as Dad about what I did.

"Oh, Perdy. You *didn't*."

"Not helping, Gran."

"I'm sorry, but didn't you think he might explode when he heard? Oh, you're definitely my granddaughter." She covered her smile with her hands.

I giggled. "It wasn't my smartest idea of all time. I'll give you that."

"So how are you getting on at the library? Been tempted to kill that nagging old crank yet?"

"Wait. You know her?"

She sniffed primly. "Of course I do. I can't stand the woman. I swear she sits at home desperately trying to figure out something new and ridiculous to complain about. Did you know she's the one who tried to ban orange flowers in the park?"

"Shut. Up."

She grinned. "Well, maybe that rumour isn't the complete truth. But if she picks on you, tell me, and I'll deal with her."

The reason Mrs. Reed didn't seem to like me became clear. "Um, no, that's okay. I'm doing fine there. No need to go granny commando on her."

She winked at me. "Good to see you in better form. Any other news?"

I lowered my voice. "Amelia came to see me at the library. Think Dad will freak?"

"Maybe today's not the best time to let that one slip," she advised.

"I know. She's different, Gran. She has a boyfriend, she cut her hair, and she seems… happier."

Gran cupped my cheek. "She must miss you if she visited you at that awful library."

I smiled. "Maybe."

***

The next morning, Dad was still ignoring me, and I was more than happy to get to work. The day dragged. I thought about Dad and Erin, about Amelia and how much she had changed, and I did my best not to think about other things.

Amelia's story about her ancestors played on my mind the most. Nathan had grown up believing his werewolf side was a curse, and I wondered how he was coping with the fact it would never go away, that it would always be a part of him, no matter what he did. Then I realised I was standing in the middle of the library, gripping a pile of books as if my life depended on it, while Mrs. Reed watched me suspiciously.

"Sorry," I said. "Spaced out for a minute." I scurried away, feeling like a servant avoiding the eye of royalty.

As long as I kept out of Mrs. Reed's way, I did fine, but if she thought I wasn't working, she began one of her lectures. I didn't understand most of it, probably because I kept zoning out, but on that day, I kept remembering what Gran had said and spent most of the afternoon imagining a senior citizen war.

Amelia hadn't turned up again, and I began to think she had forgotten about me. I was strolling home, my head in another world, when I heard a whimper behind me. I turned and almost fell over when I saw Cú bounding toward me, his lead trailing behind him.

"Cú," I practically squealed, running my hands through his coarse hair as he pressed his entire body against me, whimpering. "Oh, Cú, stop." My eyes watered at his reaction to me, and that might have been why it took me a while to realise he was unlikely to be running around alone.

"Cú!"

I glanced up from the dog just as Nathan turned the corner. My heart skittered, threatening to stop.

He was supposed to be gone. He'd said goodbye. I wasn't ready to see him, not with Cú whining at my feet. I shook my head a little and took a step back.

His hands were stuffed into his pockets, his brow wrinkled in deep thought. I saw his skin, darker than before, his hair, longer than before, and his eyes, just as beautiful. He looked right at me, meeting my gaze, seeming as surprised as I felt.

He bit his lip and stepped toward us. I panicked, took the coward's way out, and ran home.

I couldn't understand my reaction. I had steeled myself for that meeting, made a serious effort to move on, but all it had taken was one look at him, one glance at his eyes, to make it all fall away.

I burst into the house and slammed the door, tears blurring my eyes.

"Perdy?" Dad called. "What's wrong? Wait," he added as he approached the kitchen door and caught sight of my face.

"I can't," I half-sobbed and ran up the stairs, more embarrassed than anything. How could I be so immature and pathetic to completely fall apart because I had seen Nathan? I tried to tell myself I was unsettled by Cú's behaviour, but my reaction to Nathan was the real problem. I had wanted to run into his arms and forget everything else, but that wasn't possible. I had to get away from him before I let Dad down again.

About ten minutes later, there was a knock at my bedroom door. "Perdy, let me in," Dad said.

"No. Not now, Dad. Please."

"I've come up the stairs and everything. It's taken me ages. The least you can do is open the door."

I groaned and jumped up to let him in. He stood there with a sheepish look on his face.

"That wasn't fair," I said.

"I know. Worked though." He tried to smile, but he caught sight of my tears, and his face fell. "Perdy, what's wrong?"

"Now you care?"

He looked away, momentarily shamed. "I'm not... of course I

care. You're… I love you. No matter what, I love you, and I care if you're upset."

"It's nothing, anyway." I sat on my bed. "I'm fine now."

"You're obviously not fine. You've been crying."

I made a scornful noise. "I do *not* cry."

"I know. That's why I'm worried. You can talk to me."

"You'll get mad. I can't tell you anything because you'll hate me." I wasn't talking about Nathan anymore. I was talking about not being able to tell him the things *I* had done.

He inhaled sharply. "I promise not to get mad or hate you." But his grip tightened on his walking stick, his knuckles whitening.

"You *will*. Look at the way you've acted about me seeing Nathan and Amelia. If you knew the truth, if you knew what I had really done…" I shook my head. "I can't tell you anything anymore because I already know how you'll react."

"You don't trust me. What can I do to…? Wait, are we… are we talking about sex? Did you have sex with him? Is that what this is all about?" His face paled. He looked as if he were about to throw up.

I laughed through my tears. "No, Dad. I *wish* that was all it was." At least then I could talk about it to somebody. Preferably not Dad. I made a face. "Let's not have this conversation, though."

"Hey, I'm not keen on the idea either." He watched me for a couple of seconds and swallowed hard. "Please tell me why you're crying. I'll go insane imagining things."

I rubbed my eyes, deciding to go for it. "I was on my way home from the library, and I *saw* him. I got a fright. I mean, I didn't know what to do, and I wasn't expecting to see him."

"What? Who?"

"Nathan!" I hiccupped a sob. "He's back, and I actually ran away. Oh, my God." I pressed my palms against my eyes in despair.

Dad made a noise that sounded suspiciously like a laugh.

I slid my hands down a little to eye him between stretched fingers. "Don't you dare."

He held up his hand. "I did nothing. So what happened then? Did he follow you? Beg you to get back together?"

"No! I ran off, and he didn't do anything." That might have been the worst part.

"What a toad."

"Dad!"

"What? Well, he must be if he just let you go and didn't do... ah."

"Yeah, look who's talking."

"That's different. It just is," he added hurriedly. "So you're crying because you saw him? Or because you ran away? Or because he let you? I'm a little confused."

"I don't know! I didn't expect to see him right there, and Cú was whimpering like he missed me. I got a little overwhelmed, and I cried, okay? Can we get over that detail, please?"

His lips twitched. "We're over it. But you're still upset."

"Of course I'm upset. I *saw* him."

He actually looked pained. "You really like him this much?"

"Well, duh. I really, *really* liked him, but I'm trying not to. I swear, Dad, I'm trying my best to forget about him, but it's so hard, and all I can draw is him. I can't stop."

"Show me."

I stared at him.

"Show me some of your drawings. Come on. I don't have all day."

Frowning, I took a picture out of the bin.

"You throw them away?"

"I told you, I'm trying to forget about him. You demand things and then you act all confused when I follow orders."

He squirmed. "You don't have to call them *orders.*" He flattened the picture out and whistled. "This is, I mean, wow."

"Shut up."

"I'm serious. I can't believe my baby drew this. I'd prefer if it wasn't of the boy who's going to steal her from me, but I can't win every battle."

I laughed and wiped my eyes. "Nobody's stealing me. Like you said, he's a toad."

He grinned and glanced at the picture again. "No wonder you want to go to that art college."

"Not anymore."

"Excuse me?"

"You were right." I shrugged. "It's not something I can rely on. Besides, a portfolio full of Nathan Evans pictures isn't going to nab me a place on any course."

He stared at me carefully. "Are you being serious or overly dramatic?"

I glared at him.

He backed off. "Fine, you're serious. You know I want you to be happy, right?"

"No, actually. Right now, I think you want everyone to be as miserable as you."

"Ah, Perdy, that's not fair."

"The way you've been acting hasn't been fair."

He smoothed the picture again. "Maybe. Okay, definitely. I'm sorry I got mad at you about Erin. But you can't get involved in my relationships like that. Although I'm sorry you felt as though you had to go to her on my behalf."

"But I did have to. You treated her like crap, and she hasn't been back. I mean, really, what's wrong with you?"

"It's not like that. Erin and I want different things right now."

"What could be so different that you can't compromise, or you know, be nice to one another?"

He gave a small smile. "She wants a family of her own, Perdy. Maybe not now, but some day, and I'm not exactly in the best position for that. I mean, look at my track record."

"What?" I stared at him in disgust, completely offended. "I'm such a terrible daughter that it's put you off kids for life? Thanks a lot."

He held up his hands again. "Wow. That's not what I'm saying. Not at all. I'm talking about *me*, Perdy. I'm the crap parent here."

I gave him a blank look.

"Look at you. When was the last time you were happy? When your toad of a boyfriend was around doing who knows what to you?"

"He never did anything wrong to me, Dad. When are you going to start believing me?"

He shook his head. "See? Always saying the wrong thing. Always doing the wrong thing. I couldn't even raise you alone. Maybe your mother would have stuck around if I had been different somehow."

"Dad, don't say that."

"What if it's true? Look at me. What kind of a role model am I? No stable relationships, I've never owned my own home, I've lived with my ex's mother to help raise my child, and now I can't even work. It's pathetic. What kind of provider would I be to another child? What kind of father? I messed up everything with you, and now things are even worse."

"Erin obviously didn't mind."

"*I* mind. You don't understand what it's like to depend on another person so heavily. It's hard to free yourself, hard to see a time when you can go it alone. I can't do this again. I hope you never know what that's like."

"I think I have a fair idea," I admitted, thinking of how the curse made Nathan and I depend on each other in an unhealthy way.

"Everything has fallen apart, and I can't see a way out."

"I wish I could explain it to you," I whispered, tears springing to my eyes again.

"I know. You always want to fix everything, and I've been taking that out on you. I was so afraid for you when I thought Nathan had to be hurting you. Between that and the attack and your mother turning up, it's been too much for me to handle. I feel like I can't protect you."

"But, Dad, you don't have to do everything. I'll be finished with school in a year, and chances are I'll be taking care of myself. So what will you be left with?"

He stared at his hands. "I may never get better. How can I inflict this on another person? It's bad enough that *you* have to live with me."

"And what if you get better tomorrow? Or next week? What then? You'll be alone out of stubbornness."

He shook his head. "Maybe you're right. But I'm not a good person to be around right now. I feel angry all of the time, and I don't even know why."

I had a fair idea. The same reason the werewolves got angry easily. Except Dad couldn't hunt and burn off the excess energy. Dad was stuck.

"It'll be okay," I said. "I promise you I'll figure something out."

He smiled. "I love that about you. That you don't give up."

I stared at the page in his hands. "I give up."

"Will you ever tell me the truth about him?"

"His secrets aren't mine to tell," I whispered. "But he's never hurt me. He's gone out of his way to make sure I'm safe. If you can believe anything, believe that. I miss him, but I've kept my promise to you, Dad. If you don't want me near him, I'll stay away."

He wrapped an arm around me. "You're stronger than me. That's hard for a father to say, trust me. But you are. I know you'll get through everything that's upsetting you. Why don't you do something fun for your birthday?"

"You remembered?"

"I could never forget the day you were born," he scoffed. "Arrange something with Joey and Tammie. Maybe even Amelia. But not at her house. The police are still investigating, and I don't want you getting wrapped up in whatever's going on."

"Maybe. And maybe you should call Erin."

"I need time to think." He got to his feet. "I appreciate the effort you've made. I might not always show it, but I've noticed. I'm glad you're able to be mature enough to realise that sometimes what we love isn't necessarily the best thing for us."

"Are you talking about Nathan or art college?"

He groaned. "Why did *he* have to spring to mind when I said love? We're talking about art college, okay? Before you give me a stroke." But he winked at me as he left, and the weight on my shoulders grew a little easier to bear.

Chapter Eight

Nathan

She ran away from me. Did she actually think I could ever hurt her? Maybe when the curse broke, she saw what we were—monsters—and decided to keep as far away from us as she could manage. I couldn't blame her.

I had been spending as much time in the abandoned house Perdita and I had hung out in as possible. Byron, Ryan, and Amelia kept acting as though nothing was wrong, leaving me uncomfortable. Besides, I sometimes imagined I caught her scent in our hiding place.

I had gone straight home, dragging Cú with me. The poor dog had been so delighted to see her that he tried to follow her. I didn't want to get her in trouble with her Dad by being seen around her house, so I let her go and watched her walk away... again.

As I stepped through the front door of my house, I heard Byron's laughter echoing in the hallway. Curious, I kept going.

"Maybe tomorrow, then," he said in the phone when he noticed me. "We'll talk soon." He hung up.

"Opa?" I asked hopefully.

"No." He paused. "A friend."

Since when did Byron have friends?

"Well, let's get you fed," he said. "Don't want you going on the same starvation diet as Amelia."

Amelia was already in the kitchen, laughing at something Ryan had said. When she saw me, her smile faltered.

"Not too much milk," Byron said to Amelia. "Don't really relish the idea of seeing that again."

The three of them chuckled, highlighting how I no longer fit in with them. I grabbed some stuff to make a sandwich, listening to the three chatting and joking.

After another lame joke by Byron had Amelia in stitches, I interrupted. "What the hell is wrong with you? Willow's missing. Opa and Jeremy are in danger searching for her. Vin's pack could come after us at any time. What on earth is so funny?"

They all sobered, exchanging glances.

"Why not enjoy the time we have together?" Byron asked.

I shook my head. "We should be worrying. We should be planning. We should be doing something. Not *this*."

"Nathan," Byron said. "We aren't going to spend the rest of our lives looking over our shoulders. If they come, we'll defend our territory, but we're not going to run. This is our home, and we're going to relax in it."

Ryan nodded, and as I glanced from one face to another, I was startled by how solid a grouping they had become, how tightly knit. What had changed?

"Yeah, well, while you lot have been at home in comfort playing happy families, we've been wandering around getting doors slammed in our faces. There aren't enough of us to beat them."

"There are enough of us," Byron said. "And we have a secret weapon." He inclined his head at Amelia.

I almost choked on my scorn. "Amelia? A weapon? Have you lost your mind?"

"No, but apparently *you* might have." Byron's words were

coloured with amusement.

Amelia said, "If you actually let me talk to you for more than five minutes, you might know—"

I threw my hands in the air. "I don't get it. I'm going to my room."

"We hunt tonight," Byron said in his commanding alpha voice. It wasn't a request.

Once in my room, I fidgeted constantly. I was back to waiting, except I no longer had Perdita to calm me.

I had to see her.

I couldn't see her.

I argued with myself for hours, until finally, I left for her house. I didn't get to the end of the road before her face flashed before my eyes. I saw her expression from when I hadn't protected her from Amelia and when she had run from me on the street.

Ryan's words echoed in my mind. I kept her safe by staying away from her. I protected her by avoiding her. While it had once been easy to say I would do whatever it took to keep away from my mate, that was before we had met. Even if the curse was gone, even if she was done with me, my wolf still saw her as mate. I still saw her as the girl I wanted to be with more than anything.

I turned around and headed for home, but I hesitated outside my house, unable to give up on her. I couldn't go; I couldn't stay. I didn't know what the right thing to do was anymore.

Ryan approached me, and I sat on our front wall.

"You need to focus," he said, "not let yourself get distracted. This is more important than a girl. You still understand that, right?"

I shifted slightly to look at his face. Worry lines on his forehead assured me he was talking about his own family and how important it was for him to get them back. We owed him, and we still had to deal with the wolves who had torn my family apart in more ways than one.

"I'm not distracted," I said. "I just need to know—"

"She's fine. She's not your priority. Not right now. When your life is safe, then of course, deal with her. But now? Not a good idea, Nathan."

He went inside, leaving me unsettled all over again. I didn't want to hear that from him, of all people.

I strolled around to the swings and sat on one, swaying, until Amelia joined me.

"I need to talk to you," she said. "Please, talk to me."

"I'm tired of talking."

But she looked at me with those puppy dog eyes, and I couldn't walk away.

"I'm sorry I didn't warn you," she said in a low voice. "But I was trying to help. You don't understand what it's like for me. You've all hidden things from me, made me think everything was fine when it really wasn't. I was so mad about that, and I wanted to do something brave. Like Perdita. You all looked at her like you were proud of her, like you *respected* her, and I fell apart when I was needed. You all looked at me as if I were some little kid who couldn't be trusted. And you were all right. If I had been like her… maybe Mémère would be alive today."

"Or maybe you would be dead, too," I said, sitting up straight. "You can't think like that."

"But you still treat me like I'm incapable of making a difference. I *wanted* to make a difference. I don't need to be protected from everything. I'm a werewolf now, but even if I wasn't, I still deserve some credit. I can help. I don't have to be sheltered from the truth all of the time."

"That's what families do."

"No, families stick together. That wasn't what happened with us. Even now, you're still mad at me. What am I supposed to do? You would have been madder if she had died and I could have stopped it!" She walked off in a strop.

By the time for the hunt, I was more than ready for the release. We couldn't bring the dogs while the gardaí watched us in case they followed us, so we headed out for the hunt alone. The two-hour drive was silent and uncomfortable, but eventually, we came to stop in a rural area.

"Careful where you go," Byron warned. "Farmers will shoot without hesitation. Remember that if you get too close to livestock."

I was the last to shift forms. Again. The mental block infuriated me. My stress prevented the wolf from taking over. I phased slowly, painfully, listening to the sound of splintering bones. I let the wolf take over, but that was worse since I wasn't fuelled by an all-consuming anger. I lay down, giving up, and wolf howled louder than ever before. A mournful howl full of anguish and release.

Byron and Ryan lay on either side of me. Amelia lay before me and nudged my nose. My heart stopped slamming as violently against my chest. Slowly, I calmed.

The pain was ripe and new because I hadn't given wolf the chance to mourn yet. He was dealing with the breaking of the bond, the ending of the curse, the loss of mate. I might have gone wild with pain if the others weren't there helping me through it.

For the first time, we were a real pack, a real team, even with Ryan there. I understood how easily I could lose myself, one way or another, without them. I realised I needed their help to ground myself when things got tough. I was shocked Byron hadn't bitten off my tail for being such a baby about everything. His mate had died. Mine had walked away. I still had the chance to make things right. If she needed time, I would wait.

I ran then, wild and free, buoyed by a spark of hope. I was usually the fastest, but Amelia kept up with me. I held a grudging respect for her speed, but she was so small that my protectiveness didn't fade despite the realisation that my baby sister no longer needed me. There was no danger, nothing but tracks to run on and small animals to chase. It was heaven to wolf. Running with the pack healed me, but letting go of the pain helped.

Back at the car, I finally understood how comfortable I could be with the trio. Being around Opa, Jeremy, and Willow had kept me on edge. I belonged at home.

Amelia threw up. A lot. I only gagged, thankfully.

"Feeling any better?" Ryan asked on the way home.

"A little," I admitted.

"It gets easier," Byron said. "Less raw."

"Maybe."

"It's the right thing to do for her," Ryan said. "Safer for her."

"Is it?" Amelia murmured. She caught me looking at her and shrugged. "It's just that she has nobody right now. She's going through a really hard time. Her dad's still sick, she's grounded, and she has to be away from you, too." She shook her head. "I don't think she's happy."

"She's not feeling this like I am," I said. "It's the wolf making it hard."

She gazed at me in disgust. "You're such an idiot."

I opened my mouth to protest, but Byron cut into the potential argument. "It *will* get easier."

"Opa doesn't seem any better," I said.

"He's not letting himself," Amelia replied. "He wants to feel this. It's the one thing that's keeping him going. When it's over, we won't see him anymore." We all stared at her until she turned beetroot red. "I know him. He's choosing to be like this. And so are you."

"What's that supposed to mean?"

"You don't *have* to keep away from Perdita."

"Amelia, she saw me on the street and ran for her life."

Byron burst out laughing. "Sorry. It's just… sorry."

"Crap." Amelia rubbed her temples. "I hadn't told her you were back."

"You've seen her?" She hadn't even told me. Then again, I hadn't exactly been inviting conversations with her.

"Yeah. Not at her house, obviously, because her dad's gone crazy. But she's doing work experience at the library, and she's, um, helping me with something. I haven't had a chance to go see her since you came back."

I leaned back in the seat, imagining all sorts of scenarios that would have me needing to go to the library.

"You look calmer," Ryan noted.

I nodded. "I was pretty anxious with Opa and the others. Running with you lot felt much better."

"That's the secret weapon I was telling you about," Byron said.

"What are you on about?"

Amelia's cheeks flushed. Ryan half-turned in his seat. "I have a theory about your sister."

I raised an eyebrow.

"I think she's an omega. They're very rare, usually female, and I'm pretty sure it's what she is."

"Right. What's an omega?"

"An omega is balance in a pack. They say every pack needs an omega as much as it needs an alpha. You see our wolves, wild as anything, right? That's because there's no omega keeping them calm. It's like the wolf is on a different level, kind of highly strung, and if there's no omega around, we erupt at nothing. Anger, rage, pain, it's all exaggerated. The omega lowers the frequency somewhat. If we get the better of Vin's pack and have an omega, it could increase our odds of peace."

"That's kind of cool." I glanced at my little sister, shocked at the idea she could be important.

"Oh, that's nothing," she said with a grin. "There's a *lot* we have to catch up on."

Chapter Nine

Perdita

I didn't know whether to be surprised or not when Amelia turned up at the library. But I guessed if she was ever going to show, it would likely be after I had encountered, and run from, her brother.

"You saw him," she said, following me around the library.

"Yep."

"You ran."

I refused to look at her. "Kinda got caught off guard. Besides, what else was I supposed to do? It's awkward for everyone, and being near him is forbidden by Dad. It's for the best. We were crazy together. You remember that, right?"

"He thinks you're scared of him. I think he feels like you're seeing him for what he is now."

"What? The werewolf thing? Okay, it's weird, but it was always weird. That hasn't changed. I'm still banned from seeing him, Amelia. And if I had stayed there, I might have… I might have made a mistake."

"You're banned from seeing me, too."

I grinned and faced her. "Not anymore. I'm allowed to do

something for my birthday. *You* can even be there."

She clapped her hands. "I have the absolutely perfect thing! My friend Ger, you remember her, right? Well, her parents are going away for an entire weekend, and she wants to have a small party. Small as in, don't tell the whole school, m'kay? You *have* to come. It's next week, so I know it's before your birthday, but it's a party, and your dad's not going to organise anything when he's sick, so whaddaya say?"

"Um, remember to breathe? I'll ask him. Can't guarantee anything, though."

"Well, if not, we could go to the pictures or something. It's just... I'd love if you got to know my friends. I kinda talk about you a lot, and they're beginning to think I'm your stalker."

"Yeah, right. I said I'd try. Are you here to browbeat me into anything else?"

She stuck her tongue out at me. "No, I'm here for research, biatch." She cleared her throat. "Sorry, it's the Julie effect. Never mind. You'll understand at the party. So, there's something we haven't talked about yet. Ryan reckons I'm an omega, and I'd really like to find out more about that, too."

"What's an omega?"

"He says it's a type of werewolf, something the packs need to keep their cool. Like, the curse made the werewolves calm down when they have their mate? Well, the omega keeps everyone calm, all of the time."

"That would be amazing." I thought about the things I didn't like about Nathan's family, how the aggression and wildness could be easily handled if Amelia really was an omega. I was beginning to understand the anger since I was faced with Dad's on a daily basis.

"I think so, too. I don't know a lot about it, so I'd love to learn more."

"Cool. It's my break in about an hour, but we can find some books now. You can get started, and I'll join you on my lunch."

Finding suitable books was more difficult than we thought.

Everything about werewolves turned out to be obscure fairytale crap that had no bearing on reality. We eventually found two books about werewolf legends that we thought might be useful, but it was even harder to find stuff on gypsies.

"Maybe we'll just look that stuff up online."

She made a face. "I've tried that, and I keep coming up with nothing. They keep schtum, apparently. Well, this will be a start."

An hour later, she was still slogging through one of the werewolf books when I sat next to her.

"Nothing yet," she said, pushing the other book in my direction.

The book was dull and hard to read, but it contained a couple of interesting werewolf theories. Sadly, they mostly involved skin-walking and full moons. The day seemed to be a bust. Then a brief paragraph caught my eye.

"Oh," I said. "This is cool. Says here that some gypsies believed in white werewolves—white as in pure—protecting them from the dead. Back then, people were terrified of death. Apparently there were random cases of mass hysteria stemming from fear at that time."

"Fear of werewolves?"

"No, vampires. You don't think…?"

Her eyes widened. "No! Definitely not. Vampires are a total myth. Still, the hysteria thing is interesting because Kali said it was a side effect of the curse. That her people were rejected even more than they were before. Persecuted. Like some big domino effect. Kind of chills me."

"It's a pity there's not many details about that stuff. But the white werewolves would go with what you've told me about your ancestors."

She nodded. "It does fit in. It's frustrating though, not being able to learn more than what we can make out from a few random lines in a book."

"Maybe we won't find anything else."

"We'll keep trying, though, right?" she asked.

"Of course."

***

On the way home from the library that day, I felt more upbeat than usual. Seeing Amelia again made me happy. Since Dad had given the okay, it was even better.

Once we got past the initial awkwardness, having her back was a relief. I used to act like a weird paranormal junkie sometimes, desperate for a little more insight into the werewolves, for a little more involvement in their lives.

So I could get my dose of werewolf drama with Amelia, except without the danger. I was dying to know what she was going to discover about herself and her pack. The stuff with Kali had been strange enough, but finding out how to use a power that shouldn't exist would be fantastic. I was more onboard with the idea than I would ever have expected. Maybe I was opening my mind or something.

Or maybe I needed something to fill my head and take up my time.

I heard footsteps behind me two streets away from my home. A chill ran down my spine, and I turned, ready to run, adrenalin pumping through my body.

I breathed a sigh of relief. "Ryan."

The red-haired wolf nodded at me, his expression grim. That seemed to be his default face, though, so I wasn't overly concerned.

"How are you?" he asked.

"Okay. You?"

He shrugged. "Same as always. He told us you saw him, that you ran from him."

My cheeks heated up with shame. "I—"

"I'm glad," he said. "I'm here to ask that you stay away from him, no matter what he does."

I frowned. "What?"

His shoulders dropped, and he rubbed the space between his

eyebrows. "Perdita, now is a bad time. A dangerous time. Keeping away will ensure your safety for a while. And you'll stop distracting him."

"Distracting him? But I haven't—"

"I know," he said. "*Yet*. I'm asking that we keep this the way it is. At least for a while."

"But, Ryan—"

"You have plenty of time, Perdita. My daughters don't. Keep away from him, no matter what. I'm asking you for this favour. I'm asking you not to get in the way."

I shivered. "I'll… I'll keep away."

"Thank you. What is it you're doing with Amelia?"

"Um, what do you mean?"

"I catch your scent from her clothing every now and then. I need *her*, too."

"I'm helping her."

He nodded. "I thought that might be it. Make sure that's all it is."

"What the hell, Ryan? Are you threatening me?"

His jaw tightened. "I'm not threatening you. I just want you to know that I need her to unleash her power, too. But her focus has to be on the priority."

I thought of Dad and swallowed hard. "Which is?"

"Finding my girls. This isn't a game, Perdita."

I glared at him in annoyance. "I've been almost killed once or twice. I know it's not a bloody game, Ryan."

"Things change. I had to make sure we were still on the same page. Good luck to you, Perdita. Keep yourself out of trouble." He walked away, loping along like the animal I knew him to be.

I already knew what I was doing. I didn't need him warning me off or giving me hope that Nathan might want more from me.

At home, although Dad was just as short-tempered, the tension had lessened significantly, and I figured it was as good a time as any to bring up the subject of the party, except I wasn't going to use that word. Not unless Joey could come up with something really good to trade.

I brought Dad a cup of tea and some of his favourite biscuits. "So… about my birthday…"

Dad smiled. "This is going to be good."

I cocked my head to the side. "Dad, I'm a responsible teen. And I'd really like to partake in a friendly gathering next weekend in an attempt to make some new friends."

"Is Joey going?"

"I don't know. I could ask him, but I don't have a phone."

Dad gave me a wry look. "Fine. It's in the press next to the fridge. Take it. Do your worst."

"So I can go?" I jumped from one foot to another, anxious.

"If Joey goes, you can go. It's not that I don't trust you; it's that I don't trust anyone else." He grinned. "But I hope you have a great time with your cousin watching your every move and cramping your style."

"Funny." I hugged my father. "Thanks, Daddy."

He waved me away. Although he held the happy expression, there was a haunted look in his eyes, a hollow space that made it clear he was putting on a mask.

Gran gave me a thumbs-up as I passed through the kitchen, and I convinced myself that things were getting better. We were going to be okay. If I didn't think about Nathan, I could imagine life was perfect.

I called Joey to invite him to the party.

"With a gang of fourth years?" he asked.

"Technically, they're fifth years," I said swiftly.

"I don't know. Sounds kind of lame."

"What else do you have to do? Come on. You said you wanted me to get back to normal."

"Since when are parties normal for you, Perdy? Why are you so excited about it anyway?"

"Because I'll be somewhere other than home or the library. I'm bored, Joe."

He heaved a sigh. "I'll think about it, okay? And I said, *think*."

"I hope you say yes because I haven't seen you in ages, and I miss you so much."

He snorted. "Laid it on way too thick there. How are you getting on in the library?"

"She hates me, but other than that, it's fine. Sometimes Amelia pops in."

"For what?"

"To get her daily dosage of the awesomeness that is me. What do you think she's in for? To read books, of course."

"Really? To read books."

"You're so suspicious," I said lightly. "Anyway, I had better go. Text me when you make up your mind about the party. Don't forget it will be my *only* birthday celebration."

I hoped he wasn't too interested in what Amelia was doing in the library.

Chapter Ten

Nathan

An excessive amount of perfume wafting from my sister's bedroom indicated she was going out. With a boy. I decided to wait outside to see if he was picking her up or not. He did arrive—I grudgingly gave him a point—but he showed up with a group of friends, which automatically lowered him in my estimation.

I sat on our gate, and as the group approached, one of them spotted me and whispered something to *the* boy. They all hesitated, glancing at each other nervously, leaving wolf satisfied by the petty win.

He moved forward, closely followed by the rest. They pushed together, narrowing the group as if they were a herd of frightened deer. I let the wolf show in my expression, in my smile, and the boy swallowed hard.

Surprising me, he held out his hand. "Connor," he said, and his voice only trembled a little.

I gave him a real grin and shook his hand. "Nathan."

Two girls and three boys, probably none of them more than fifteen or sixteen, stared at me as if they couldn't believe I existed or something. Their wide-eyed interest made me want to laugh.

If Perdita had been born a month later, she would have been in their year. If I hadn't messed up so badly so many times, hadn't moved around so frequently, I might have bypassed school in Ireland altogether. Ifs and maybes could have kept Perdita and me apart until after the curse had broken. I couldn't help wondering how that would have gone down.

Two teenage girls giggling and whispering together distracted me, and I wished Perdita was with me to see the lot of them. They were in absolute awe. Why? I had no idea, but I suspected Amelia might have told them some untruths to impress them.

"Where are you heading tonight?" I asked Connor.

"Just into town to grab a bite to eat. Maybe hang out at the arcade."

"How are you getting there?"

He hesitated. "Um, a bus?"

I raised a brow, and his cheeks flushed with colour.

"I mean, we could get a taxi if… if—"

Amelia came up behind me and punched my arm. Laughing, I almost fell off the gate.

"Stop trying to freak him out," she scolded.

"I'm just sitting here." But I got down and opened the gate for her.

"I'm going out," she said, as if challenging me.

"I can see that."

"Yeah, well…" She glanced at her friends. "We should be going."

"Have a good time," I said, but I stared at Connor.

His eyes twinkled, and I saw he understood. He wouldn't hurt her, even if I wasn't around. That settled me down. Not that any of them were likely to have the strength to physically harm Amelia anymore.

My sister hesitated, watching me with worried eyes. "You can come with us if you like. Instead of hanging around here."

Instead of moping about Perdita, she meant.

"I've got some stuff to do tonight," I said. "Seriously, have a good time."

"You can come to my party next weekend," a girl with an impossible amount of freckles said. "I mean, if you wanted."

"Yeah," her friend said eagerly. "You should definitely come."

Amelia rolled her eyes and grabbed their arms. "We're going. Tell Byron I won't be too late."

I watched them walk away; Connor took her hand as soon as they were a safe distance away from me. It was so normal for her, and I desperately wished I could have given that to Perdita.

Ryan was gathering the dogs when I returned to the house.

"You don't have to do that," I told him.

"I need time to think," he said. "I'm worried about Willow. Need to think about what Vin might do next."

I shrugged. "They could be on their way back and haven't had the chance to call."

"I doubt that."

Cú stayed behind, and I made him lie on the sofa while I sat on the floor next to him.

"I think that's the wrong way around," Byron said from the doorway.

"He's not well."

"He's doing better than he was."

I stared at him. "Why's Ryan staying here?"

"You expected him to live in a hotel? He's pack now. Got a problem with that?"

I almost smiled at the protective tone in Byron's voice. "It's not that. I'm just baffled by the way everyone trusts the dude after ten minutes."

Byron showed his teeth. "It took longer than that. He stood next to us, possibly forsaking everything he holds dear. He protected Perdita when you couldn't. I think he's earned his place."

My ears burned as the blood ran straight to my head. Boiling with anger, I spluttered something, but he held up his hands to stop me.

"Don't," he said. "Don't even say it. That's the point of a packmate: to do what you can't when the time comes, to have your back. He did what he had to do, and you should be grateful he was there."

"But how can he be pack if he's not family? I mean, it's always been family only."

"Family, and a pack, is more than what you're born into, Nathan. He helped us. When you ran, he stayed and helped me with Amelia. He defended the house with me. He's kept watch over Perdita while you've been gone, just in case. Don't tell me he isn't family when he's done all of the things a family member would do."

I looked away, chastened.

He sat on the floor next to me. "It's okay, Nathan. Nobody's expecting you to be strong every second of every day, but the point of a pack is to be able to lean on each other, to work together to protect all of us. I'm still learning that myself, so don't feel bad if it takes you time to get used to it."

"That's what I'm mad about, though, that he was the one who protected Perdita. Why did I freeze? Why couldn't I move? She looked at me like…" I ran my hands over my face. "I'm like some idiot kid who doesn't know what he's doing. I've brought trouble, and I wasn't there when it counted. I can't take that back, and I don't know what to do about it."

"She's alive. That's what matters. I couldn't save Diana. Nobody else could either. There was no doctor who could keep my wife alive. I couldn't save your parents. I couldn't save my own parents. I couldn't keep my son by my side. And I wasn't a teenage boy for any of those things."

"It wasn't like that. You can't blame yourself for any of that."

"Then you can't blame yourself either. You're so much like your father—always seeking perfection. It doesn't exist. It never will. You'll drive yourself mad looking for something that isn't there. You have to make the best of what you have."

"I don't know what that means," I said sullenly.

"It means you have to stand up and be the person you're supposed to be, instead of the person you think you should be. It means that you can't keep pining after what the curse gave you, or what it took away, when you could be making the most of what's there now."

I sighed. "I knew what the curse meant, though. I knew what I was getting into. Now, there's so much uncertainty. I don't know what I'm doing."

"You still care about her," he said.

"Of course I do."

"Then what's the problem? Why can't you try again, this time without the curse?"

"It's not that simple. It's... I've done things only the curse could make her forgive. I've acted stupidly. And I'm afraid to ruin whatever she has going on now. Maybe too much time has passed. Maybe she's disgusted with what I am now that the curse isn't glossing everything over."

"Are we still talking about what happened when Amelia changed for the first time? You were in shock. I doubt the girl would hold that against you."

"It's not just that. I've been working with the wolves who stalked her and hurt her father. I told her that I wasn't going to stop hunting the werewolves until I made sure they couldn't hurt anyone again. I made it sound like I was... the kind of person she wouldn't like. I think I've ruined the way she sees me. I was so angry, and I don't think her perception of that will change again."

"Don't you think she deserves the choice?"

"I told you she ran away from me. I'm terrified she won't ever want to see me again, that I've messed up for good. I don't know anything for sure anymore."

"That's the way it's supposed to be. No destiny, no guarantees. It's normal. Healthy. And you need to stop moping about. Learn to have fun without her. She can't always be around for you, even if you are together."

"I know that, but what we had was a certain way, and I don't think I know how to have normal now. She hated the way the curse made us feel. She kept trying to fight it. And she's still that same stubborn girl, except now there's no magic forcing her to be with me. Maybe Ryan's right about keeping her safe this way, and maybe I have no right to try and push this life on her. Maybe I should be giving her time. I don't know anymore."

No matter what I said, I still couldn't convey how I really felt. What if my life would never be close to normal? What would I be dragging her into, even if she were willing? I wished I could talk to her, but I knew her dad had major hate for me. I didn't want to make life harder for her.

***

Amelia came home earlier than expected.

"Something wrong?" I asked my sister as she flung herself into a chair.

"Nah. Just tired. Been worrying about you."

"Why?"

"You look so depressed all of the time. You should have come out with us."

I snorted. "To be stared at like a performing monkey all night? No chance. Besides, your boyfriend would have pissed himself if I had said yes."

"No, he wouldn't have. The others, maybe." She grinned cheekily. "They're just in awe of you because they saw you beat up Aaron, that's all."

I stared at the floor, uncomfortable with the memory of losing control at school.

"You could come to that party, though. They only asked because they wanted sixth years there, and they thought you could produce them."

"Charming."

"It might be fun."

"Maybe," I said, still thinking of my conversation with Byron. Maybe he was right. I needed to know what it was like to have time away from werewolves, curses, and destinies. I knew Perdita wouldn't be there because she was grounded. "Maybe I'll bring someone."

Amelia's face lit up. "Really?"

I shrugged. "Why not?"

I didn't want to go to the stupid party, but I had been such an idiot to my sister that I felt I should do something to make it up to her, and at least I could drag along the few friends I had left to make it slightly more bearable. "Maybe it will be good to do something normal before the summer holidays are over."

"Enough of that talk. Plenty of summer left."

The sound of the front door opening drew our attention. Hearing voices, I followed Amelia out into the hall to see Opa and Jeremy dropping their bags on the floor. No Willow. Ryan stood next to Byron, his eyes alert as he waited for news.

"No sign," Jeremy said. "We couldn't find a trace of her. We came home in case she talked, told them how we had split up. We thought we should be together."

"For her sake, I hope she talked," Ryan said, and his pronouncement chilled me to the core.

Opa and Jeremy both looked exhausted, and I felt guilty for leaving them.

"Go get cleaned up while we get a meal ready," Byron said. "We can talk over food."

The pair trudged up the stairs, and the rest of us followed Byron into the kitchen.

"Do you think she's okay?" Byron asked Ryan.

He shook his head. "Hard to say. Last time I took her punishment for her. This time… let's just hope she isn't in their hands. She's not worth enough for Vin to care about."

We speculated while we prepared the food, and when Opa and Jeremy were ready, the lot of us sat around the kitchen table.

Jeremy dug into his food eagerly. "What's with the police car outside?" he asked between bites.

"Keeping an eye on us. Hoping to catch some wolves," Ryan said.

Jeremy's eyes narrowed, and I wasn't sure if it was because of the answer, or who had responded.

"That's probably played into our favour," Opa said. "But Vin holds all of the cards. He likely has Willow and knows the curse has broken, and he surely knows that Amelia's a werewolf."

"Which ups her value," Ryan said. "He has my daughters, too. Don't forget."

"Nobody knew anything about them," Opa said. "We asked along the way."

"Except for Malachai," Jeremy said.

I swallowed hard. I hadn't told Ryan about that for a reason.

"Malachai?" Ryan asked.

"The last wolf we saw. Willow knew him, and we think there's a good chance they took her at his place. He's the one who took your girls." Jeremy stared Ryan down, waiting for his reaction.

"You knew?" Ryan asked me.

I nodded. "I didn't know how to… what good it would do to tell you that right now. He's gone, too."

Ryan jerked his head forward a couple of times, taking deep breaths. "Remind me what he looks like if he ever reappears."

A tense silence reigned for a couple of moments. Amelia shifted uncomfortably in her seat.

"We run together tomorrow," Byron said at last. "To cement the pack."

Jeremy's fork fell. "With him?" He jerked his head at Ryan.

"Yes, with him. He's stood with us. That makes him one of us."

"But he's not blood," Jeremy said, sounding way too much like me. I cringed at how whiny I must have sounded to Byron.

Byron stared at his son. "Pack is more than blood. It's time we started living the way we're supposed to." He gazed around the table. "And that means one alpha."

Opa leaned forward. "And that's you?"

"You know it's me," Byron said steadily. "But if anyone wants to challenge me, do it now so we can save ourselves some time."

Nervous silence filled the room until Byron spoke again. "Good."

"I still don't trust him," Jeremy said as if Ryan wasn't in the room. "The places he and Willow sent us to were mostly empty. Abandoned. Vin was nowhere to be found. How do we know he isn't setting us up?"

"You weren't supposed to be looking for Vin," Byron said, his voice rising slightly.

"We had to try," Opa said.

"And his info was crap," Jeremy added.

"Did you really think Vin would hide out in a place I've been? A place I've heard about? He isn't stupid. Don't underestimate him."

"Stupid enough," Jeremy muttered.

"Stupid enough?" Ryan echoed, holding Jeremy's gaze. "You think you know more than him, pup? You think you've seen as much as him? He's one of the most intelligent werewolves I've ever met, and don't you forget it. He may be cruel and sadistic, unbalanced even. He may make decisions based on the kind of logic that would never apply to a normal person. But never mistake how intelligent he is when it counts."

Jeremy leaned forward, and the tension racketed upward. "Whose side are you on anyway?"

"My side," Ryan said. "My daughters' side. Anyone who shares the same enemy as I do. This is about survival. It's not a pissing contest, pup. It's about time you took this seriously."

Jeremy leapt to his feet, Ryan following less than a second later.

"That's enough," Byron bellowed. "Nathan, deal with Jeremy."

"Nathan?" Jeremy gasped as Byron led Ryan away. "*Nathan...* deal with me?"

Byron fixed a chilly stare at his only son. "You heard me. Remember who's in charge here, son. And remember what we're all here for. It's not to tear each other apart."

Byron turned his back on Jeremy, and I jumped in the way to block Jeremy's lunge.

"What the hell are you doing?" I hissed as he slammed me against the wall.

Opa walked out of the room as if nothing was happening. Amelia stood at the door, and I wanted to tell her to run, but I had to remember to stop treating her like something delicate that needed to be protected.

Jeremy pressed his thick forearm against my throat, and I pushed back until I had him backed up against the fridge. Jeremy was strong and angry, and it was all I could do to keep him in the room.

"You need to calm the hell down," I said when he finally stopped struggling.

"Because you say so?" he spat bitterly. His blue eyes were cold and cruel, and I remembered how he had acted in the mountains.

"Because your alpha says so," Amelia said quietly. She pressed her hand against his shoulder, and he relaxed almost instantly. "Look at the bigger picture, Jeremy," she said, still in that soft voice. "Byron's right. You know this. We can't afford to turn on each other. We need to protect the pack. How are we supposed to do that if we can't even be in a room with each other for more than five minutes?"

Jeremy pushed us both away from him and sat down to eat his food as if he hadn't been about to go wolf on us. "I'm just frustrated. I can't stand having to come back here and wait around to be attacked again. I can't stand not knowing what happened to Willow. And every time I come home, everything's changed again. I have no place here. That man can call me *son* all he likes, but he's never been a father to me."

"You go," Amelia whispered to me. "I want to talk to him for a bit."

As I left the room, I heard Amelia speak to Jeremy in that same hypnotic tone of voice again. I went straight outside to the back garden where Byron and Ryan were having a discussion. They got quiet when they saw me.

"Amelia calmed him down properly," I explained. "I think you might be right about this omega thing, Ryan. It's bizarre, but she definitely had some kind of effect on him."

Ryan nodded, a muscle ticking in his jaw, and I wished she would come outside and do the same thing to him.

"So she's basically a werewolf whisperer," I said.

Ryan laughed, the tension falling from his shoulders. "Pretty much. But she can't make Jeremy accept me."

"He'll come around," Byron said.

"I'm not so sure, to be honest. He's... he's not like us." I scratched my head, unsure if I should continue. "Things got a bit out of hand when we were away together."

Byron clenched his jaw. "What do you mean?"

"One of the last places we went to, well, it got rough. Opa and Willow were acting weird, so Jeremy and I went for a run. He took me far out, and we ended up running close to a place we'd been turned away from, a hut in the mountains. I... we... like I said, it got out of hand.

"I ended up fighting the werewolf who lived there, but then... then I realised Jeremy was running after the humans—an old man and the wolf's mate. Jeremy tried to... I stopped him. Nothing happened in the end, not really, but it could have." I inhaled sharply as I recalled the scene. "It could have been a *lot* worse. I thought... I didn't know what to do. Put it this way: he hasn't been happy with me since then, so that probably didn't help back there."

Bryon turned away and stalked up and down the garden.

"Give him a minute," Ryan advised, putting a hand on my

shoulder.

"Have you really been watching out for her?" I asked.

"Who? Oh. We can't just leave her running around alone. Luckily, her father has made our job a lot easier." He gave me a rare smile. "I owe that girl a lot. Did you really think I would let her get into trouble?"

"I didn't think. I mean, you're kinda still the wolf I saw about to attack her in the woods."

His face fell. "I know. If I could change what happened... but I can't. My daughters' lives are in your family's hands. If it's any consolation, I can't find a moment's peace."

"It is, actually." But I shook his hand. "Welcome to the pack."

Byron joined us again. "It's my fault. If I had been more of a father to your kids, everything would be different. When all of this is over, when we've won, we're going to be the family my mother always wanted us to be."

I saw how determined he was, and I understood. I had my own promises to keep.

Chapter Eleven

Perdita

Amelia whispered the gossip to me as we read through the same books again on my lunch break.

"So even though Opa and Jeremy are home, we're none the wiser really. We're back to waiting for Vin to make a move, if he ever does. I mean, now that the curse is broken, he might just give up, right?"

"Yeah, but will your grandfather?" I asked.

"Probably not." She bit her lip. "Ryan thinks Vin will want me. They tried to take my mother, and they meant to take Mémère before she died. What if they come for me?"

"Nobody's going to let them near you."

"Yeah, but what if I go willingly?"

I slammed the book shut. "Don't even joke about that, Amelia."

"I mean it, though. What if that would end everything? Maybe it wouldn't be so bad."

"Are you freaking kidding me right now? Haven't you heard Ryan talk about those people?"

She blew out a breath. "I know, but—"

"But nothing. That would be idiotic. Never even *think* anything like that again."

"Never think what?"

Both of us jumped at the sound of Joey's voice behind us.

"Seriously," I whispered to Amelia. "Use your nose every now and then." She made a face, and we both turned to greet my cousin.

"What are you doing here?" I said as brightly as I could manage.

"It's the library. What do you think?" He shrugged. "What are you two up to?" He reached to pick up the book I had been reading. "Werewolf legends? What's this about, then?"

"Uh, a school project," Amelia said quickly.

"In the summer?"

Amelia rubbed the back of her head. "It's... I missed a lot of school and stuff, so..."

He frowned. "A school project, in the summer, on werewolf legends. That's the best you can do?"

"It's not just werewolf legends," I said. "It's about Romani gypsy... culture and... and..."

"The Ukraine," Amelia added. "In the eighteenth century. And mass hysteria and a whole lot of other stuff."

I rolled my eyes at her.

"Then why aren't you looking in the historical section?" he asked.

I looked back at him. "Um, what?"

He sighed. "It sounds like you would be better off looking in the historical section rather than the mythology section."

"That might be a good idea, actually," I said to Amelia.

"Ridiculous," Joey said.

"We can't all be natural-born geniuses, Joe," I said, stretching.

"I'm not a genius. I work my arse off to learn whatever I can. It's called hard work. It's not like somebody beams shit into my brain while I sleep."

I smirked. "Settle down."

"Wreck the head. Wait here." He was back within five minutes with a huge pile of books. "We can order in some books because there isn't that great of a selection here, but there are some decent websites that might have the kind of information we're looking for."

"Hold on a second." I held up my hands. "We?"

"Oh, yeah," Joey said. "You can lie to me all you want, Perdy Rivers, but I'm your cousin, and I'm going to find out what's going on whether you like it or not."

"Nothing's going on," I said, flustered.

"Great, then you'll have no problem letting me help."

"I, um, I don't think…"

"Good," Amelia said. "Should get this project finished a lot quicker. You could email us those websites you were on about. What did you mean about ordering in books?"

"Mrs. Reed will order in books we need. She still has all of her budget for the year left."

"Mrs. Reed knows the word *yes*?"

"Ha, ha. *Not*. Watch and learn, girls." Joey sidled up to the counter to charm Mrs. Reed.

I watched in surprise, and with a little terror, as a beaming smile lit up her expression. She appeared to write down a list, and she patted Joey's hand before he rejoined us.

"What the hell was that?" I blurted.

"She likes me. I'm here a lot. Sometimes Mam bakes cookies and stuff for her. I buy her chocolates on special occasions. We're friends."

I narrowed my eyes. "That's unbelievably creepy."

"And yet useful. We might be related, but I'm not her arch-enemy's grandchild."

"I knew she hated me!"

He laughed. "She told me you look like Ruth did back in the day, right around the time she stole her boyfriend. Sorry about that."

"Did she say that before or after you roped me into work experience here?"

He grinned, and I glared right back at him.

"Um, okay," Amelia said. "Back to the books. Is she going to order them?"

"I gave her some keywords, so she's going to see what she can find. She's quite the googler."

"That sounds so very wrong," I said. "Joe, are you coming to that party with me or not?"

"Oh, yeah," Amelia said. "You should totally go."

"You're just saying that because Perdy can't if I don't."

She smiled at him. "I would never be so sly and manipulative."

He studied the book in front of him. "Only if Tammie can come."

Amelia and I exchanged a glance.

"Oh, don't be so bitchy," he said, looking up. "She's been through a lot lately, and she's tried to say sorry to you, Perdy. Give her a chance."

"What's she been going through?" I asked.

"Thought you didn't care about her anymore." He smiled as if he had won something.

"Shut up. Bring her, then. So I can tell Dad we're going?"

"Go on then. But it better be good." He eyed Amelia. "And warn your annoying friend not to bother me."

She looked at him blankly.

"You know," he said. "The loud, excitable one I keep seeing you hanging around with."

"Julie? Oh, don't be so bitchy," she mocked.

He grinned and took a seat. "Might as well get started now. Prepare yourselves for some serious research, ladies."

"Yeah, well, my lunch is nearly over," I said.

"You can bring books home with you, then," he said. "So what exactly are we looking for?"

Amelia passed him our list of search words.

"Chovihani, gaje, gypsy magic, werewolf curses, omega? What the hell kind of—"

"Just read," I snapped, opening a book and widening my eyes to ensure I didn't fall asleep out of boredom. Research was not my strong suit.

"Wait a second," he said and disappeared behind the stacks again. He threw a book in front of me.

I checked out the cover. "Wolves?"

"Look up omega in the index," he said before promptly diving into another book.

I read an entire chapter on wolf hierarchy. "So it talks about alphas and omegas, but I don't know if it's right. I mean, if it applies to werewolves. Or the legends, rather," I said, my cheeks heating up.

"What does it say?" Amelia asked.

"Okay, it says that there's a dominant couple who are the alphas, and then there's a beta. The beta is like, second-in-command and the next alpha. The rest of the pack are subordinates, except for the omega."

She arched a brow. "And?"

"Well, it says the omega is basically picked on by the rest of the pack. They take their tension and aggression out on the omega, and it keeps the pack peaceful. If an omega dies, the rest of the pack can get depressed for a while."

Her face paled, and I slammed the book shut.

"Wolves aren't werewolves," I said softly.

She nodded, but any time I glanced at her after that, she was busy staring into space with a frown creasing her forehead. The pair of them read through books past my lunch break and until closing. We walked home together as they discussed what they had found.

"There's not a whole lot on gypsy culture," Joey said, "at least not the Romani kind. But there was a really interesting section on their beliefs. They believed the dead would taint them. They apparently had this big thing about cleanliness."

"Yeah, they had *marimc* taboos, like the women would be in trouble if a man touched her skirts even." Amelia sounded extremely excited.

"I think I read some of that. The stuff about the dead though... they believed the dead could basically come back if they buried them, and that was why bodies were burned. They believed in hell and all kinds of monsters being able to escape from there."

"Oh," Amelia said, "Perdita read something about the gypsies believing in white werewolves protecting them from the dead. I mean, if they believed the dead came back, then obviously, werewolves would be valuable."

I zoned out from the conversation, but they seemed really into it. With Joey's help, we might actually get somewhere on the research. We had already found way more than we had without him, and maybe the websites he mentioned would be more interesting than a couple of dusty old books.

I watched them stroll away from my house, still chatting animatedly together.

Dad opened the door. "Was that Amelia with Joey?"

"Yeah." I yawned. "He's helping her with a project. They were in the library for a few hours."

"Oh? What kind of project?"

"Some kind of history thing. I wasn't paying a lot of attention. Too busy working."

He smiled. "Ah, is this part of the guilt trip effect in order to persuade me about that party?"

I stuck my tongue out at him. "Nope. Joey's going, so now I am, too. Just like you said."

"You need to stop bullying your cousin into doing whatever you want."

"What are family for? Anyway, he and Tammie are going to go. Reluctantly, yes, but we're calling it an early birthday celebration."

"Maybe next year, on your eighteenth, we could do something special."

"What, like a party?"

"Maybe. I could DJ for you."

"Tempting, but no. Thanks, though."

He chuckled. "You know, David and I used to be in a band. Maybe we could get the whole gang back together for the night."

"Dad, you're scaring me. It's bad enough to find out my cousin regularly flirts with the octogenarian librarian without you donning a bass guitar."

"I was on drums, I'll have you know."

"So weird."

"You're fine with your grandmother being a club singer, but your dad can't have had a life ever?"

I giggled. "Gran is cooler than you."

He held his chest as if struck through the heart. "Harsh."

"I like you better when you're not trying to be down with the kids."

"Go to your room."

"That's more like it."

We laughed together until Gran came home, and when she saw us, her face lit up. We were definitely going to be okay.

Chapter Twelve

Nathan

Amelia ate dinner with her nose in a book.

"Interesting reading?" Byron asked.

She laid it down, her eyes shining. "Yes, actually. We've been looking for something that might help me figure out Kali's power. And the omega thing."

"We?"

"Yeah." She glanced at her food. "Me and some friends."

"You told them?" Opa asked in a shocked voice.

"Of course not! I said it's for a school project." She shrugged. "I just want to know more about our heritage, and who knows? Maybe I'll find something that will help us. There's still the fact that Perdita's dad is ill to deal with, remember?"

"We'll deal with that when the time is right," Opa said impatiently. "There are more important things than books right now, Amelia."

"But there could be something useful. The omega thing—"

"Ryan, stop filling her head with nonsense," Opa said. "It's a myth; that's all."

"I believe in it," I said, harsher than I intended, but that was because of the mention of Perdita's dad.

"You're a child—" Opa began.

But Byron interrupted him. "I think it's important. Keep looking, Amelia. We need all of the help we can get."

She grinned and turned back to the book, but Opa looked absolutely disgusted.

"Maybe I can help," I said to my sister as we cleaned up after dinner.

"Would you?"

"Yeah, why not? I saw you with Jeremy, how you calmed him down."

She hesitated, twisting her bracelet around her arm. "The omega in a wolf pack is the lowest-ranking member, the one who gets picked on."

"That's not the same thing. I won't let anyone pick on you."

She gave me a sad smile. "And the beta is the next in line to be an alpha. Kind of like the vice-president. Who would that be in this pack? Jeremy? You? Because I feel like Ryan is the new vice-president."

"Ryan can't be alpha."

"How are you so sure?"

I shrugged. "I just don't feel it. He's not dominant. Jeremy, yeah. Even you're more dominant than Ryan."

"Omegas are the least dominant. Wolves fight with the omega so they don't fight each other."

"I think you bring peace in other ways. Seriously, when you calmed Jeremy down, I realised there's something to that omega stuff, after all."

She raised her chin. "And what about the other stuff?"

I shrugged, unable to commit to an answer.

She shivered. "It's all true. Everything I've told you about us, about our ancestors. It's important we remember. I don't want Kali invading my life again if she reckons we've forgotten her story already."

"Yeah, okay. I just don't see how it can help us. That's all."

She bit her lower lip. "I can think of lots of ways. I'm getting closer to answers, Nathan. I can just feel it. It's like this is what I was meant to do. It's in my blood. Mémère even thought so. If it wasn't for Opa, this stuff would probably already be part of our lives."

"I get that you're excited about it, but there's so much going on right now."

She turned to face me. "I *am* sorry about what happened. Well, not that I broke the curse, but the way I broke it out of the blue like that. We didn't get a chance to deal with it, not any of us. It feels like there's been no closure or anything."

"I know you didn't mean everything that happened. I was just pissed. I still am sometimes, but since I've come home, I've felt better."

"I wish you'd talk to her."

I shook my head and turned to go to my room.

"No, please, don't walk away. It just seems so stupid to throw everything away like that."

"You don't know what I've done. I've been everything she despises. I'm no use to her this way. Maybe someday, when everything's over and my head's in the right place."

"What if it's too late?"

I shook my head. "Then that's something I'll have to deal with."

***

"This is ridiculous," Opa said as he stared out of the window at the police car parked discreetly down the street. They weren't there all of the time, but we never knew when they would show up. "What do they think is going to happen?"

"You'll get used to it," Ryan said. "They'll move on as soon as something more important comes along."

Opa grunted. "Not soon enough."

"We run tonight," Byron said as if nobody had spoken. "We need to be seamless if we're attacked, and that's not going to happen unless we hunt together."

"We need a proper plan of attack," Jeremy said from the corner, sounding slightly less sullen than usual.

"You're right," Byron said. "Maybe you could work on that with me."

They held each other's gazes until Jeremy finally nodded. I could almost taste my cousin's surprise, but I was glad Byron was making an effort. Jeremy was angry at his father—that was obvious—but it was up to Byron to bridge the gap he had forced upon his family.

"I think we should move on," Opa said, and all of us turned to look in his direction. "Get rid of this house before it's too late. We're sitting ducks here. We can't run freely. We need to drive hours away to hunt. It's not working for us anymore. I'm tired of waiting for Vin to come after us and trying to figure out how he'll come at us next. We need to move on, travel Europe, and really make an impact on his pack."

"Amelia and Nathan have school," Byron said.

"We'll hire tutors. This is more important than education."

"I don't want to leave," I said.

Amelia shook her head. "Me either."

"We do what's best for the pack," Opa said, and he picked up a newspaper from the table.

"We're not leaving," Byron said.

"We'll see." Opa's response sounded more like a challenge than anything.

Amelia signalled for me to follow her outside, so I did.

"Do you think he'll make Byron leave?" she asked, sounding frantic.

"Byron's the one in charge," I said. "But Byron could change his mind."

"We can't leave. I don't want to move again. I'm *happy* here. It's the first time I've ever felt like I fit in somewhere, and I want to have a home, Nathan. This is where I have to be."

I frowned. "I know. If it comes down to it, we'll stick together. You and me. I won't let anyone force you to go anywhere you don't want to."

She looked so surprised that I laughed. "Oh, what now?"

"I'm just… I didn't think you'd want to stay with me."

"Shut up," I said, not unkindly. "Yeah, I was mad at you, but that doesn't mean I'm going to ditch you. If things get worse, we may end up on our own, but you're my sister. Like I said, we'll stick together." I started moving a little further away from the house.

"Opa's losing it," she said, walking next to me. "I'm afraid he'll drag everyone down with him. Even I can't help him now. He's too far gone. He doesn't *want* to feel better."

"I know how he feels." Seeing her expression, I added, "Don't give me that look. It's hard to lose what your wolf wants. It's hard to… I don't know, deal with the loss for both sides of you."

"There are no sides, Nathan," she said impatiently. "It's all you. Everything you feel is yours. Blaming the wolf only makes it harder to deal with."

I shrugged. "Maybe you're right. I've gone so long thinking of the wolf as a problem that I can't get my head around the fact this is for life."

"We were meant to be this way. To be a pack. But keep an eye out when we're running together later. I have this feeling that something's going to happen. I don't like it."

"Hey, relax. We're going to hunt together to cement the pack, like Byron said. You'll see the difference in everyone after that."

She frowned. "Here's the thing. This feeling I have is like… under my skin. I *know* something's coming. I just don't know what. Last time I felt this and ignored it, well, things got furry."

"Next you'll be predicting thunderstorms."

"Oh, shut up!" But she laughed along with me.

We left soon afterward for the hunt. I travelled in the car with Byron, Amelia, and Ryan, while Jeremy and Opa brought the jeep and the dogs. There were no police cars outside, but we still travelled far away, just in case.

Ireland had plenty of small, tight cities, but a lot of the land surrounding them was lush and green. Forests, fields, farms, and open land were a pleasure to run on.

There were a lot of choices, but we still had to be careful. Farmers could shoot, and we didn't want to disturb livestock, but wild things were fair game. Travelling around meant we didn't upset the balance, something that Opa had never been overly concerned about.

We drove past endless fields of cows, my eyes blurring as everything melded into one long stretch of green and yellow. Byron seemed to get a kick out of finding new places for us to hunt, and he manoeuvred through dozens of tiny, winding tracks that couldn't exactly pass for roads, what with the grass growing in the centre of them.

We finally pulled in before a steep hill shrouded by forestry. I could smell horses nearby, and I worried we would set them off, but all was calm. Still, I kept an eye on Amelia, her nerves triggering my own. I felt ill at the thoughts of what could happen in the middle of nowhere.

We trekked through the trees, stripping to phase, and I was off before anyone else, closely followed by Amelia. She nipped my tail before she outpaced me, and I urged myself onward, hoping to outrun her.

We left the others behind, chasing, fighting, and nipping at each other's tails. She was good. *Really* good. She already had stamina and was as agile as I was. I didn't have to worry about her strength either. She rolled me over a number of times, which was embarrassing.

Still, it was fun to have someone new to run with. She wasn't a grownup, and she took pleasure in everything wolf. We played, and wolf choked on his own laughter whenever he managed to trip her up. It was probably the closest we had ever been. I had always been protective of my little sister, but she was right: I had never treated her like an equal. She equalled me as wolf.

Byron howled in the distance, and we both raced back to him, me winning by a nose. She snapped aggressively, and I batted her snout, barely avoiding the clamping of her jaws. We had all run wild for a while, forgetting everything, but it was time to eat. The hunt was tense, and I kept my eye on Opa and Jeremy, worried for reasons I wasn't even sure of.

Amelia's comments about something coming played on my mind, and I had to admit that even my wolf was unsettled during the hunt. Something about the way Opa stayed at the back of the pack set me on edge, some look in his eye, some feeling in the air. I couldn't relax.

Having become a larger pack, we doubled up on some of our roles. Byron sniffed out the prey, but Amelia and I forced the creatures into the path of the rest of the pack. Byron and Ryan took care of the killing, and Jeremy and Opa kept to the edges in case anything escaped—or something came too close.

Byron ate his fill first, a statement to the rest of us. We all waited patiently, but I could see a tremor in the corner of my eye: anxious movements, very slight, from Opa and Jeremy. Steeling myself, I prepared for anything.

Byron made a sound that let us know we could join him. Opa crept up behind Byron, looking ready to pounce. I growled in warning, and Byron turned in time to meet his father's attack. I made to move forward, but Ryan got in the way, warning me back with a growl.

Jeremy paced, while Amelia lay down and waited for the challenge to be over. Opa was smaller than Byron, but still tough and fuelled with more than just anger. They snapped at each other aggressively, but I could tell Byron held back. Opa kept pushing, trying to pin Byron and force him to show his belly.

My heart pounded. I felt desperate with the instinct to help Byron, but Ryan had been right to stop me. It wouldn't do any good to interfere. Amelia glanced at me with knowing eyes, and we watched as Byron pinned Opa, forcing my grandfather to submit. It was painful to see, but if Byron didn't assert himself, we would be stuck with Opa as alpha again. I would have challenged Opa myself to avoid that.

When it was over, Byron acted as though nothing had happened, and we all shared the meal. Opa avoided looking at Byron, and when we took one last run together, everything felt smoother.

We wouldn't have to move.

Perdita

The party had more of a kid's sleepover kind of vibe. When we arrived, Ger's parents still hadn't left, so Ger made Joey walk around the block a couple of times.

"Really?" Tammie hissed.

Amelia held up her hands as we huddled together in the living room. "I didn't know," she said, barely containing her laughter.

"Joey's going to kill you. Just so you know," I said.

"I'm kind of glad to get a minute alone with you two," Amelia said. "I really want us all to get along, and I thought this might be the place to clear the air, you know?"

"I'm up for that," Tammie said, surprising me. "There's no reason for us to fight. We need to be there for Perdy right now."

Amelia grinned. "Agreed. I can move on if you can."

They shook hands, and Ger's parents finally went out the door.

"I thought they were never going to go," a hyper girl named Julie exclaimed as soon as the door closed.

"Shush," Ger hissed from the window, watching her parents drive off to their weekend away. "Fine, they're gone. Music, please?

Everyone, text the boys and let them know the coast is clear."

The boys, including Joey, arrived, and everyone paired off. I was the extra wheel, yet again. God, I needed some new friends.

Amelia paraded her boyfriend in front of us. He didn't look like anything special to me, but they definitely had some chemistry, and it was kind of sweet to see them together. They weren't nearly as vomit inducing as Tammie and Joey.

"What do you think of him?" Amelia whispered to me as her new beau ran, literally, to get her a drink from the kitchen.

"He seems lovely."

She smiled back, but something caught her eye, and her face fell. "Oh, no. What is he *doing?*"

Confused, I followed her line of sight. Abbi walked in with Nathan, Dawn following right behind them. My lungs decided working properly was too much trouble, and I sucked in a dry gasp of nothing.

"I'm so sorry," Amelia said. "I invited you both, but I didn't expect him to turn up with *them.*"

His gaze locked onto mine, and I couldn't break free.

"I need air," Tammie murmured. "Wanna come with?"

I nodded, still staring at Nathan. Amelia kept whispering to me, but I couldn't hear her because I was tumbling through space as everything came rushing back at once. I had fallen for Nathan, no matter what they said about curses breaking, and I couldn't switch off the feelings.

Even if *he* could.

Maybe Ryan had been right. Maybe my drama was a distraction that Nathan didn't need. As it was, his face had drained of colour, and he had stopped talking mid-sentence once he saw me. I turned away, following Tammie outside, relieved to get some space from the situation.

Even though a tiny part of me had hoped he would be there, I wasn't ready to see him and not be with him. I wasn't ready to deal with how it had ended, how we had been behaving *before* it ended. It didn't feel right for us to be in the same building and not even say hello.

"That was so incredibly awkward," Tammie said as the two of us moved to stand at the side of the house.

"Just a tad." I smiled wryly. "At least it's done now, though."

She eyed me warily. "I still don't see the attraction. He never made you happy."

"I was happy. Other stuff got in the way, and it made everything go bad. But he didn't make me *un*happy. Why did you always dislike him so much?"

She shrugged, picking at the nail polish on her thumb. The shade matched the newly dip-dyed purple ends of her hair. "He looked at you like he owned you, you know? He was always looking at you. And listening. I could tell. He was always trying to listen in on our conversations. He's probably listening right now."

We both glanced toward the door then burst out laughing. The door opened, cutting off our laughter, but it wasn't Nathan. Worse, it was Dawn and Abbi.

Dawn approached us, Abbi whispering frantically in her ear. I groaned, wondering what drama they would start.

Dawn edged up to Tammie, her expression absent of her usual sneer. "I heard what happened. I'm sorry for you."

I glanced at Tammie in confusion.

Her face paled, and she nodded jerkily. "Thanks." Her voice trembled.

Dawn gave her a grim smile before walking away with Abbi, who looked as confused as I felt.

"What was that about?" I asked.

She stared after Dawn, wrapping her arms around her torso. "It's nothing."

"Didn't sound like nothing."

Tammie looked away. "Let's just say I'm an idiot."

I touched her arm. "Come on, Tams. Tell me what's going on."

"I didn't want to tell you here. I wanted you to have fun."

"Well, I think that's blown out of the water," I said with a little laugh. "So you might as well spill."

She hesitated before nodding. "Come up here." She pointed behind us. "Where it's quieter."

I followed her until she stopped and picked at her nails, roughly this time, completely ruining her nail polish.

"It's… remember years ago, when Dawn and I were friends?"

"Yeah, of course." They had lived in each other's pockets until one day they seemed to hate each other on sight. I had been only too grateful when Tammie decided she was my friend instead.

"Not many people do, but it all started then. Our parents were good friends, so we were together a lot, and we told each other everything. I mean *everything*. So anyway, one day she told me a secret and said I couldn't tell anyone. I worried myself sick about it, so sick that Mam knew something was wrong, and she made me tell her."

"What was it?"

Tammie took a deep breath. "Dawn's mam and my dad. She caught them *together*. And I told. It caused so much unbelievable shit, but Dad told Mam that Dawn was a little liar, that she never saw them together. He begged me to back him up. Dawn's parents were already splitting up over it, and I didn't want the same thing to happen to mine, so I… I did what he asked. I called her a liar, said she was always making things up. I even said she admitted lying about it to me, and my parents stayed together. That's why she hates me so much. I know I let you think she was just a spiteful bitch, but she had a reason for it. Can't really blame her, right?"

"That's so screwed up. How could your dad—"

"That's not all of it." She looked as though she might vomit. "Months ago, I saw them together. Kissing. On the street. Right out in public. I mean, it must have been going on for years. I was in bits over it. I couldn't bring myself to tell you, to tell anyone, apart from Joey. He always knows what to do, you know?"

I nodded, my own stomach turning.

"I wanted to tell you—I did—but you were with Nathan or Amelia all the time, and I got pissed about it. At first, I didn't want to talk, but then it seemed as though you were turning to Amelia instead of me. I felt like I had nobody, except Joey."

"Oh, no, Tams. It wasn't like that for me."

"Yeah, well, it all got wrapped up in my head. I couldn't deal with it, so I unloaded it all to Joey. He told me to confront my dad, to make sure I hadn't made a mistake. So I did, and Dad… he started crying, said it was all a big misunderstanding, that he didn't mean it. He said he was comforting her out of pity. That he felt *sorry* for her."

She kept her eyes on her fingers. "That's when I first realised that Joey would stay with me if he pitied me. I knew he didn't like me the way I liked him. I knew it, and I didn't care as long as I was with him, as long as I had *someone* for myself. It sounds stupid now, stupid saying it out loud, but at the time, I needed him. I needed someone, and you weren't there anymore. No, I'm not blaming you. I'm just saying it was a bad time for me."

"But what happened with your dad?"

"He made me promise not to say anything. He said Mam would kick him out, that he would have nowhere to go. So I agreed. I still didn't want them to break up, but I felt like a little kid again. I was terrified, like, all the time. It was ridiculous, and my head kept getting all screwed up over it."

She exhaled shakily. "I couldn't blame Dad because he would get mad at me and make a million excuses, so I blamed everyone else. I took it out on everyone, pretty much. Especially you." She shook her head, looking disgusted. "But then he started getting me to lie for him, to cover for him. I mean, he made a fool out of Mam, and he used *me* to do it. I was so stressed out that I'm pretty sure I failed my summer exams."

She quickly wiped her eyes, but when she spoke again, her voice grew stronger. "I wanted to talk to you, but you've been really distant for a while. You had stuff on your mind that you weren't telling me, and I was kind of scared to know what was going on with you. I couldn't handle any more, you know? And sometimes, I would be afraid that you knew already, and that's why you avoided me. I started thinking that Dawn knew, and she told Nathan, and he told you, and you were all having a good laugh about it behind my back." She gave a humourless laugh.

"I would never do that to you, Tams," I said softly.

"I told you, my head was screwed up. You wouldn't believe the stuff I've been thinking. I couldn't handle it, and I was so paranoid about every little thing. I do that, though. That's my thing. I get fixated, imagine things." She sighed and shook her head. "I picture it happening in my head, and then I get mad because I convince myself it's true. But this was worse, and I swear, I thought I was losing my mind for a while there. So anyway, I ended up telling Joey everything. The truth this time, and I'm pretty sure he really is sticking around out of pity. We're going to split up. Soon, I think. He's biding his time, and I don't know how to make him change his mind. Sometimes I want him to leave me alone because we're connected with everything bad. I'm sick of worrying about when he'll end it. I told you. My head's messed up."

I saw the tears in her eyes and the trembling of her lower lip, and I realised I hadn't been there for her through any of it. She hadn't trusted me, just as I couldn't trust my own father, just as I couldn't trust Tammie or Joey. So many secrets and lies. We both knew what it was like to deal with something alone, and I felt a pang of regret for her. "I'm sorry I wasn't... I'm just sorry."

She made a face. "Like you said, I pushed you away."

"So what happened with your parents?"

She gave a watery smile. "I told the truth, and Dad freaked out. He called me every name under the sun and told Mam I was looking for attention, that I was jealous and spoiled and that nothing was ever enough for me. My sisters all believed him, and none of them talked to me for weeks. Some of them still won't. But Mam asked me out straight, and I told her everything. She just nodded, her mouth all tight. She made him leave, said she might have forgiven him for betraying her, but she could never forgive him for what he had done to me, how he had torn the family apart."

"I'm so sorry," I said, fully aware of how inadequate my words were.

"Don't be. I got what I deserved, didn't I? I thought Dawn would tell everyone, that she'd really make my life hell over this, but she didn't. I can't believe it after everything I've done to her. I… I actually made myself believe she was lying years ago. I made myself hate her, but she's a much better person than I am. She should have told everyone. I deserve it."

"You don't deserve any of it. You were just a kid back then."

"Maybe," she said. "At first, yeah, definitely. But the rest of it? All on me. Worst bit is that I'm just like him. Mam's always said it, and now I know it's true. You were right before about me treating you like crap because I knew you'd take it. Just like Dad did to me. Apple doesn't fall far from the tree."

She sounded absolutely disgusted with herself, and I felt horrified that so much had gone on with her that I had been completely oblivious to. Life had gone on for everyone around me, and I was at a standstill, wishing everything could go back to the way it had been.

"You were manipulated by your own father. He's the one in the wrong."

"You're lucky," she said abruptly. "Your dad would never ever do anything like that to you. I used to think he was annoying, but now I'm kind of jealous because at least you know he cares about you."

I stared at her, startled by the truth in that.

"I'm going to apologise to Dawn." She swallowed hard. "And I really think you need to talk to Nathan. The way you look at each other… it would be a waste not to at least talk. I mean, even if you don't get back together, you could still be friends, right?"

"I don't know." I hugged her. "Thanks for telling me

everything, Tams."

She gripped me tighter. "I've missed you lots, Per. I know it's hard to be a friend to me, but thanks for listening. I don't deserve it."

"Course you do."

She hurried away, a new expression on her face, almost as though she was relieved to have gotten it all off her chest. Sometimes, I wished for that relief. I wished my father knew everything so I could stop that tight, choked-up feeling in my chest whenever I had to lie to him and pretend that everything was okay. That *I* was okay living with what I had done.

The circle kept coming back to me, to the things I had done... or hadn't. I couldn't believe I had been so self-absorbed that I hadn't realised something was terribly wrong in Tammie's life. I hadn't thought about considering *why* she was acting the way she had. Or that Dawn had a reason for disliking Tammie. That made me no better than anyone.

Worst of all, I had been so concerned with werewolf business that I had neglected Dad, Gran, and even Tammie. I had messed up so badly in every area of my life.

There was still one thing I could fix. Nathan had looked so guilty when he saw me, and once I had laid eyes on him, I could almost forget about the reasons why we shouldn't be together. But they still existed, and he needed to be able to go about his business without feeling at fault for having a life after me.

We needed some kind of closure, at least for the moment, and I needed to get rid of that ache in my gut whenever I looked his way. I would find him, I would talk to him, and I would give him an excuse to move on, because until he did, I couldn't.

Nathan

Seeing her changed everything. *Everything.* Gone were my resolutions to forget about curses and soul mates until after we had sorted out pack stuff.

Looking at her felt like home.

"Can I speak to you alone for a minute?" Amelia demanded rather than asked, completely ignoring Dawn and Abbi. I had asked them to come with me for moral support, but judging by Amelia's expression, that had been a bad idea.

"Go ahead," Dawn said. "I need to speak to someone anyway."

"What are you doing?" Amelia asked as soon as they walked away. "Are you completely stupid?"

"I haven't done anything wrong," I reminded her.

She stuttered something I couldn't make out before closing her eyes and taking a few deep breaths. "Bringing *them* was wrong," she said in a slightly more level voice. "I asked you and Perdita both to come here so you could talk to each other away from anyone who might interfere. You just ruined that, genius."

"I get that you're trying to help, but she doesn't want to talk to me."

"If I thought that, do you really think I would make her see you? Come on!"

"Ryan said—"

"Forget what Ryan said! I like Ryan, but keeping you two apart is what's best for *him*. I miss having Perdita around, and you obviously do, too, so why not man up, speak to her, and figure out what's going on?"

"It's not that simple anymore. After everything that's happened, she's finally free. She can walk away from me."

She frowned. "What if she doesn't want to, Nathan?" She turned on her heel and joined Connor.

Connor rubbed her back absentmindedly as he spoke, and I felt a pang of something. Almost like homesickness. I wanted to talk to Perdita, but I was afraid for a million reasons. What Ryan said made a lot of sense, but it wasn't what I wanted, and I realised I had no idea what *she* wanted. The days of certainty were over. Even before, she had always found ways to disagree with me or get mad at me. How would it be when there was nothing magical keeping us together? I was terrified to find out.

But I *wanted* to find out.

I wandered outside, disinterested in the party itself. I had only turned up because a tiny part of me had hoped she would somehow be there. No matter what happened, she was still at the forefront of my mind. Even being away for a while hadn't helped me switch off that part of my brain. She should be with me. I just needed to figure out a way to convince her of that. She had looked mildly horrified when she saw me, so how could I force my presence on her without coming off like a complete dick?

I sat on a bench on the patio at the back of the house. The neighbouring houses were all quite nice, and I wondered why the area was such a ghost town. It had been pretty much crime-free, at least before we werewolves invaded.

"I wondered where you got to," Abbi called out, joining me on the bench.

"I needed some air," I muttered.

"Sorry about you and Perdita. You both looked pretty uncomfortable back there."

I laughed in spite of myself. "Understatement, Abbi."

"Maybe it's a good thing, seeing each other before school starts back. Means you have a chance to get over the awkward stage before Aaron can make it so much worse."

I grinned. "Thanks for putting an upside to it. Doubt he could make it much worse than it already is."

"It's not so bad. I mean, she's not all psycho outraged ex, is she? And we'll hide you if she is."

I glanced at her, seeing a hint of worry in those smiling eyes. "She's not like that, Abbi."

Her smile faltered. "I was just kidding around. I hate seeing you so unhappy. She's nice enough, but you were miserable most of the time you were together."

I clenched my fists, my inner darkness fuelling my rage. "I wasn't miserable. Not with her."

She looked confused. "Then why aren't you together?"

Why indeed? I shrugged. "Lots of reasons. Right person, wrong time, maybe."

She laid a hand on my shoulder and squeezed. "What if it was the wrong person, right time?"

That confused me, and my entire body froze as she leaned forward, glancing at my lips. I closed my eyes, wondering if I could even do it, but my wolf howled inside with displeasure, and I pushed her gently away before she got close enough to kiss.

The door closed softly behind us, leaving behind a trace of the scent I liked most in the whole world.

"I'll be back," I said, jumping to my feet.

Abbi grabbed my hand. "Nathan, wait."

"Just… Abbi, give me a minute. Give me two minutes, okay?"

She nodded, and I ran after Perdita for what felt like the

umpteenth time in my life. I caught her in the kitchen, her face paler than I liked.

"Let me explain," I said hurriedly, moving too close to her, judging by the way she backed away.

"There's nothing to explain. You're a free agent. I'm not... I'm not going to try and get in your way. Don't worry." She said it in a kindly way. I would have preferred a scream or even a slap in the face. But not a smile. Not with those words.

"She tried to kiss me," I said, unsure of what to say in the face of her calmness.

"I saw. I didn't mean to. It just happened in front of me. I tried not to look, but... you know." She shrugged. "This might be good for you. You need something normal, something drama-free."

"I don't need anything else," I said, confused again.

Her lip trembled a little. "I've felt so bad for you. That you thought... listen, I'm not your responsibility. It's not your fault what the curse did. You don't have to... you don't owe me anything. I can deal with it. You don't have to feel embarrassed about moving on. It's just the way it is." She was gone before I could form an answer.

I started after her, stopped, and couldn't move again.

"I swear to God," Amelia snapped, coming out of nowhere. "If you listen to what she just said and didn't hear what she was really saying, I *will* bite you."

"I'm not going crazy, right?"

She laughed in spite of the dark look on her face.

"Should I run?"

"Yes, you div!"

I ran.

I found Perdita on the next street, and I got ahead of her, my heart threatening to explode out of my chest. "Wait," I gasped. "Now, just wait a minute, okay?"

She froze, obviously startled. Recovering quickly, she made to move on, but I grabbed her arms and refused to let go.

"You can't say stuff like that and not even give me a chance to reply."

She opened and closed her mouth a couple of times, and her eyes glittered. "I'm not supposed to talk to you."

"So I'll take the punishment from your dad. I don't care. Just talk to me, please."

She fell silent, looking stunned and unsure of herself.

I wasn't above taking advantage of that. "I'm letting go of your arms, but you can't walk away until the conversation is over."

She nodded, her eyebrows rising.

"Good." I grinned. "Thanks for being cooperative."

She gave me *that* look.

I hurried on. "Here's the thing. I don't want to move on. Not with anyone else. I keep telling myself that staying away from you will keep you safe, that I can try to make things up to you, prove that I'm not who you think I am, *after*."

"After?"

"After. When all of this werewolf crap is over and done with. But anything could happen, and I'm sick of missing you."

"The curse—"

"I don't care about the stupid curse. So it's over. Fine. Done. That doesn't mean we have to be. I still care about you, Perdita, and I still want to be with you. I know you hated the influence of the curse hanging over us, but that's over, so it'll be just me and you from now on. We can handle anything, but if you tell me to keep away from you, I will. Okay, I'll *try*, anyway."

The corner of her mouth twitched.

I carried on, barely taking a breath. "But I have to make sure you know that nothing's changed for me. I need you to know that us being over isn't what I want. It's never what I wanted, and I know I acted, well, like a cretin, but I promise you I'm not like *them*. I could be, trust me, the opportunity has arisen, but I kept thinking of you, of how you'd think, and I always backed off. I'll always be darker than you like, but it's important that you don't think of me like a monster, like someone who could hurt you because I... I could *never*...

Perdita, I'm still the same person who saw you for the first time in a classroom. I'm still the same person who made you mad, who you danced with, who you kissed. The curse ending hasn't changed *any* of that for me."

She stared at me, and my brain stopped functioning.

"So, um, has it changed for you?" I asked.

She looked away and shook her head as if confused. I began to lose hope then, but she turned back to face me with a look I knew well in her eyes.

The rest of the world fell away. She took one step closer to me and cocked her head to the side. "Not one bit."

It sank in after a couple of seconds, and a grin spread across my face, a weight lifting off my shoulders. "Are you sure you can deal with the other stuff?" I asked.

She took my hands, entwining her fingers with mine and gifting me with a smile I hadn't seen in too long. All of my fear drifted away. Pulling her arms around my back, I let go of her hands and cupped her cheeks. Wolf growled at me to get on with it already, but I was nervous. There were no certainties anymore. I couldn't tell what she was feeling. At least, not exactly.

Brushing her hair out of her face, I tipped her chin upward and leaned forward to kiss her, relishing her taste, the warmth of her skin, how her fingers gripped at my shirt as if she wouldn't ever let go, and the way her pulse raced against my fingertips.

It was as if we had never been apart, as if the curse hadn't been broken. And I realised none of that had ever mattered. Not deep down.

We swayed toward a garden wall, and I lifted her to rest on top of it, lost in the kiss. Maybe we had attributed a little too much blame to the curse because I wasn't ready to let her go any time soon. Her hands found their way to my hair, and I shifted her closer to me, forgetting we were in public. Not really caring, if I was honest with myself.

She broke away abruptly, her eyes wide with guilt as she

slipped off the wall. "Nathan, it hasn't changed for me, but Dad's still—"

"So I'll wait," I said hurriedly. "I'm sorry if I came on too strong. I get that it's not the same anymore, but I missed you. And I'll wait. I'll talk to him. I'll do whatever it takes. *This* is worth it."

She moved up on the tips of her toes, putting her hands on my shoulders. She kissed me, and warmth flooded through my body. Wolf relaxed, and the constant pressure behind my temple eased considerably. I pulled her close, and everything was okay again.

She stepped back, her cheeks flushing. "Abbi…"

I covered my face with my hands. "Ah, crap! I told her I'd be back. Not to… I meant to explain to her properly that I could never…"

"Go on, then," she said, laughing. "I have to go home anyway. I need to talk to my dad. I have to be honest with him about this."

"I want to be with you. I'll go with you."

"Well, let me talk to him first, so he doesn't have a nervous breakdown at the sight of you. I just… I don't want to waste another minute, so if you're serious, come over later and face Dad, too. For me. I want him to know he can trust me now."

I kissed the corner of her mouth. "This is *not* a goodbye kiss. No more of those, just in case. We have a lot more to talk about. I will be ten minutes tops. Tell the others I left, okay?"

"I will."

She turned to walk away, but I called her name. She looked back at me quizzically.

"I missed you."

She smiled, colour flooding her cheeks again. "I missed you, too."

I sprinted back to the party, shouting at Amelia to let Joey and Tammie know Perdita had left. Abbi was still on the bench, looking miserable, and a wave of guilt hit me.

"I'm sorry," I said. "You're a great friend. It's just—"

"I know," she said. "It's her."

"It's always been her," I said softly.

She sniffed, and I knew she was pissed. "Good luck, I suppose."

I made to leave, but three figures stood before the front door, waiting for me.

"What's going on?" Amelia asked, her eyes bright with excitement.

Joey and Tammie didn't look quite as pleased.

"We're going to talk to her dad. Try to convince him to let me see her sometime in the next year, I suppose."

Joey's frown deepened. "This better end well," he all but growled.

I might have laughed, but he and Tammie both wore venomous expressions, "You better not hurt Perdy, or we'll kill you, and nobody will ever find the body" kind of looks.

"It's going to end well," I insisted. "It will. Everything's going to work out. We're doing what we want. We're not listening to what anyone else wants anymore." My anger rose at the scornful look on Tammie's face. "I care about her. What more do you want?"

"Then go get her," she said, surprising me. Joey scowled at her, and she shrugged helplessly. "She wants this. Let her have it, Joe." She opened the door for me, and I ran, unable to do anything else.

I couldn't wait, not even my guilty conscience about Abbi could slow me down. I sprinted, buoyed by excitement, even at the thought of facing Perdita's dad, but as I approached her house, a warning sounded, loud and clear.

Something felt *wrong*.

I assumed it was nerves until I got closer to her home and saw that the front door was wide open. Afraid, I sniffed the air as I walked into the garden.

I smelled it. The scent of werewolf. *Enemy* werewolf.

I gasped as I called out for Perdita, but I smelled her blood when I stepped through the doorway.

She was gone. She had been taken. Furniture was flung around the place, just like the flat in Lyon. I smelled blood again. Not just hers. She had fought. Hard.

Wolf felt pride. Wolf felt *anger*.

"What on earth are you doing?" Perdita's dad asked from the open front door, keys in hand.

"Something's happened here," I whispered. "Something's happened to Perdita." I wanted to vomit.

He shouted her name, struggling up the stairs. She wasn't there. She wasn't in the house. They had come for her, and I hadn't been there to protect her. Again. I found it hard to breathe. I moved around the room blindly. They had taken her from right under my nose. I could still taste her on my lips, but she was gone, ripped away from me all over again, except it hurt much, much more.

I had been with her. I had left her alone. I had led them straight to her.

I stepped out of the house, panicking so much I couldn't see straight. I collapsed to my knees, struggling to control the ire of my wolf. Wolf was beside himself with rage at the loss. What he had felt before was nothing compared to his current fury.

With shaking hands, I rang Amelia. When I told her what had happened, she promised to pass the word to the others. I said I would wait, that I would do something. What, I didn't know. The world was still blurry, and my head was too full of the scent of her blood.

My own blood boiled in my veins. I would kill them. I would kill every single one of them.

I heard Perdita's ringtone, and I glanced around, hope blooming.

Perdita's father stumbled out of the house, holding her phone, his face deathly pale. "There's blood on the wall," he murmured, looking as sick as I felt. "What did you do to her? What did you *do*?"

I wanted to throw up. Horrified, I stared at him. "I just got here! What are you talking about? I would never hurt her. Never! She's only been gone a few minutes. She was at the party, and she left. I followed her to talk to her… to ask her about getting back together. She said she had to speak to you first. I went back to the party. I was supposed to follow her here to talk to you. But… but when I got here, she was already gone. They took her, but maybe I can find her scent."

I leapt over the wall, fully aware I was leaving an utterly confused man behind. I chased her scent, picking it up once my head began clearing properly. I smelled her everywhere, but the scents were old. No good.

Then I caught the smell of werewolf again. It cut off abruptly, and I knew they had taken a car. But where?

I ran toward the main road, unable to think of what else to do. I had been running for less than five minutes when Byron pulled up next to me.

"Get in," he called out. "Phase, and I'll keep the window open. Amelia told me. You must be… just get in."

I hopped into the backseat. "Ryan said they'd leave her alone." I began removing my clothing. "He said she'd be safe if I stayed away."

"Then what were you doing at her house?"

My cheeks warmed. "It was the first time. They couldn't have known!"

"We'll discuss it later. We can't let them take her. Stay focused."

I shifted, and he kept driving on the main road. I snarled in his face as I caught a scent. He pulled over, opened the door, and let me out. I bounded along the edge of the road, trying to find what held her scent.

Her bracelet. A small amount of blood was smeared on the clasp.

Byron followed me, and he picked up the bracelet, sniffing deeply. "Good girl," he muttered. "Back in the car, and we keep driving. No need to snarl in my face next time."

We got back into the car, but I shifted back so I could talk.

"She left that on purpose, I bet," I said, excited. "She's trying to show us the way."

"They'll notice eventually. And they could easily double back. They could prevent her from trying to get herself noticed, too."

"So we'll keep driving until we pick up another scent. I'm not going home without her."

"They likely won't hurt her," he said, but he didn't sound convinced.

"It had to be Willow."

"They played this too well," he said. "How could they have known when to take her? As soon as we think she's safe…"

"I'll kill them! All of them. I'll do anything to get her back."

"We'll play it smarter than them," he promised. "We'll get her back."

I glared out the window. If we didn't, I would become something much worse than Vin. They would regret *everything* they had done to us.

Perdita

I awoke in the middle of a nightmare, clutching myself as the visions of blood and gore faded. Then I remembered. Reality wasn't a whole lot better.

After seeing Nathan, I had walked back to my house as if floating on a cloud. Everything was working out. I was getting the people I cared about back, one by one. When I heard footsteps behind me, I assumed it was Nathan.

But when I turned to greet him, I saw a stranger's face. There were two more behind him. I spun back to see another in front of me, standing there, watching and waiting. Breathing deeply, I walked as normally as possible until I got closer to the one in front of me.

At the last second, I dodged out of his way, under his outstretched arms, and sprinted to my house, four werewolves on my heels. I knew I didn't have a chance, but I couldn't give up.

I ran into my garden and even managed to get my front door open, but one caught the door before I could slam it shut. He burst through the doorway, almost knocking the door completely off its hinges with his supernatural strength.

He grabbed me as I ran into the kitchen, the carving knives just out of reach of my outstretched hands. I wasn't fast enough or strong enough, but I was desperate to get away. I struggled out of his grasp, his surprise my only advantage as I refused to let him get a good hold on me.

He hadn't expected a fight. I managed to grasp the edge of a plate left on the table, and I swung and smashed it across his face. Stunned, he stumbled. Brushing past him, I ran for my life.

Three more werewolves blocked my way as I tried to run upstairs, and I skidded around the closest one. Another took a quick step after me and slapped me across the head, not even full strength, but the force knocked me against the wall, and my head cracked against the hard surface. I slumped to the floor, unable to stop the room from spinning, but I kept crawling away, knowing I couldn't stop. I took my phone out of my pocket. I needed to ring Byron or Ryan, but one of the werewolves kicked the phone out of my hand.

"Careful," a deep voice warned as the one who had struck me lifted me by the scruff of my shirt.

"Let them smell her blood," my attacker snarled.

They half-carried me to a car and tossed me into the back seat. A werewolf sat on either side of me. I tentatively touched the back of my throbbing head, wincing as my fingers came away wet. I was grateful Dad and Gran weren't home and that nobody else had gotten stuck in my mess. I wished Nathan could see the car, but I didn't want him to face all of the werewolves alone. They would kill him. Of that, I was certain.

But I had to leave a trace.

"I feel sick," I said. "I need to sit by the window, or I'll throw up. I get carsick, I swear, and... and everything's spinning." I made a gagging sound.

"You hit her too hard," one of them drawled.

"Well, she's not throwing up in my car," the one in the driver seat said. "Not unless one of you is gonna clean it up. Move over, Dar."

The one to my left, a skinhead named Dar apparently, reluctantly wound the window down slightly, then switched seats with me. "Make a sound, and I'm locking you in the trunk," he warned as he closed my seatbelt.

When he bent over me, I saw blood trickling from the corner of his eye. He was the one I had hit with a plate. I gagged in his ear, and he backed off in a hurry.

"Where are you taking me?" I asked, and then bit my lip at the expression on his face.

"What did I just say?" he bellowed. His blue eyes darkened into black, and I was too afraid to speak after that.

Gazing out of the window, I fiddled with the clasp of my bracelet until it opened. I pretended to retch again. Apparently I was pretty convincing because Dar reached over and wound the window down the rest of the way.

"Out there if it happens," he pointed, looking disgusted. "Quiet now. Draw any attention to yourself, and there'll be blood on your hands."

I stuck my head out of the window, gripping the door and gagging loudly. The bracelet slid easily from my fingers and dropped to the ground. I flinched, sure someone would notice, but they were too busy speaking amongst themselves in a language I didn't recognize.

I expected them to take the motorway, but they took a longer route, the less obvious one, as if they knew exactly what they were doing, had planned the entire thing out in detail. When the car slowed at a traffic light, I snapped the seatbelt latch and opened the door in almost one fluid motion. Flinging myself out, I rolled from concrete to grass, scraping my skin against the pavement. The car squealed to a sudden stop, and before I could get to my feet, a heavy hand gripped my hair, pulling me back.

I screamed, tears springing to my eyes as my scalp burned, and I saw a movement in the distance: a woman in her garden, hiding behind the trees, peeking around to stare at us in horror. I screamed again to make sure she knew I was being taken against my will, and I was piled into the boot in a hurry.

I didn't care. I couldn't outrun them, but I had left my scent, and I had been seen. The more traces I could leave, the more chances I had of being found.

Dar hovered over me before they slammed the boot shut, his face distorted with anger. He swung back his arm and punched me right in the face. I couldn't gather myself enough to feel the pain for a couple of seconds. Dizziness overcame me, then a searing pain in my jaw, but the agony faded as I lost myself to the dark.

***

When I first awoke, the darkness fooled me into believing it was night. But as my eyesight adjusted, I noticed pinpricks of daylight coming through the window above the cot. I listened for breathing, or any sign of another person in the darkness with me, but heard only silence. I got to my feet shakily and slid my hand across the window. My fingers came away smeared with peeling black paint.

The bed shifted easily, folding neatly inward when my knee brushed against it. I inched my way around, but there wasn't much space, and I realised I had to be in some kind of mobile home, a modern caravan maybe.

There was little furniture, and I soon found a door. I tried to open it, but it was locked. The caravan could have been surrounded by werewolves, but I would rather risk an escape than sit around and starve, or worse, wait for them to come to me.

I fumbled around in the dark, feeling past the bed. There had to be something I could use to free myself. I found a small stool hidden under a pulled-out foldable table and decided that was the best I could do. Determined, I took off my cardigan and tore it into jagged pieces, fear for my life giving me strength. I wrapped my wrists and hands as best I could then stood before the largest window. If the window broke, *if*, I needed to be ready to run.

Using the stool, I whacked it against the window. I cringed at the noise and paused to listen. Nobody came running, so I kept hitting until I heard a nice cracking sound. I could almost smell the freedom. Again and again, I lashed out at the window until it finally shattered. I cleared away as much glass as I could before climbing out and half-falling to the ground. I only scratched myself a little on the broken shards.

Ignoring a pain in my ankle, I ran, blinded by the sudden light and still unsteady from everything else. I heard nothing and saw no movements, so stopped a moment to take in my surroundings and try to figure out a hiding place, somewhere to go.

The place appeared to be abandoned. I had been locked in a small neglected camper on a space of grass surrounded by shrubbery. Nothing was familiar. I felt as though I were in the middle of nowhere and might never find life again.

I slipped into the shrubbery, hoping to eventually find a real road or a house. I avoided the dirt track in case the werewolves came back that way in the car, but I tried to follow the general direction of the track to find my way out to a main road somewhere.

I kept moving, sweat running down my back as I listened for movement. After a while, I entered a copse of trees. I wasn't sure if I should try to cover my scent or hope to expose it. I had no idea how long we had been driving. Had they ditched me?

I pushed on, an unbelievable stitch in my side. I breathed too loudly and stumbled too hard. My head felt swollen beyond belief.

I heard a snarl before I saw the shape approach.

Werewolf.

He crouched as if to jump, and I held my breath. Despite the pain, I ducked out of the way as he leapt into the air. He came at me again, and I fell, kicking out at his face repeatedly, somehow rolling out of the way of his fangs.

I pulled myself up by a tree, landed one good kick in the werewolf's face, and heard him whimper. He was small, I realised, young. He definitely wouldn't be alone.

Launching into a desperate run, I only made it a couple of yards before two strong arms wrapped around my waist and dragged me off my feet. I flailed, struggling to get free, but when the hands released my waist, one yanked my hair before I could regain my balance. Whimpering, I froze as an iron grip held my throat.

Dar again. I recognised the earthy smell from his hands.

"Bloody nuisance," he growled.

I automatically clawed at his fingers, trying to remove his grip from my neck, but the darkness came before I could win that particular battle.

Nathan

We headed home without her. Without any further signs. Without any hope of finding her.

"Why did they take her?" I kept asking. "Why now?"

I knew Byron didn't have any answers, only unsatisfying speculation. One person knew what was going on, the one person we still hadn't found. If I had stayed with Opa and kept searching for Vin, if I had gone after Willow's scent instead of giving up, if I had done something different a million separate times, Perdita might be safe.

Back at the house, Amelia seemed to be spinning around the room, she paced so fast around us.

"What happened?" she demanded. "She'd only just left. I don't understand!"

"Neither do I!" I shouted. "I was only a couple of minutes behind her. I don't get how she could just vanish without me even hearing anything." I paced for a couple of seconds, trying to think. "They had a car. There are one-way streets around her estate, so they may not have driven past me. I don't remember any cars passing me, but I... I don't know."

"We found her bracelet close to the motorway," Byron said. "She must have left it there on purpose."

"This might not be our business," Opa said.

"He scented werewolves at her house. Of course it's our business," Byron said firmly.

"Ryan," Amelia said, "you're a tracker. You found her before, so you can find her again, right?"

"It's not that simple." He shook his head, looking distressed. "I have to be given a clue."

"What kind of clue?" I spat. "A bloody postal code?"

His lips tightened. "Vin works with humans who see things the rest of us don't. Psychics, maybe. All I know is that I would be given a location, and I would have to work it out from there." He glanced at Amelia. "This could be your chance."

"I have no idea where to start," she said, her face paling.

"You've been with her lately," Ryan said.

"Yeah, she's been helping me try to find information on the whole gypsy thing. But we hadn't gotten anywhere. Joey found some websites, but I haven't had the chance to look properly yet."

"If you can trace her, I may be able to track her the rest of the way," Ryan said. He turned to me. "Does your wolf still see her as mate?"

"Yeah, of course."

"Good. That may help. We should all go to where you found the bracelet, drive around, and split up to cover more ground. She could have left other traces on her way. If she was able to get away with a bracelet, then who knows what else she did? We have to stay positive, but we can't let them get further away. If they do, then the only way to find her will be to rely on Amelia, and that might be too late."

"Don't say that," I whispered.

"If Vin has her, it's for a reason. He may play his hand before we can get to her. Be prepared is all I'm saying." Ryan's face hardened. "We should move before the scents fade even more."

"Right," Byron said. "Amelia, you stay—"

The front doorbell rang. Repeatedly. We all glanced at each other, a wave of fear thundering through the room.

A scent wafted through the air. "It's her dad," I said. "He thinks I did something."

"Come on," Byron said in a weary voice, and we followed him toward the front door. "We need to deal with this."

Stephen Rivers stood on our doorstep, apoplectic with anger. "Where. Is. She?" He ground the words through clenched teeth.

"We don't know," Byron said. "But we're going to help look for her. The dogs are good at picking up scents. We'll help you find your daughter, Mr. Rivers."

"Goddamnit, you people did something to her. Something you're involved in. Where *is* she?"

"I swear to you, if we knew, she'd be back," Amelia said, getting in front of the rest of us. "Have you called the police?"

"Of course I've called the police. I've to go to the station and make a proper report and convince them that she hasn't run away with her idiot boyfriend." He glared at me. "They're going to come here, you know. You lot will be top of the suspect list. If she's here… if she's…" He bowed his head, and all of the fight left him.

"I'm going to find her," I said. "I'm going to get her back, no matter what it takes."

His phone rang, startling everyone, but when he answered, all of our ears pricked up.

"What? Where? Yes, yes, of course. I'm on my way." He hung up, breathing heavily. "The police got a call from someone claiming to have seen a girl matching Perdy's description. I have to go with… with pictures. To make sure."

"To the station?" I asked.

"Screw that," Mr. Rivers snapped. "To the place they saw her." He turned and ran back to his car.

"We need to follow him," I shouted.

"Nathan, Ryan, Amelia, with me," Byron called out. "Dad, Jeremy, take the dogs and follow us. Be ready to run."

We jumped into the car and followed Perdita's dad. He drove toward where we had found the bracelet, then he kept going and turned off onto a smaller road, one I had never been on before. A few homes were scattered here and there, and in the distance we saw a police car parked outside one of the houses. Perdita's dad pulled in behind them, and we followed suit.

Another car appeared before we all got out, and Joey and a man who looked like a chubbier version of Perdy's dad jumped out, both of them glaring at us.

"What are *they* doing here?" Joey asked loudly.

A policeman who had been to my house before to question us beckoned us over, but Perdita's father got to him first.

"Are you taking it seriously now? Are you treating it the way you should have after my first call?" he yelled, gripping his walking stick tightly.

The policeman didn't bother to even look his way. He kept his eyes on us, and his lips barely moved as he spoke. "Mr. Rivers, this isn't the first time you've called us about your daughter. She's a young adult. She has a history of running. We treat every case with the level of seriousness it deserves."

"She doesn't have a history of anything!" Mr. Rivers spluttered. "How dare you imply—"

"We follow procedure. Sir, I'll have to ask you to step aside. I need to ask these men some questions and figure out what happened here. If you want your daughter home, I suggest you allow me to do my job."

Byron and I bristled at the garda's rude tone.

"Are these the men you saw?" the garda asked an agitated woman next to him.

She glanced at us. "What? No! Weren't you listening to me? Four men. Big ones. Two fair-haired, one with longish brown hair, and one skinhead. The car slowed at the light up at the end of the road there, and the girl barrelled out of it. I didn't know what was going on, if it was a couple of teens messing about or not, but one jumped out right after her and grabbed her by the hair." She shivered. "It was so violent, and she screamed like nothing I ever heard before. I ran into the house to get my phone, to get help, and as I was waiting to speak to someone, I looked through the window. I couldn't see very well at that distance, but they packed her into the boot, and I saw one of them..." She gulped. "He closed his fist, and it looked as though he hit her. I was never close enough to make out the car reg."

"Was this her?" Perdy's dad showed her a couple of old photos of Perdy.

The woman frowned. "Maybe. The hair colour is the same. I mean, it was all so quick."

"Wait," Amelia called out. "I have a newer photo of her on my phone." She showed the woman. "Think. Is this her?"

The woman stared at the picture for a couple of seconds. "I... I think so. Oh, she's so *young*."

"Which way did they go?" I demanded.

The garda lost his patience. "All right, that's it. Everyone back off. We'll speak to all of you in turn, so wait by your cars, and do *not* leave." He turned his back to us.

"Small-town idiots," Byron muttered.

As we walked away, we heard the woman give a description of the car and the direction it had gone.

"I'll ring Jeremy and let him know so they won't stop here," Byron whispered.

Joey pushed against me when we got back to the cars. "I know there's something going on. I know it. You better not be hiding anything that would help find her."

"Nothing I can tell you will help," I said. "*I'm* going to find her. As soon as the coppers let us go, I'm going to find her."

"I'll go with you, then," he said.

"I... I can't let you do that."

"Dodgy as hell," Joey muttered. "Amelia, come on. This is all my fault."

Her expression softened. "It's definitely not your fault."

"She wouldn't have gone to that party if I had just said no. I said yeah, and then I let her go home alone. If I had been with her—"

"Then you would have been hurt or worse," she insisted.

"You're acting like you know what happened. Talk to me. *Please*."

She glanced at me. "I don't know what I can say, Joe. But she trusts us. You know she does. Can't you just try to trust—"

"Trust? Trust people who are only honest about the fact that they're lying to everyone? Look at my uncle. Hasn't he gone through enough?"

Perdy's dad looked broken. Already ill from Willow's attack, he was the lowest I had ever seen him. Guilt and frustration and pain poured off him, but how could I explain when I already knew it was something they would never believe?

"I'm sorry," I said. "You'd never listen in any case."

Joey turned to storm off, but Amelia got in his way, laying her hands on his chest to stop him. He seemed startled—by her strength, probably—but he didn't push her away.

"Help me," she said. "I need you to open your mind for a minute and understand that Perdita already knows what I'm about to tell you. Okay?"

He nodded.

"Good. You know we aren't working on a school project. But what I'm working on could help me find Perdita. I need you to keep helping me. Even my family doesn't trust that I can do it, but I can."

"What are you talking about, Amelia?" he whispered. "What are you saying?"

"I'm saying I need you to figure it out," she answered. "And I need you to help me find Perdita. The stuff we've been looking up, you don't believe in any of it, but what if I said I could do things you don't think are possible?"

He backed away, shaking his head. "Don't *mess* with me, Amelia. Not today. Don't even try." He headed back to Perdita's dad, who was still talking to the man who had arrived with Joey. I could only assume he was Joey's father. Joey stood by his father and uncle, his face sullen and dark with anger.

"What are you doing?" I asked Amelia.

"Taking a chance," was her only reply.

Byron and Ryan rejoined us. "They're going to go straight on," Byron informed us. "Opa reckons that road is an old one, leads one way only. They probably took the less travelled roads to stay out of sight. Didn't bet on Perdita not giving up without a fight." He grinned as if proud of her, but I wanted to punch him. I wanted to hit anyone at all just to see if it felt better than standing around waiting while the werewolves got further and further away.

"We need to go," I said, my voice hoarse. My spine twitched, and I struggled to keep hold of the wolf.

"It's important we deal with this first, and then we'll join them before the police can start a search. We can park somewhere, go on foot. We'll be done before they can organise anything. You heard her father; there isn't even an official missing person report yet. They still aren't entirely convinced that she didn't just run away."

"There was blood in her house. Signs of a struggle," I protested.

"We know the significance of it. They aren't aware, so we need to move quickly and get the girl home before anyone innocent gets involved."

"Someone innocent is already involved," I said.

Byron looked at me with sympathy. "I know. I'm just trying to keep it from escalating. I'm sorry you're going through this."

"They killed my parents." I barely breathed out the sentence. "Now they have Perdita. It's not me going through it."

He laid his hand on my shoulder, but I shrugged him off. "Nathan…" He shook his head. "We'll find her first."

"What do we do when we find her?" Amelia asked, trembling.

147

"We get her out of there, by any means possible," Ryan said, his own voice tight. "Vin could be here."

"Why would he be here?" Amelia asked.

"Because he knew your grandfather was searching for him, perhaps. Maybe he needed more collateral. But if he's here, then there's a good chance my daughters are, too." He shook from head to foot, barely able to stay in the one spot. "The time's coming. We get Perdita. We get the girls. We get them as far away from Vin and his werewolves as possible. And then we end this. Once and for all."

We all stared at Ryan, and I felt the same anger as his growing in my gut. We would end it. We would definitely end it.

A garda approached. "Strange how your family members seem to involve themselves in every kind of drama in this town of late." He smirked. "Sadly, we've no evidence to make an arrest, but I'm sure we'll find something eventually. So, the girl, where is she, then?"

"If we knew that, she wouldn't be missing," Byron said, and his expression was a challenge. The officer stared him down.

"We have plans," Ryan said, interrupting the staring contest. "Is this going to take long?"

The garda asked us frustratingly similar questions that seemed to have little to do with Perdita's disappearance at all. When he turned to me, I was livid over the time we had already wasted. Murderous werewolves were getting away with my mate while the patronising idiot kept me standing around for nothing.

"So let me get this straight," he said after he had asked me variations of the same questions three times. "You were the last one to see her."

"No, the people who abducted her were the last ones to see her."

"No need for the attitude," he murmured, scribbling notes in his stupid little book.

I fantasised about ripping it out of his hands and tearing it to shreds. Then moving on to his Adam's apple... "There's every need. You're. Wasting. Time," I said through clenched teeth.

Amelia laid her hand on my arm, but I moved out of her reach, unable to bear anyone's touch.

The garda eyed me. "And you've had a relationship with this girl."

"Have," I said. "I *have* a relationship with her, which is why this is so bloody stupid. I can look for her. We can all look for her, so why are you hanging around here? *Do* something!"

"And you've rowed with her. You left the country to get away from her."

"What? No!"

"You didn't leave?"

"I didn't... give me a break. We haven't rowed. We got back together today."

"Did you?" He crowded me, his voice rising with every word. "Or did she turn you down? Did you follow her home from that party and teach her a lesson, Nathan? Did you go too far? Lose that temper of yours again? Because I've heard stories about you. Breaking noses and hearts, eh? Did your family help you hide her body?"

Byron had his arms around me before I could connect with the policeman's nose.

"I would never hurt her, you—"

Ryan clamped his hand over my mouth, helping Byron pull me back, whispering for me to calm the hell down before I made everything worse.

Joey's father stormed over. "Why aren't you arresting anyone? Who else could have taken her?" He pointed at me, his eyes narrowing. "If you've laid one hand on my niece, I'll—"

"Settle down, the lot of you," the copper said, but he didn't exactly sound bothered.

"I have *never* hurt Perdita," I insisted.

"If you have any evidence at all," Byron said, his voice suspiciously calm, "or anything that suggests we've done something illegal, then please, go ahead and make an arrest. Question us after we've consulted with a solicitor, if you like. But until then, we should be free to go." I sensed his tension, sensed his wolf coiling up as if ready to strike.

"I have a few more things I'd like to clarify." The garda flipped through his notebook. "Perhaps a different theory is more accurate, Mr. Evans. After all, a gang of disgruntled dog fighters who had been promised money or dogs to blood might be mad enough to hurt a young girl to get to your family. What do you think?"

"I think you need to concentrate your efforts on reality rather than fantasy," Byron replied sharply.

And so it went on.

By the time the police let us go, wolf simmered under the surface, desperate to escape. They clearly wanted to look no further than my family, and that meant it would only be us taking the time to look for Perdita properly.

We sped off as quickly as we dared, Perdita's dad shooting daggers at us as we left. We drove in the direction the witness had mentioned and found ourselves on a small road that seemed to go on forever. We passed fields and forests, and eventually, we saw the jeep that Opa and Jeremy had taken. We parked next to it and got out of the car.

"We run on in the woods," Byron instructed. "They can't stay on the road after being seen, so we run as wide as we can and try to pick up any scent or any sign of an abandoned car or Perdita. We split up on my say so. Meet back here at dark. Howl if you find anything. Twice if you're desperate. Are you all ready?"

I was more than ready, and for once, I was the first to phase. The four of us ran through the trees, and Byron let out a bark before running across the road, followed by Ryan. Amelia and I stuck close together, ready to split up if needed. They couldn't keep Perdita hidden in the car after being seen and couldn't move her far on foot. We still had a chance.

We ran for a long time, trying to pick up any scent of Perdita or werewolves. We hurtled past an endless number of trees, fuelled by determination, until we rushed into a clearing.

A chill ran through me, despite the sweltering day. I stopped short when I spotted an old woman sitting on the step of an old-fashioned gypsy wagon. She was warming her hands by a fire.

The caravan was painted in faded, once-garish colours, but there was no horse or car attached to it. The vehicle was planted in the middle of the clearing as if it had dropped from the sky. The old woman crooned softly and beckoned us over without looking in our direction.

I glanced at Amelia, but she was already trotting over to the woman. The scents in the air were in no way familiar to me.

"I'd say what you're looking for passed me by a few hours since. Straight up the road, you'll find a dirt track that at first glance appears unused. Follow it, and you'll see what's there. But you may be too late." She lifted her head and looked directly at Amelia, but her eyes were sightless, a cloudy white shade. "You'll be back to see me, little cousin. The journey never ends, you see."

The old woman reached out her hand, and Amelia moved close enough for her to touch. I wanted to growl, but my throat had closed up as soon as the woman began to talk.

She brushed her fingers against Amelia's fur and nodded. "I feel it cooking away. Ready to boil over, I reckon. Best run now. It's later than I thought."

I ran, but when I looked back, Amelia was still there, staring at the woman. I made a harsh-sounding bark, and Amelia followed me. I howled as we ran, hoping family would hear and follow.

The woman knew what we were, but she wasn't afraid. That and the fact that she knew we were looking for something, for *someone*, had the hairs on the back of my neck standing up. I tried not to think about the words *too late*.

Amelia found the dirt track first, and I saw marks from the wheels of a car—fresh ones. Encouraged, I ran faster and soon heard barking from one of our dogs. They crashed through shrubbery, followed closely by Opa and Jeremy. I let out a sound, but it didn't matter because the stink of werewolf was strong.

We'd made it off the track and were running through some trees when Byron and Ryan caught up to us. Byron moved into the lead, and I pushed forward, but Ryan nipped at my tail to pull me back. Something inside me wanted to challenge him, both of them, but the sensible part of me knew I wasn't ready for that.

I caught the scent of blood. Perdita's blood. Again. I imagined them torturing her. How else was her blood everywhere? We slowed, sniffing around the area. Some of the fauna had been flattened, and I knew something had happened there.

We kept going, catching stronger trails of both Perdita's scent and that of some werewolves. If we faced them… I only hoped I had the chance to face them.

We came upon another clearing with a broken-down motor-home. The window of the vehicle was smashed, but when I ran inside, I smelled my mate so strongly that I whimpered. Her blood remained, but her scent was fading.

The others ran around, searching, but it was too late. They were already gone. They had moved on, and we had wasted too much time.

I wanted to scream, to destroy something, but that wouldn't help Perdita. That wouldn't get her back to me. After we had followed scent trails back on top of each other, we returned to the dirt track and pushed on in the other direction. We found ourselves on the road and next to a burned-out car. I knew the vehicle was the one they'd used to abduct Perdita. Did that mean she had been taken in another vehicle? Did it mean she was alive or dead? Had we wasted too much time on foot while they got away?

Amelia and I raced back toward the old woman to try to find out what else she knew, but she was gone. We couldn't find the clearing. There were no signs that anyone had been in the area at all, apart from us.

Perdita

I awoke to the stares of two similar-looking girls in their early teens at most. One observed me with interest, the other with suspicion. The floor was cold and hard, and everything came back to me in a rush.

"Oh, crap," I whispered, pushing myself up into sitting position.

Both girls sat huddled together. We were in a tiny room with a dirt floor and no windows. The girls both had strawberry-blond hair and strange amber eyes. Ryan's eyes. Their skin was tanned and freckled. The open hostility in the older one's expression shook me. She couldn't have been more than thirteen or fourteen, but she looked at me with such hate, I grew embarrassed under her stare.

"You must be Ryan's girls," I said.

The older one's shock changed her face dramatically.

The younger one leaned forward eagerly, and I realised she was even younger than I originally thought. "You know our daddy?"

"Yeah, I mean, a bit. He helped me. He told me about you. How are you doing? Have they hurt you? I mean, are you—"

"We're fine." The older one set her jaw defiantly. "Who are

you, anyway?"

"My name's Perdita. Perdy. I'm... I mean, I *was* caught up in some werewolf stuff. There was a curse; I was a soul mate. It's complicated. Anyway, Ryan made a deal with *my* werewolves. We... *they* are supposed to help get you away, bring you home. But I was taken, too, so now I don't know what's going on."

"He's trying to get us back?" The older glanced at the younger one in confusion.

Beaming, the younger gripped her older sister's hand. "I told you they were lying. Daddy would never, *ever* leave us here. He would never forget about us."

"Forget about you?" I asked, shocked. "He lives for getting you home. All he's been doing for the past couple of years is working on getting you out of here."

The older one looked away, frowning. "I'm Rachel," she said at last. "This is Meg. They took you?"

"Yeah, they dragged me out of my house. It was *not* fun." I touched my swollen jaw.

The hostility left Rachel's expression. "They took us while we slept in our beds. We haven't seen our dad since, and they told us all kinds of things about him."

"He's doing his best, and he's helped me before. I think he's a good person."

Meg grinned proudly. "He's the best dad in the world. I told you, Rach. I told you he'd come get us."

"He's not here yet," Rachel said under her breath.

"He hasn't been able to find you. But we're all here together, so maybe something's going to happen. Any idea where we are?"

They both shook their heads.

"They don't tell us that stuff," Meg said. "We move in the night. Sometimes we're asleep for a long time."

"They put something in the food when we're going to move on," Rachel confided. "One time, they didn't put enough, and I woke up in a coffin. I thought I was going to die."

"That's awful. I'm so sorry for you," I said, appalled. "If Ryan knew—"

"Oh, don't worry," Meg said. "If he doesn't already know about it, he will. And he'll deal with *everyone* who's hurt us."

"Do they... do they hurt you? I mean, what's it like with these werewolves?"

"They're mean," Meg said. "And hateful."

"Not all of them," Rachel added hurriedly, her cheeks turning pink.

Meg made a face. "Just because Micah smiles at you doesn't mean he isn't like the others."

"But have you heard anything?" I butt in before a sisterly war started. "Have you any idea what they want? What they're doing?"

"We don't see many of them. We have to work sometimes." Rachel looked thoughtful. "Most of the people are pretty normal. I mean, they're not werewolves like Dad. Although we didn't even know that about Dad until we were taken."

"Seriously? What happened?"

Rachel's lips twisted into a semblance of a smile. "They let us know exactly what a werewolf is." She shrugged. "They aren't all bad, though. Some of them were taken, too. We see them some days. Other times we're stuck in rooms like this. It depends on who's around. The faces change a lot."

"I like it better like this," Meg added. "At least we can talk here. They don't like it when we whisper outside, and I don't like how they look at us. The werewolves anyway."

They knew so little, and I wasn't sure what kind of details I should share. I didn't want to warp their minds any more than had already been done. "Well, we need to get out of here."

Rachel shook her head sadly. "We can't. They could be right outside, listening. Stop saying things that will get us into trouble."

"What happens when you get into trouble?"

Rachel's face paled. "Somebody gets hurt."

I walked around the room, trying to figure out a plan. Maybe we could run for it, but I didn't fancy our chances against werewolves. "What do you do every day? I mean, what's the normal routine?"

"Usually, if we're locked in, then someone comes to let us out to use the bathroom or whatever. Or brings food in. And if we're out there, we're with the rest of the people, doing whatever they're doing."

"So they don't watch you?"

Meg shrugged. "Where are we gonna go?"

"Do you know people by name? Faces? Who's in charge?"

"What's with all the questions?" Rachel asked sullenly.

"I need to know *everything*," I said.

"Leave her alone, Rach," Meg said, but she bumped her hip against her sister affectionately. "We only know a few names and a few faces. Most ignore us."

"Well, it won't be for long," I murmured, moving to try the door, but Rachel pulled me back.

"Stop it!" she hissed. "If you get my sister hurt, I'll rip out your hair."

"Jesus," I said. "Calm down. I'm not going to do anything, okay?"

I moved to sit back down, eyeing her. There was a darkness in her eyes, and I wondered if she would turn werewolf some day.

She watched me carefully, but Meg asked me questions. When I answered without getting back up, Rachel relaxed. We spent the next couple of hours chatting about inane things. They didn't get to watch television, and old celebrity gossip seemed to be at the forefront of their minds. I didn't blame them, but I preferred it when Rachel grew confident and asked about Ryan. That made me less likely to think she had gone Stockholm on me.

"Have you tried to run?" I asked, lowering my voice.

"No!" Rachel said. "They're always watching. Bad things happen when people run."

"Are there *really* other people like you? Trapped here?"

Rachel picked at a hangnail. "Not like us. Not exactly. But

trapped here? Yeah."

"They can't watch you all of the time, though," I said, thinking hard. "If we could figure out a way, would you come with me?"

"Yes!" Meg said immediately.

But Rachel still seemed reluctant, although she had calmed a bit. "I swear I'm not making it up. It would be dangerous. But what if—"

She was interrupted by the door swinging open.

An older woman walked in with a tray of food. "Eat that and quieten down. Don't want none of your chatter today."

She refused to look at me, so I thanked her loudly, trying to make her think of me as a person.

My plan backfired. Her expression changed immediately into one of violence and fire. Her pupils dilated, clueing me in to her werewolf side.

"You think I want your thanks? You're nothing more than a thief to me. If I could kill you now, I'd rip your throat out. But there are better things coming your way." She smiled, but there was no warmth to it, and it drew terror from every cell in my body. "Your days are numbered and good riddance." She left the room, and I heard her mutter something about pathetic humans as she slammed the door after her and locked it.

"They all like that?"

Rachel shrugged, and we ate what little food was there in silence.

"Who was she?" I asked, unsettled by the eerie quiet.

"They call her a beta," Meg said. "Behind her back, anyway. They say it in a mean way, like it's a bad word."

A beta was supposed to be next in line for alpha. How was that an insult?

"Seems like she hates my guts," I said, trying my best to remember everything I had learned about wolf pack hierarchy. Nothing I could think of seemed useful.

"You're one of *them*, aren't you?" Rachel asked, her eyes

widening.

"Them? You mean my boyfriend's family?"

"I dunno," she said. "They talk about other werewolves a lot. Sounds like they hate them. You sure my dad's hanging around with them? They don't sound good."

"They are," I said harshly, and she shrank away. I felt immediate remorse. The girls had already had a rough go of it; I shouldn't be making it worse. "I didn't mean to snap. I have a headache."

"They talk about war sometimes," Meg said. "Dad's on the other side is all, Rach."

"So do you know anyone else out there?" I asked. "How many there are? Is Vin here? Willow?"

They both gazed at me blankly, and I sighed with frustration. They were basically growing up in captivity, and it was probably beginning to seem normal to them that they knew so little. That would *not* do.

The old woman returned a few minutes later, and I couldn't resist talking again.

"What am I doing here?" I asked. "What do you want with me?"

She hacked out a genuinely amused laugh. "You're here so we can get what we want." She pulled out a pair of rusty shears.

I imagined a million things when she pulled my hair, but none of them ended with her cutting off my pony tail.

"Thank you," she said in a mocking voice. She picked up the tray and left. When she locked the door, I heard a cheer followed by laughter outside. I couldn't make out how many different voices there were, and I was beyond frustrated.

"What the hell was that about?" I said.

"Don't speak to her," Meg said with a worried expression. "She's one of the worst ones. She's worse than *him*."

"Him? The alpha, you mean? You've seen him?"

Meg nodded. "He's in charge. They lay down at his feet as he walks past them. They push us down, even put our noses in the mud, and he doesn't ever look at us."

"How can she possibly be worse than him?"

"Don't," Rachel hissed. "You need to be quiet, or we'll all suffer for it."

"I'm sorry," I whispered.

The girls dozed on the floor until a young male wolf entered. I wondered if he was the same one from the woods. His hair was long and scruffy, and his grey eyes focused on Rachel at all times.

"Hi," I said. "She's pretty, isn't she?"

He blushed a deep red. "Get on out."

Meg giggled. "That's Micah. He takes us to use the bathroom."

Rachel thumped my arm as we went outside, and I grinned at her.

Micah led us behind a tree, and Rachel said that was where we had to pee. It was humiliating, given that a group of strangers circled us the entire time. Micah tried to lead us back, but I brushed past him and strode right up to the one who appeared to be in charge, a muscular dark-haired man. He flinched with surprise when I approached.

"I want to see Vin," I said. "Right now."

He threw back his head and laughed. "You do now, do you? All right, princess, let's go see Vin."

He made a face, and the men around him all laughed. He gripped my shoulder to lead me away. I didn't recognise any of the people, but they all seemed to have a job to do: skinning small animals, watching us, chopping wood. The place practically bustled with life despite the relatively small numbers.

We passed tents and caravans, heading for a building that looked more like a converted barn. People formed groups and watched us walk. Some whispered while eyeing me with suspicion, while others gazed at me with something akin to pity.

I guessed Vin had been taking entire families. But there didn't seem to be a pack, not like Nathan's family. There were groups here and there, and people seemed more suspicious of the group closest to them than of me, judging by the evil looks they threw at each other.

"Watch yourself, lads," the werewolf leading me shouted. "The werewolf killer is demanding an audience."

People came from every direction to stare at me. Men and women alike glared at me. Children stared at me with wide, scared eyes as if I were the monster from their nightmares. Some laughed and others jeered, but I held my head up high, meeting their eyes with a challenge. That didn't go down well, and the man holding on to me had to bark out a command to keep the werewolves away. I spotted Dar again, staring at me with darkness in his eyes, and I hoped the werewolf holding on to me could keep Dar away, too.

I was losing hope. Nathan's pack hadn't been able to find Vin, or even Meg and Rachel. How would they find *me*?

The werewolf led me up to the door of the small building, and when he knocked, the old woman who had cut my hair opened the door.

"What is this?" she asked, looking me over with disgust.

He spoke rapidly in French, but I couldn't understand a word of it, despite Joey's tutoring.

She grinned, and I had to force myself to remember I had faced down a werewolf before. I told myself I wasn't scared.

It didn't work. I was terrified.

She caught hold of what was left of my hair and pulled me inside. As the door slammed shut behind us, a feeling of dread sent sweat trickling down my spine. She dragged me into a room and shoved me forward. The room was dark, but as my eyes adjusted, I finally saw him. He sat in a ripped armchair. When his eyes met mine, he looked slightly confused for a couple of seconds.

"She wanted to see you," the she-wolf said mockingly, and I got the impression it wasn't me she was mocking. "So I brought her in for a visit."

He rose to his feet, displaying a bare, muscled chest that only showed the mildest hint of his age. Seeing him sent me into a panic, and I struggled to get away. I didn't want to look into those eyes anymore.

"Enough," he called out as I squirmed. "Little interest in you."

The woman stilled me easily in any case, and I stood there, panting, watching him warily. As if watching him could prevent anything—he could rip out my throat before I made it halfway across the room, and the darkness in his eyes had my knees wobbling with fear at that unwanted image.

He was handsome, despite his wild and rugged appearance. I imagined he had probably been a bit of a stud in his younger years, if he hadn't scared everyone away with his craziness.

"So this is the next generation," he said languidly, his eyes running over my appearance. "This is the one to bring the next Evans wolf into the world. Does my old friend Jakob approve?"

"Vincenzo," the woman said. "Let me throw it back in its cage."

"Get out, Martha!" he bellowed.

He ran his fingers through his shoulder-length grey hair as she hesitated, but one look in her direction had her running from the room, leaving me alone with the beast.

He paced, avoiding my gaze. I knew I would likely provoke him, but I needed to see him. I needed to see the person who had brought all of the trouble on us. He had sent wolves to scare me, to attack my father. He had destroyed all of us in some way. And there he was before me.

"My mate sometimes forgets to be obedient." He held his arms close to himself. "The wolf knows too well who the mate is. Who the mate will always be."

I stared at him, utterly baffled by his words.

"You've spent time with them? With Jakob and his family?"

I nodded, startled backward by his speed as he rushed at me. He put his arm around my waist, and I squeezed my eyes shut. But no pain came. I opened them again warily, surprised to see him sniffing me.

He released me. "You don't smell like her. I hoped you might."

I shivered, wondering what exactly was happening.

"What was she like when you knew her?"

"Who?"

"Lia!" he bellowed in my face.

I shrank from him.

He closed his eyes, took a step back, and nodded, his finger tapping his temple. "Lia. What. Was. She. Like?"

"Beautiful, until you killed her." I didn't know where I'd gotten the nerve to say that, but my words worked like a strike against him.

He flinched, horror colouring his expression. "I didn't," he whispered, shaking his head. "It wasn't me. It could never be me." He sat back in his chair, and his expression turned ugly. "But at least now he knows what it's like. He can suffer as I did. His mate is gone, and he will never be whole again. Now he'll understand what it was like for me when they ran, when he wouldn't let her say goodbye. He couldn't even give me that. He took her, but now he'll know what it feels like to lose your heart."

"You have a mate," I said in a croaky voice. "That woman—"

"That woman is *nothing*. A name. The strongest female, so it made sense to try. The wolf won't recognise her. Not anyone. Only Lia. The wolf has been dying for years, but now, now we're fading because she's gone for good. Except I can't give up yet."

"Lia and Jakob were soul mates."

"No." He sounded so distraught that I almost forgot he was the monster ruining my life. I almost pitied him in spite of myself. "She was mine. She was *my* mate. *I* found her first. *I* protected her. *I* saved her. I challenged the alpha to keep her safe when I knew *he* couldn't. Jakob acted the hero, and she was loyal, but he stole her away from me."

He raked at his arms with his fingernails, reminding me of how Nathan had described Willow.

"Did you know," he said, closing in on me, "that I tried to turn her wolf to protect her? To keep her safe. Give her the strength to defend herself in case I wasn't there. I did it because he didn't have the balls, but he ruined it. He filled her head with nonsense and actually made her believe that I would try to hurt her. Me, whose heart she tore into pieces! As if I could ever hurt her. He only did it to steal her from *me*."

"You can't steal a person in that way. They have to *want* to be taken."

"You child." His voice trembled, but it was wild and hoarse, as if he hadn't spoken in years. "You small-minded child. Do you know so little of the world? Of course you do. It took you too young, this curse of yours. The curse that ruined my life."

"It's gone. It's over. No more curses. Lia's dead because of this. Isn't that enough? They don't want your pack. They never have. Can't you leave them be now? Can't you leave all of us alone?"

He got up and prowled toward me. "It wasn't my fault. I just wanted her with me again. I wanted to see if... to see if it was still there. Everything we felt before."

"And now she's dead," I said bitterly.

He sank to his knees and stared at me, his eyes widening with either shock or madness. "I don't care about anything else. I only ever wanted her. All of this has only ever been for her, but I'm surrounded by *beasts*. Beasts with no brains and heavy hands. Bad-blooded fools. I promised the pack so many things, and now *they* want to kill us for it."

"They're not murderers," I said. "They won't come in here and take anything from you. They don't want it."

He looked at me as if I were the one consumed by madness. "You don't understand. You can't understand, can you? The wolf who loses his mate is lost, is dying. He will do anything and everything, and nothing will ever be enough. I had to take another mate just to hold on to my control. Jakob has *nothing* now. He's lost it all, and he won't stop until he repays me. We're all going to suffer for it."

What would my death do to Nathan? I shuddered. "You could make peace. Byron... Byron would accept it. I know he would."

He laughed humourlessly. "The son? After what happened to his brother?" He shook his head, his eyes losing the room and finding another place.

I shifted from one foot to the other, uncomfortable and terrified and confused. How was this man controlling our lives? He could barely control his own thoughts.

"Another mistake," he barked. "I only wanted his wife with me to force Lia to come for her. But even when they died, even when their son died, Jakob never let her. If she had come to me, all of this could have been prevented. So no, I don't believe the other son will be quick to forgive."

"Byron's sensible. He's not like Jakob, but he's in charge. He wants everyone to be safe. He wants this all to be over. You don't have to keep going, keep making everything worse. Enough people have died. And for what? Lia would never want this. Deep down, you know this would make her hate you. She would never, ever want people to die because of her. It will destroy everything, stain the very memory of her if you let that happen. You can't do that to her. If you ever loved her, truly loved her, you would stop this."

He sat back in his chair, his eyes moving rapidly from side to side as if he were running through sequences of events, of possible endings to his story. "Maybe it would work. With you there, I could even—"

"Don't listen to her," Martha said from behind me. I hadn't heard her come back in. "She's spying on you for them. She would tell you anything to make you complacent. They want to kill us all, but we'll die fighting, won't we?"

"No," I said. "There's no need for anyone else to die."

"It's the only way, Vincenzo," Martha whispered.

"Yes!" He stood and thumped his bare chest with his fist. "We will take them down with us before we kneel at that animal's feet."

I stared at the floor. There was nothing anyone could do. Both Vin and Jakob were mad and delusional. Both were suffering from grief and loss, and it meant nothing could ever end peacefully. We were all being sucked into a supernova of pain and anger, of sorrow that could never heal, and none of us could break free. Not until death cured the madness.

The madness was so infectious that I found myself laughing. My laughter became louder until even Vin looked freaked. I couldn't stop, and when the tears finally came, they flooded out of my eyes with a power I didn't think I had anymore.

Nathan

Our barking dogs woke me. All of them were going absolutely crazy, especially Cú. He had a new lease of life, and according to Jeremy, he had been leading the other dogs in the search for Perdita. Our family's bond with the wolfhounds was often a tad spooky, but at the moment, I was glad of it.

When I heard Cú's bark above the others, I raced outside to see a car speed away beyond the driveway.

I ran, shouting for my family, but the car was gone by the time I made it to the road. I stared after the speedily retreating vehicle until I caught a certain scent in the air. Following it, I found a box on the ground inside our garden wall. I lifted it onto the top of the wall and opened it.

Long auburn hair. Perdita's. Swallowing hard, I held the bundle tightly, struggling to stay on my feet as the world spun on its axis. I wanted to vomit. Voices were all around me, shouting, arguing. Amelia's hand gripped my shoulder as she whispered for me to calm down, and I realised I was one of the shouting voices.

I shook my head and glanced up to see Perdita's father roaring at me, his face purple, his eyes darkening like a werewolf's. I couldn't even hear what he was saying. I just kept thinking, *why*?

And then I saw the note. "It's not in English," I said numbly.

Opa whipped the slip of paper out of the box. Everyone was around me: my family, Ryan, the dogs, even Perdita's dad, who must have been outside the house, hoping to catch a glimpse of his daughter.

"They want to talk," Opa said. "They want us to meet this afternoon, outside of town. We're all to come. All of us." He glanced at Perdita's dad. "She'll be there, too."

"What's going on?" Mr. Rivers demanded. "Is this a ransom note? Someone tell me where this came from."

"Didn't you see who left it?" I asked.

"I just got here. Someone call the police, for God's sake!"

"No," Byron said. "The police won't be able to deal with this." He glanced at me. "But we can."

Mr. Rivers' eyes became wilder. "Where is she? Who has her? Tell me what's happening!"

"Come inside," Byron said. "I'll talk you through it."

"No!" Opa exclaimed. "What are you thinking?"

"He has a right to know," Byron said wearily. "It might have saved us some trouble if he'd known a while ago."

They tried to take Perdita's hair from me, but I couldn't unclench my fist.

"He'll be okay in a bit," Amelia said, leading me into the house with firm hands. "You'll be okay, Nathan." Her voice sounded strange, as if my hearing was muffled.

Byron made me sit in a chair in the kitchen. Amelia made coffee and served some to everyone. Perdita's dad drank some with shaking hands, but he never stopped glaring at me.

"Mr. Rivers," Byron said. "Has your daughter told you anything about us? Anything at all?"

"No, she won't talk." But he looked eager, as if he had been waiting for that particular discussion his entire life. "Where is she?

You know where she is, don't you? That's why the note came here. This is all about you. This has always been about you people. What have you gotten Perdy involved in?"

"You're right," Jeremy said in a firm voice. "This is about us. But we haven't touched your daughter."

"There is a man," Byron began, "who despises our family for reasons out of our control. He sent people after your daughter when he found out she and Nathan were involved. We tried to protect her as best we could, but a man died."

Mr. Rivers recoiled. "You killed someone?"

"No," Amelia said softly. "Perdita did. To save my grandfather."

He shook his head, his face paling. "What are you talking about?"

"The man she killed had a daughter," Byron continued as if Perdita's father wasn't freaking out. "This daughter was one of the people who came here after Perdita. She wanted revenge, so she attacked you at our house, partly to send a message to us, but mostly to punish Perdita."

"She set her dog on me?" He looked so confused that I felt badly for him.

"No, *she* attacked you."

"I don't... I don't understand what you're saying."

"I'm saying that Perdita's in the hands of dangerous people. Uniquely dangerous people. My family are the only ones who can get her back."

"What are you, terrorists or something? None of this makes any sense."

Byron laughed. "I know. That's why I'm going to show you something that will hopefully explain everything." He began to open his shirt, and Perdita's dad looked more horrified than ever.

"It's okay," Amelia said. "Perdita already knows all of this. Remember that. Everything she couldn't tell you, everything you didn't know, today is the day. But Perdita needs you to focus, to stay strong. The only way we're getting her back is if we all keep control. Can you do that? Can you stay calm?"

He had been watching her the entire time, drinking in her words as if trying to hear something that would finally make sense.

"Look," I said, pointing at Byron the werewolf. "There's your answer. *This* is the real reason why you shouldn't let your daughter near me. *This* is what you should fear. *This* is what took Perdita."

He stared at Byron in silence for so long, I thought he might have had a stroke or something.

"I need to get out of here," he said at last. "I think I need to go back to the hospital or something. I think I need to…" He got to his feet and stumbled, but Ryan caught him.

"You need to listen," I said. "You need to hear what Perdita's wanted to tell you. We're werewolves. The people who have her are werewolves, and the only difference between them and us is that they don't give a crap about hurting anyone. Do you understand? She had to kill one of these werewolves to save my grandfather's life, to stop them from coming after my little sister next. Their pack stalked Perdita for months. She's been carrying all of this on her shoulders, and now she's in the hands of the people who murdered my parents and my grandmother. She's in *danger*."

"Nathan, easy," Jeremy said. "He's freaking out."

And he was. Perdita's father opened and closed his mouth like a fish, looking as if he wanted to vomit. "This isn't real," he said through clenched teeth.

Byron changed back and dressed hurriedly. "It's very real," Byron said. "We're running out of time. They want to meet this afternoon. They'll have your daughter with them. If we can attack, somehow get—"

"And risk her life?" her father bellowed. "This is my daughter you're talking about. If any of this is anything less than some… some weird hallucination, then you're not going to put my daughter in harm's way. Do you understand me?"

Byron smiled, and nodded. "Of course. Do you have any

questions?"

"Of course I have some damn questions!"

And so began the retelling of our entire lives and histories. At least, the quick version.

"So she's been miserable because she hurt somebody?" Mr. Rivers finally asked. "This is what she couldn't tell me? And yet... it sounds so familiar. Like a dream or something."

I cleared my throat. "She kind of told you everything when you were unconscious in the hospital. Right before you woke up, actually."

He shook his head. "Goddamn kids. My poor girl struggling with this alone, and there was I, keeping her away from everyone as if that would help her. And they still took her. She was never safe, and I had no idea." His face turned red again. "How dare you? How dare you people put her in danger and not even warn me, not even let me know I needed to protect her? If I had known... if I had done something differently..."

"If you had been there, you'd be dead," I said bitterly. "They wanted her for a reason, and nobody was going to stop them. They were going to keep trying until they got her. I guess we'll find out what their reason is at the meeting."

"I'm going with you," he said.

"Mr. Rivers, we—" Byron began.

"Call me Stephen, for heaven's sake. You don't show a man your bare arse and then call him Mister."

Amelia covered her laughter, and even Jeremy shook silently. I shook my head in disgust. As if anything was worth laughing at.

Byron's cheeks turned pink. "Right. Stephen, then. I don't think it would be safe for you to be there."

"I need her to know!" He waved his hands. "I'm sorry, but I need her to know I don't blame her, that I'm not angry with her. She needs to know that I would forgive her anything, given the chance, that she can trust me to be there for her. If these people are as bad as you say they are..." He paled, swallowing hard.

"We'll get her back," I said. "There's no other option."

"Is this… is this why I'm sick? Why nobody can figure out what's wrong with me? Is this what she meant before when she said… is this why I'm so bloody angry all the time?"

"I believe so," Byron said. "The blood transfusion you received altered something, stopped the natural process. It's something to do with your blood, Perdita's too, that you both have the *potential* to become a werewolf. The wolf in us angers easily, but we soothe that by hunting, or finding our mates, or maybe even by having a certain type of wolf nearby. You can't do any of that. The transfusion corrupted it and made it linger in your system somehow. You have to understand there's a lot we don't know. We're on our own, and we're different. What we have came from a curse."

"A *curse*." He sounded sceptical, despite everything we had just told him.

I laughed. "*That's* too much? You just saw my uncle turn into a werewolf."

"I need to understand. I still don't know why they took Perdy." His eyes were desperate, and I knew the feeling.

"We don't know for sure," I said. "All I can tell you is that this started because of the curse. We are, we *were*, rather, cursed to search for our soul mates, to be unable to keep away from them. We would fall for them, and they would be taken away. Killed. Amelia broke the curse, and I thought… I thought Perdita was safe. But she's still my mate. Do you understand what that means? I *have* to find her. I can't let anything happen to her. It will destroy me if she gets hurt out there. That's how you know I'll take care of her. That's how you know I'll bring her home."

He caught my gaze and nodded. We were definitely on the same page. "I need to call people. Tell them *something*. Her grandmother, and I think her mother's on her way back here. I can't deal with them all."

"You should call Erin," Amelia said. "She could help you."

"Yeah. I really should." He nodded. "I'll go do what I have to do, and I'll be back. Don't leave without me."

"We won't," I promised.

Once Stephen had driven away, Opa exploded. "Have you all lost your minds?"

"What's the point in letting the man suffer?" Byron asked. "Don't you remember what it was like with Louis? How not knowing was worse than... worse than knowing."

"He has no business with us. We need to fight. We need to face Vin and rip out his throat."

I knew Opa's anger had nothing to do with Perdita.

"If we can, we will," Byron said. "But there won't be a challenge unless I say so. Does everyone understand that?" But it was me he looked at.

"Fine," I said. "If we can't take her safely, then we won't take her. Yet."

Ryan was strangely silent, and that worried me.

Perdy

Something was happening. Everyone was moving and nervous. I felt as though every bone in my body might crack with the pressure.

An unwanted thought popped into my head. *Today could be the day I die.*

I heard a constant ebb and flow of voices outside, and I waited for someone to come to us. We hadn't been fed, hadn't seen anyone since the morning. Something was rumbling under the surface, and I itched to know what was going on. I exhausted myself by fretting over it, and eventually, I sat in the corner, closing my eyes.

Finally, the door was opened. Micah walked in, and Rachel's day was made. They gazed at each other longingly, Rachel blushing prettily under Micah's stare, and my heart grew cold.

"How can you stare at her like that, knowing you're forcing her to stay here to be murdered?" I spat, and he took a couple of steps backward. "You like her, don't you? But you'll let them kill her. My mate would rather die than let somebody hurt me. What kind of *wolf* are you?"

His eyes grew hot, just as I wanted, and I knew he would think of my words later. His expression turned stony, all wolf and anger, and it took everything I had to keep regarding him with such scorn.

"You're all wanted by the alpha," he said in a low voice, beckoning for us to follow as he turned to leave.

"What are you doing?" Rachel whispered as we trailed after Micah.

"Hopefully, saving your life," I replied under my breath. "Something big is happening. You need to be aware."

We were led into Vin's barn, pushed into the dusty darkness as Micah retreated in a hurry. Vin appeared as on edge as everyone else, pacing the room and clutching at his throat. Had the Evans family found us? Were we running?

Rachel and Meg huddled behind me, and I held their hands, hoping that if I stayed strong, the girls wouldn't lose it. They were kids. They shouldn't have to go through this kind of thing over a problem some unstable adults had with each other.

I watched Vin stride before us, unable to look away. He remained constantly on edge, like a live wire that had been cut, ready to spring and burn at any second. He could kill us whenever he liked. But he hadn't, which meant he needed us alive. But for what?

He glanced in our direction and came to an abrupt stop as if he had just noticed us standing there. He sniffed the air, seeming more canine than man, and moved toward us in that way of his, making it seem as though he were about to pounce. He didn't, but the feeling never quite went away. Waiting to be attacked was infinitely worse than anything else.

"We'll see your mate today," Vin whispered to me, circling around us. It killed me to let him out of my sight. "Do you think he's gone as mad as I yet?"

I swallowed my fears and held up my chin. I refused to look afraid, no matter what happened. I would not let them have that. I couldn't fight back, but the stubborn part of me refused to let them win everything.

Vin didn't appear as cocky as he sounded. His fingers constantly moved, fidgeting and twitching, and I realised what it was about him that made me jumpy. He didn't seem entirely comfortable in his own skin. It was the werewolf equivalent of reluctantly wearing a tie but constantly pulling it away from the throat. He hated to be human. Wolf was the one usually in control.

He made us stand there while he muttered under his breath. Sometimes I picked up a few words I understood, either in English or even a little French, but most of it was a stream of murmuring sounds. Too harsh to be lilting, too terrifying to be comforting, Vin's voice never quite sounded human.

"When are we leaving?" I asked, bolstering my nerves.

Vin exploded. "Do not interrupt! Get out. Get out! Martha! *Martha!*"

In no hurry, Martha sauntered into the barn, and I wondered if she had driven him even more demented than he would have naturally become. She shoved at us soundlessly, acting as though Vin wasn't there. We had only taken a few steps when the muttering began again. I took one last glimpse at Vin before we went outside. He had curled up in the corner, rubbing his forehead.

Outside, Martha made us stand together right next to the barn. I listened to gossip and got the gist of what was going on.

Nathan's family were coming.

"We're going to see your dad," I murmured to Meg and Rachel. "Don't make him worry for you, okay? Be strong. Know that he's nearby. We won't be here long."

Vin's mate slapped my face, and I stumbled to the ground. A couple of people laughed nervously, but I had been counting werewolves in the dark eyes I provoked. There were a lot more non-wolves than anything else. Those people were in danger, and they probably knew it.

In fact, as I observed the people running around us, I realised that what I saw in their eyes wasn't anger. It was tension, fear, and wariness of the unknown. Maybe that was why so many of them hated me. They knew my presence was bringing trouble their way. They knew I was calling the Evans werewolves to them, and there was no running from that.

We all knew *something* was happening, that *something* would soon change, and an unsettling fear licked my insides. There was a pattern in the movements of the people. Everyone had their own job, and when it was finished, when everyone stopped rushing around and the nervousness stank in the air, they stood near us, ready to leave, probably. Most weren't fighters. I was certain of that. They were thin and haggard, mostly, or else too young to be of any use. Nathan had told me once that if he didn't have a mate, he would somehow be a lesser wolf, that finding me had made him the wolf equivalent of a man. How many of these werewolves had a mate?

We were soon surrounded by the beefiest-looking werewolves, and I knew nobody was getting near us without them knowing it. I tried to work out how many were with us. As I glanced around, I noticed a bloodied woman being dragged by a leash to the front of the crowd before us.

I gasped aloud. "Willow?"

She turned her head slightly, gnashing her teeth. Her arms were tied tightly, the skin turning blue. Although her neck was heavily bruised, the collar hung loose around her throat. I looked away, horrified. I hated Willow, but that wasn't what I wanted. Pity ricocheted through me. Her eyes... she was lost. She was ready for oblivion. For the first time, I truly feared for my life, for what might happen before death came.

We were thrown into the back of one truck, Willow in another.

"Did you see her?" I barely made out Meg's shell-shocked words.

"She must have turned wolf with the collar on," Rachel whispered, wrapping her arms around herself. "That's why they tied her arms so tight. So she couldn't do it again. Did you see her? What they did to her? That's why we can't run."

"That's exactly why we have to," I replied, my eyes dry despite the lump in my throat.

We drove for what felt like an eternity, rocking against each other whenever the vehicle turned a corner. Meg cried every now and then, but nobody spoke. We sat uncomfortably in complete darkness. I had no idea where we were, but I was comforted to know I would soon see Nathan. Maybe I could figure something out. Maybe they were going to give us back.

Wishful thinking.

When the truck stopped for the last time, we sat for a long time before the doors were pulled open. A couple of men, Dar being one of them, gazed in at us, laughing and joking amongst themselves.

"Why let them be comfortable?" was Dar's parting shot in English as they dragged us out of the truck.

I blinked rapidly, my eyes adjusting to the sudden light as I glanced around me, desperate to find something familiar. We were surrounded by grass, at least a couple of acres. Further out were trees, but there was nothing I could pinpoint or identify, nothing that would help me say, "Ah, I am *here*."

Dar pushed me onward, and I glared at him without meaning to. He slapped my cheek, not hard by a werewolf's standard, but my legs were so cramped by the journey that I tripped and fell. Micah helped me to my feet, coming out of nowhere it seemed. His Adam's apple shook as he addressed Dar.

"Vin warned us not to hurt them. No marks," he said.

Dar growled before pulling Micah toward him, and I sucked in an anxious breath, expecting violence. Dar held him by the scruff of the neck, but he ruffled Micah's hair. "Get on, you."

Micah fled, and I gave him a grateful smile as he passed. He glared at me in return. Maybe my plan wasn't working out so well.

Dar made the three of us stand in the middle of the grass alone. He and his friends watched us, but kept their distance.

"What's going on?" Meg whispered, her eyes darting around nervously.

"Maybe they'll give us back," I said hopefully. I stamped my feet a couple of times, trying to get some feeling back into my legs. "Stay calm, though. Don't provoke anyone today."

"You mean like you've been doing all day," Rachel snapped.

"Rach," Meg said reproachfully, "don't be mean."

"I'm not. I'm just… I'm *scared*."

"You've made it this long," I said. "If anything was going to happen to you, it would have already." I hoped I was right.

We stood there for at least an hour. My feet had gone numb again. A group of werewolves covered the view in front of us, discussing something under their breaths. Soon the men moved in on us again.

Each of us had two werewolves shouldering us, and I wondered what would happen if anyone came close. Would they attack, would they protect, or would they kill? I couldn't imagine what their orders were, or if they would obey them.

My stomach growled. I was about to ask for some food, but a howl rose up in the distance, and then another, somewhat closer. The werewolves shifted uneasily, and I lost my appetite.

Vin stepped forward with a confident stride, a direct contrast to his earlier behaviour. A massive contrast to the behaviour of everyone else. The fear in the air remained ever-present. Vin walked past us, closely followed by his mate. Martha turned back to look at me, and a wolfish grin lit up her features.

"It's going to be okay," I said out loud, hoping Meg and Rachel heard me. "It's going to be fine."

The werewolf to my left hushed me, but he trembled. These people, these scary enemies, were all terrified themselves. It gave me a moment of relief until I remembered that people made crazy, disastrous decisions out of fear. This was a bloodbath waiting to happen. All it took was the wrong word, the wrong signal, and everything could end in a sea of blood and pain and anguish.

Two vehicles drove up and parked half a mile away. As figures got out of the cars and approached us, I counted an extra one. Then I noticed the limp. Then I spotted the walking stick.

"No," I whispered, wanting to cry all of a sudden. *Dad.* It couldn't be.

"Close enough," Vin called out.

My father, Ryan, and the Evans family stopped walking.

Vin took a couple of steps forward, asserting his authority. He held out his arms. "Well, here we are. How nice of you to visit."

Byron stepped forward, the same way Vin had, as if he had no concerns. He didn't even look my way. Not one of his family had shifted into a werewolf, and I grew uncomfortable at the number of wolf forms surrounding Vin.

"What do you want?" Byron called back.

Vin motioned with his hands. I was led forward first, and I saw Nathan and my father move as if surprised. I was close enough to see the relief on their expressions until Vin began to talk.

"I'd like to make an exchange," he said. "This one for that one." He nodded in Amelia's direction.

Nathan pressed his fists against his eyes, and I sensed his pain as if I felt it myself.

"No!" I shouted, pulling away from the werewolf behind me. Martha walloped me in the face, knocking me down. Nathan tried to run, but Jeremy swung him back around, and Amelia rested her hands on his shoulders as if holding him there. I was lifted back to my feet by a muscular werewolf.

Vin motioned again. "We could always add to the pot," he said, and Ryan's daughters were led to my side.

I heard Ryan's mournful cry as he saw his daughters again for the first time, but I had a bad feeling about how the day was going to go.

"Three for one," Vin said, sounding ecstatic.

Byron stared at him scornfully. "We don't trade in people here."

But Ryan shifted restlessly, and again, that ominous feeling stabbed at my gut.

"Really?" Vin asked. "How about I add this one to the mix?"

Willow was led to Vin's right. She lifted her head, but her eyes were blank. She saw nobody.

Byron shook his head, swallowing hard. Martha whispered rapidly into Vin's ear. I couldn't make out the words, but his easygoing expression hardened into something terrible before my eyes.

"No deal?" he asked. He shrugged, took a step to the right, and snapped Willow's neck before anyone could move.

A scream pierced my ears, and I tried to reach Willow—I wasn't even sure why—but a hand clutched my throat, choking me to a stop. The werewolf leaned against my back, forcing me to still, making sure my father and Nathan could see the hand on my head and the one covering my throat, a hint of how close I was to Willow's fate.

Dad was white with shock, and Ryan was on his knees, holding his head in his hands. Nathan was wild. His face had turned purple with rage, and I knew he would lose control if he wasn't careful. I tried to shake my head as I caught his eye, and he took a couple of ragged breaths.

"Oh, don't come any closer," Vin warned. "You had your chance. Now the deal is pick one, or they all die. Take one more step, and I'll rip out their throats right here, right now. They'll be dead before you reach my first line of wolves, and trust me, these girls are more precious to you than anyone here is to me. You're the only ones with something to lose. Make your choice."

I heard shouts of alarm, and from Ryan's strangled cry, I guessed his daughters were being threatened by a werewolf. But I couldn't move, couldn't look around, couldn't do anything more than take a guess.

"You have twenty-four hours to make a choice," Vin said gleefully. "The werewolf, the daughters, or the mate. Tick tock, my friends. Leave now, unless you want to see how pretty their blood will look sprayed all over you."

The wolf holding me—Dar, I realised—squeezed my throat a little too tight, and my eyes watered. I could barely see straight, but I heard my father's yells, heard arguments and shouting from the people I knew. Vin had just pitted them all against each other, and that was his plan, working out perfectly.

They dragged Ryan's daughters and me back, and I desperately tried to catch my father's eye to see if I could tell what he thought was happening. I couldn't imagine he knew the truth, couldn't imagine one reason why he would believe in any of what had happened, but if he knew, then he knew what I had done. We were whisked into the truck before anyone could make a move—or a mistake.

Even from inside the truck, we heard voices shouting and pleading, accusing and begging. I didn't recognise all of the voices, so some of the pleas for mercy were coming from Vin's own wolves. Both Rachel and Meg sobbed as we listened. Eventually, my father and the others all must have left because silence fell over us. Vin's wolves got us out of there in a hurry after that.

Again, we drove for hours, but we must have been going faster than the previous trip because the shaking and rocking worsened, and I knew we would be covered in bruises before the truck stopped. When we returned to the camp, Vin made the girls and me sit on the floor in his room as he brooded.

"Do you think I upset him?" Vin asked. "Who shall they choose? That's what interests me. Obviously, they'll want to keep their little wolf-bitch, but will they fight each other? Will the boy come alone? Will Ryan beg for his daughters' lives? I can't wait to see how this turns out."

"Will you live that long?" I spat, and he glared at me. "You said it yourself: werewolves without their mates go crazy. Insane. They'll do *anything*, anything at all. I'd say you're the one who's screwed right now. You just provoked the strongest werewolves in existence. I feel *sorry* for you."

His glare transformed into some kind of acceptance, some acknowledgement that I was right. My lips trembled at the idea that he had no hope, that he never had, but I refused to cry, even when

Martha dragged me back out to the shed by the hair. The girls were soon ushered in after me, clinging together and weeping about what they had seen and about their own uncertain futures.

I glared at them. "No crying." I hardened my heart. "We have to survive this, and I need you to be strong. You saw what he did to Willow. I can't let that happen to us. Vin doesn't care anymore. Not about his wolves, not about survival. He doesn't want us walking out of this. This isn't a negotiation. It's a suicide attempt. I know that now. So we have to get out of here ourselves. And I need your help with that."

Nathan

My eyes weren't on Willow when her neck was snapped and her life ripped away as she stood trapped and defenceless.

I was trying not to breathe through my nose, and my gaze was steady on Perdita. That was the way I had been since I'd caught her scent and found her in the crowd as we approached the meeting place. It took everything, *everything*, in me to stay still, not to run to her. I couldn't risk her getting in the way of a werewolf shifting. It killed me that I couldn't protect her, couldn't take her home with me.

She didn't look afraid, and wolf grew proud. I knew she was doing it for us, but her strength lessened my anxiety slightly. I wanted to stay calm, didn't want to mess things up for anyone. Seeing her standing there, looking as though she hadn't slept and with her hair hanging around her face in jagged edges, left me with the desire to kill something.

Preferably the wolves who had taken her from me.

My eyes fell on the alpha again, my nostrils flaring with anger at his presence. My first glimpse of Vin had brought to mind the word *unimpressive*. He wasn't intimidating; he wasn't that large. He was fit—that was obvious—but his sinewy muscle was lean rather than bulky. He wasn't particularly tall, not so young anymore, and he didn't come across as dangerously aggressive.

Until he murdered Willow without a second thought.

All of the stories I had heard about him, and it still came as a surprise that he would kill her. Ryan had told us Willow held little value for Vin, but she was part of his *pack*. I couldn't believe he would go through with it, in public, for everyone to see.

I blinked a million times, trying to fix the image, but Willow's body crumpled to the ground all the same. If he would do that to his own pack, his own werewolves, his own *people*, then what could he possibly have in store for Perdita?

Time stood still. I heard the snap, but I saw Perdita's horror and outrage. I waited for her to cry, but she didn't because she was strong. Stronger than I was. She was thrown to the ground with a strike, and I wanted to run over there and rip out hearts when I saw her fall. I knew her father wanted the same thing. I knew we couldn't do anything.

At least not yet.

A man yanked her roughly to her feet. I committed that were-wolf's face to memory and promised myself I would tear him apart, one limb at a time. A gush of sound swallowed me up then. It was as if someone had pulled a plug. Everything changed in a split second.

Perdita's father was going into some kind of shock. Jeremy danced around, ready to run, trying to hold himself back, fighting with his wolf over what to do. Opa kept a stony gaze on Vin, and Byron swallowed hard, his spine twitching as he struggled to keep his focus.

It was Ryan I felt sorry for. He had tried to help Willow, to protect her. And her life had been torn away in a split-second by the same person who had stolen his daughters. Vin meant business. And he had my girlfriend next to him, too close to a limp body on the ground.

"He's messing with us," Jeremy said. "He thinks he can..." He looked away, biting his knuckles in an attempt to lock in whatever he was feeling.

Opa remained silent, and I knew he was the one to watch. He was liable to run right at Vin. That was probably why Amelia kept hovering next to him.

Even though Vin was supposed to be talking with Byron, he had kept his eyes on Opa the entire time, taunting him, tempting him to approach. Every word was directed at my grandfather.

Vin was bat-shit crazy.

And he had Perdita.

Then he opened his mouth about choosing only one of them, and any sign of unity within our family fell apart. I barely understood what he was saying at first. It made no sense. The direct change in approach. Then I realised. It made perfect sense.

Ryan and I faced each other, and I shook my head.

"*Two* girls," he spat. "Two girls are worth more than one."

"That's the stupidest thing I've ever heard," I said with a growl. "I'm not giving up my sister *or* Perdita. Not for anything."

He gripped my shirt, and I pushed back.

Byron got between us before anything escalated. "Enough," he commanded. "Stop giving him what he wants."

"We only get one choice," Ryan reminded him, his teeth gnashing together dangerously.

"So we change the game," Byron said under his breath. "We take everything from him."

"We can't leave," Stephen insisted, pushing into the conversation. "I'm not leaving without my daughter."

"There are too many of them around the girls," Amelia said. "Werewolves who would kill them before handing them over. They'll never let us take them like this. You saw how quickly Willow…" She turned away, her eyes glassy.

"We need to get out of here and come up with a plan that gets everyone home safely," Byron said.

"Or I could take him on now," Opa said, his first words since we had arrived.

"No!" I shouted. "Didn't you hear? They'll kill the girls before you reach him."

He didn't care. I could tell by the slackness in his jaw and that mean look in his eye. He focused on Vin only. He didn't give a crap about the innocent people standing in his way. He would willingly plough through them to get whatever he wanted.

Byron stood in front of him. "We need to leave. *Now*. Dad, did you hear me? Get in the car."

Amelia and Jeremy pushed Opa toward the car, but Stephen wanted to chase after Perdita.

"Stop it," I snapped. "You'll get you *and* Perdita killed. Is that what you want?"

"I can't leave her there, Nathan. Did you see her? Did you see what they did? How can I leave my little girl and walk away from this?"

He looked as destroyed as I felt, but I gripped him by the scruff of the neck. "Get in the car. I promised you I would bring her back, and I will. But I can't if you get her killed today. Do you understand me?"

"Nathan, stop it," Amelia said, pulling me away.

I swallowed hard, trying to control myself. I had been too close to the edge. I was still dangerously close to losing myself to the wolf. It would make things easier for me, but it could provoke a battle that wouldn't end. We all had to be careful. "I'm sorry," I said. "I'm just… I'm sorry. I'll get her back somehow. I will."

Ryan was the hardest to persuade to leave. "I won't let you sacrifice my girls," he insisted as Byron shoved him toward the cars.

"We won't," Byron kept saying. "We'll get all of the girls home, but we need to surprise Vin's pack to do it. The girls are too close to danger right now. Our time will come, Ryan. We're keeping all four girls alive. I swear it. The only ones who are going to get hurt are the ones who took the girls. We'll deal with them together. Are you with me?"

Ryan sagged in Byron's arms, but he let my uncle lead him to the jeep with Opa.

"My daughter," Stephen practically whimpered as Amelia and I pushed him toward the second car. "She'll know we're leaving her."

"You saw him!" I shouted. "He would have killed her without hesitation. And she knows that. She isn't stupid. She understands!" I seriously hoped I was right.

"Poor Willow," Amelia said, hiccupping a sob as we all climbed into the car. "I should have gone over there. I should have given myself up to him."

"So he could kill you, too? Don't be so bloody stupid," I snapped.

"That's enough," Jeremy said from the driver's seat. "This is exactly what he wants. For us all to turn on each other. Ryan must be…" He shook his head. "This is going to take some dealing with."

"There has to be a way of finding their camp," Amelia said. "Surely someone in the country will have heard of a group of people camped out somewhere near here."

"They could be anywhere," I said. "Didn't you see how pale Perdita and Ryan's girls were? You saw those trucks, right? They could have been driving all night, for all we know. They might not even have a camp. They might drive around constantly."

"I have the registration of one of the trucks," Stephen said. "I can give it to the police, see if they can find something on it."

"And what are you going to tell them?" I asked. "That you saw a werewolf? If they did find the girls, what's to say the wolves won't kill Perdita *and* the police? We're not dealing with normal people here. And what's a kidnapper going to do, hand the girls over to the police? No, they're going to get rid of them first."

That I was speaking the truth only made it all the harder to stay in the car and not freak the hell out.

Chapter Twenty-One

Amelia

I stopped listening to the others. Something crawled across my skin, a feeling, a premonition. Ever since I had turned into a werewolf, the feeling of *something* squirming under the surface, struggling to break free, had relentlessly strengthened until I couldn't ignore it.

Sucking in a breath, I closed my eyes and tried to concentrate. A thudding swept over me, violent and blackened red behind my closed eyes, and I snapped back to reality.

"Stop the car!" I screamed, startling Jeremy into slowing down. Just in time because the jeep swerved in front of us before stalling out.

Swinging open the door before we came to a full stop, I leapt out and ran toward the other car. Ryan was out of the vehicle and running back the way we came before I could grab him. I chased him a couple of yards before latching on to his arm and dragging him to a stop.

He was trying to run back for his girls. I saw it in the desperation smoking his eyes, the way his fingers stretched out as if he could reach them.

"I'm so sorry," I whispered, trying to calm him. As soon as I touched his skin, I felt the wildness under the surface, the way the burning madness was always ready to take him because he had no mate. He needed his family back, and I hated to be the one who kept him away, but we had no choice. We couldn't afford a mistake.

"I'm so close," he whispered. "So close to them."

"I know," I said, overwhelmed by his anguish.

Opa and Byron joined me, and I worried that my grandfather's aggression would trigger something in Ryan. The wolf stared out at me through Ryan's eyes.

I nodded, keeping my voice as calm as possible. "We're going to get them home. We need to do it safely. We need to make a plan and figure all of this out. We need *you*." Something in my wolf soothed Ryan's, soothed everyone's in some way, but with him, the change was direct, forceful, and immediate. I used that to my advantage. I kept talking, saying the things he needed to hear, and slowly, his breathing calmed, and his pupils stopped dilating.

"I know," he said hoarsely. "I know."

Influencing the werewolves was irresistible. There wasn't a better word to describe it. It was power, but in a less obvious way. Half the time, they didn't realise I was doing anything to them, not even my brother. I had calmed him so often, it became a full-time job, but it didn't take anything out of me that I didn't have to give. It made the pack better, helped us be around each other, and that was the smallest thing I could do to make up for everything. The only one I couldn't get through to was my grandfather.

I wasn't sure why that was. I had no idea what I was doing really, but I knew one thing: Not even my omega-ish power could keep the werewolves calm now. Vin knew exactly what he was doing to us. I needed to help track Perdita before it was too late. Ryan remained on edge, despite my efforts, and I knew it would only take something small to set him off again. I couldn't even think about Nathan.

As Byron spoke to Ryan in an attempt to reassure him, a thought occurred to me. An old gypsy woman had told us where to look for Perdita. If we could find her again, who knew? She knew me, recognised what was inside me, and that meant she knew how to use it.

I tried not to think about how strange it was that she had been alone, apparently settled in for the evening, and then she had vanished without a trace. We were desperate. Even the smallest hope was worth chasing.

"Byron, I have an idea," I said and quickly told him what I wanted to do.

"Sounds like a bit of a wild goose chase," he said.

I looked at Ryan. "We have to do something. This person knew about me. Maybe she can tell me more, help me find the camp."

Byron thought about it briefly. "We'll make a quick journey that way. If you don't find her, we're leaving. Understood?"

"Of course." I jumped back into the vehicle, trying to explain it to the others.

"So we're looking for a little old lady now?" Jeremy asked, sounding confused.

"She might be able to help me find Perdita," I said firmly.

Nathan nodded, making me grateful for his support. "It's worth a try."

Stephen didn't appear convinced, but he didn't argue, and I sensed his despair as we clutched at straws.

I fidgeted for the rest of the journey, trying to remember exactly where we had found the woman. But it wasn't until I had phased and was running through forestry that I remembered the way, as if it were a puzzle a human mind couldn't decipher.

I heard someone following me and realised it was Nathan. He couldn't wait. I barked impatiently, but I knew we weren't far off.

We came into the clearing quicker than I expected, and at first, I couldn't see anyone, but then a laugh from behind startled us both. *Who sneaks up on werewolves?*

"I've been waiting for you," the old woman said.

A crackling fire appeared out of nowhere. It couldn't have been there before. The sky was suddenly dark, when a few minutes before, there had been daylight. I smelled magic in the air, felt it crackle against my skin like electricity. I had been right to come there. I edged closer to the woman, but she refused to look in our direction, her blind eyes fixed upward on something I couldn't see.

"Little cousin, haven't you opened it yet?"

Opened what? I thought, fascinated.

"That third eye of yours," the woman said, chuckling as I stepped backward in fright. Had she read my mind? "That's what you're here for, isn't it?"

The power, I thought, wondering how she was managing to communicate with me directly. *The chovihani essence. Is that what you mean?*

"That and more. The greatness your bloodline has been waiting a long time for. The balance the earth needs. This can be your time," the woman said.

Greatness? I don't deserve that. The thought came fully-formed before I could stop it.

She cocked her head. "None wake up deserving it. They earn the right to keep it. To make up for their wrongs. And they can only keep it by sacrificing a piece of themselves at a time." She stoked the fire and turned her blind eyes to me. "This isn't a gift. It's a burden. To keep it will take from you, over and over again. Only the tainted hearts need to prove themselves, little cousin. You owe debts that only you can repay. Some of those debts aren't even yours, but your line's greatest fault has always been that selfish streak, so you're weighed down by generations of wrongs. Now it's your turn to learn from it. Even a deaf little Romani thing like you should understand the truths you've already heard."

But I don't understand. How do I use it? What do I do with it? How can I—

"It's in your blood. I am but a guide. Only you can open up your final path. And from one witch to another, it's about time you woke up." She blew ashes in my face, and I choked out a cough.

Lightning struck, and when my eyes focused again, the woman was gone.

Nathan growled, a constant stream of rumbling sound. All I wanted to do was figure out what had just happened. I ran back to the car, knowing Nathan was following, and I tried to shrug off the excitement in my blood. Something had changed. I felt it.

Once we had phased and changed back at the cars, I tried to explain what happened.

"It was like she was reading my mind or something. We were communicating mentally. It was…" I glanced at the faces staring at me with interest. "Actually, I'm not sure she was real," I confessed.

"What are you talking about? I *saw* her," Nathan said.

I shrugged. "I've read similar stories, and I think she might have been some kind of spirit guide."

Nathan groaned. "Just once, I'd like to wake up to a normal day."

"Keep hoping," Jeremy said. "Is this for real?"

Ryan frowned at me. "Do you feel different? Did something change?"

"I think so. I just don't know what. It's hard to describe because everything is new for me now." I screwed up my face, realising nobody was taking me seriously. "Let's just go," I said, tired of the scepticism.

When we got back, Joey was sitting on our doorstep, a bunch of papers in his hands. "I couldn't stop," he said before yawning. His eyes found Stephen. "You in on it, too?"

"Sort of," he said. "You?"

"Nah, they won't tell me anything. Where's Perdy?"

"She's in big trouble," Stephen said.

"Let me see," I said impatiently, yanking the pages out of Joey's hands. The adults all wandered inside to discuss how to negotiate with Vin. I scanned the pages, important words popping out at me as if there were neon lights flashing around them. "This actually might help. Scrying, why didn't I think of that before?"

Scrying was probably the best way to find a person, but did I even have the power to do something like that? Maybe I needed a little guidance. This was my perfect chance to make things up to Nathan and Perdita, to show everyone in my family that I could be relied upon, that when it mattered, I could do something useful and important. Fear built up inside me at the thought of the pressure mounting on my shoulders, but I pushed it aside. Perdita needed me.

"Nathan, Joey, there's something I want to do, but I need both of you. Will you help me?"

"Do I earn the truth then?" Joey asked wearily.

"Yes," I said. "But remember, you can't unlearn what you hear, so make sure you really want to know. When we're done here, I'll need you to meet us at Perdita's house. If you could bring Tammie and persuade Perdita's gran to take part, that would be great. I'm going to do something a little unusual, and I need the extra power. Will you both do it?"

"If the doc is in on this, then I'm not backing out," Joey said.

"Anything," Nathan said. "Can you find her?"

I paused. "I might be able to give Ryan a clue. Maybe even a bloody postal code." I grinned at my brother, and for the first time since Perdita had been taken, I felt a glimmer of real hope. I had a plan. "Come up to my room, both of you."

They followed me upstairs and watched apprehensively as I gathered some candles.

When I produced the spirit board, Nathan held up his hands. "Are you sure this is such a good idea? I mean, after last time?"

"What happened last time?" Joey asked.

"She tried to kill Perdita," my brother said, but there was no malice in his words, only worry.

"It's different now," I said. "I promise. There are more of us, and I know what I'm doing. I'll be the one controlling the situation this time. Besides, it might help Perdita. Wouldn't you try anything?"

Nathan nodded, and we both looked at Joey.

He stared at the spirit board, his eyebrows needling together into a frown, but he shrugged when he caught my eye. "I'll try anything to get her back safely. She trusts you. I have to, too."

I nodded, pleased with his reaction. I set up the candles and the spirit board and urged both of them to place their hands on the cup. "Don't let go. No matter what happens. Try to keep an open mind." I blew out a breath and closed my eyes, focusing on clearing my own mind.

I spoke the words I needed to protect us and kept breathing deeply until I sensed something change in the air, ripples of power and strength coming from Nathan and Joey. I could use that, use it to open a channel I hadn't opened properly the last time.

"I need help," I said in a low voice, startling Joey. "I was told to open my third eye. I need more guidance than that. I need to be sure. I need somebody to help me figure out how to—"

The cup flew across the board.

Ask.

Joey's breathing grew louder, and I whispered for him to calm down. My brother, too. Nathan was on red alert, and I needed him to contain his fear and anger in order to truly *hear.*

"Can I find Perdita?"

Yes.

"It's not too late?"

Almost.

"Who are you?"

Blood. Family.

"Kali?"

Not that family.

Exhaling loudly, I pushed on. "How can I find her? Can I scry? Is there magic that I can use? Can I use Kali's power?"

Her power is your blood.

"How do I use it, though?"

Open all eyes.

"I don't understand," I hissed, frustrated.

You know.

"What do you know?" Nathan asked.

"I've no idea. Whatever Kali and that old woman in the woods told me. I don't know where to go from here, not really."

See.

"I don't know how!"

Draw the power from the circle. Use everything you have. Give up a part of yourself.

"I'm not sure I can—"

Sacrifice.

The cup flew from the board and slammed into the bookcase. I leaned away from the board. It was over. The presence was gone, and I was exhausted from keeping that channel open.

"That was..." Joey shook his head. "Maybe I don't need to know every detail of Perdy's life."

"What did it mean?" Nathan asked me. "Can you do it?"

"I can try," I said. "It's better than nothing. If there are enough of us, maybe anything is possible."

"So you still need me to gather everyone in Perdy's house?" Joey asked, his paling features the only outward sign of his distress.

"Yeah, definitely. We can do this. I just need to prepare."

"Fine. I'll go try to sort that out," Joey said, looking relieved at the thought of leaving. "And, Amelia? Do your best, okay? Whatever that means."

He left, and I sat there staring at the board.

"Who were you communicating with?" Nathan asked.

I shrugged. "Not sure. I'm guessing somebody from Mémère's bloodline."

"Were they even being truthful? I mean, can we trust some random spirit?"

"It could have been someone trying to screw with us, but it didn't feel like that. The presence felt familiar. Comfortable. I think we can trust this one. I need to figure out exactly what it is I have to do. I need a little more time, but maybe some of the material Joey brought us can help."

Nathan and I joined the others, ready to tell them what I believed I could do with a little help, but we were interrupted when Stephen got a phone call from the local gardaí.

After he hung up, Stephen said, "The police didn't give a crap when I reported her missing, but now, after that witness called them, they've decided to arrange a search party because they've apparently gotten a lot of volunteers needing something to do. What if they end up getting in the way?"

"She's not anywhere near where they'll be searching," I said. "If she were, we would have found her already. Maybe it'll be a good thing if it keeps people busy for a while."

"They're going to think it's strange if none of us go along," he said.

Nathan shrugged. "Chance we have to take. You can go if you want."

"Not a chance," he scoffed. "I may not be any help against were… whatevers, but I'm going."

"It might be better if you stay back, though," Nathan said. "Maybe keep the jeep running in case we have to run. She'll need to get away. No matter what else happens, Perdita and Ryan's girls all need a way to get away safely from whatever we have to do out there."

He nodded. "Fine. As long as I'm there, I don't care what I have to do to help."

"Well, before that, you can help me," I said, my cheeks warming with embarrassment. "I need as many eyes on this stuff as possible, just in case I'm missing something. I'm not completely sure how to go about this, but I feel like that's what that old woman was trying to tell me."

"Who the hell was she anyway?" Nathan asked.

"An Irish gypsy, I think. Not quite the same as our ancestors, but there have to be similarities. That's if she was real."

"Do you have any idea where to start?" Stephen asked, seeming to take what I said in his stride.

I shrugged, trying to think. "I know that I need something. A link."

"Something belonging to Perdita?" Nathan offered. "We found her bracelet if that's any help."

"It is, but I kind of need vibes. I know it sounds weird, but when we used the spirit board, I was able to channel energy from you and Joey to open up a line safely. I think the same thing would work with scrying, but I'll need as many people who love Perdita as possible to help me find her. The more we have, the better the connection to her should be, and the more accurate the scrying will turn out." I swallowed hard. "I hope."

"I could call her grandmother," Stephen said doubtfully.

"Joey already agreed to handle her," I said.

Stephen frowned. "I'll try Erin. But no matter who comes to help, they'll want to know more."

"Maybe they'll believe that this is just something we do when there's a problem. The way people say they'll give their prayers for something. If they know you and Joey are involved, then maybe they'll want to feel as though they helped in some vague, out-in-the-universe sort of way."

"Good will, karma, luck before the search," Stephen muttered. "Got it. Are we doing this here?"

I shook my head. "Your house would make more sense. I'll try to find everything I need, and we'll follow you over when you and Joey have everyone gathered there."

He nodded grimly. "I'll get on that." He hesitated. "Thank you. Both of you. For helping her and for being there for her when I wasn't."

"I care about her," Nathan said earnestly. "I know you aren't going to approve of us, and I get that I might have to wait around for her, but I do care about her. That doesn't change. She can always count on me."

"Good. I'll head on. Let me know if there's news."

He left, and Nathan and I read up on scrying to make sure we had everything we needed.

"Okay, so I might not know what I'm doing," I said as we gathered things in my room. "But I can make my own way. There's something inside me, under the surface. Becoming who I was meant to be is going to help it release."

"Are you sure?"

"No." I hesitated. "What else can we do apart from trust our instincts? Ryan's trying to contact all of his sources, Opa's brooding, Jeremy's ready to kill someone, and Byron looks as though we're all about to die. We have to do something before the deadline runs out."

"All right. Let's go talk to Byron."

Nathan led the way, but Byron wasn't alone, so I had to tell everyone where we were going. My announcement was met mostly with disbelief.

"Let them go," Byron said. "It's better than being around the arguments."

We left them discussing the merits of indulging in my *interests*. Nathan and I took Cú and headed to Perdita's house, where everyone was already waiting: Erin, Perdita's grandmother, even Tammie. They were all willing to help, despite the strange request. Erin and Joey helped us clear the living room so we would have enough space.

"This is kind of weird," Tammie said, peeling away her nail polish.

"Do you care about Perdita?" I asked.

"Of course I do."

"Then shut up and join in with everyone else. I need your energy."

Tammie stared at me. "I always knew you were creepy."

"That's enough," Joey said. "We're all here for Perdita. If it doesn't work, it doesn't work. At least we tried."

"We should be out there looking for her," Tammie insisted.

"We've tried that," Nathan said. "Trust me. We know she's not there. They're not going to stick around in the one spot."

"Fine," she said. "But let's hurry. My mam agreed to drive around with me and look for her."

Erin and Stephen stood close together, but they didn't speak, and she didn't question what we were doing.

I laid the map on the coffee table. "I have a couple of them. We'll try a larger one, and then if it works, we'll use the detailed maps to get a more accurate location." I hoped, but my nerves churned in my gut.

I lit purple candles with trembling fingers, resting the candles on the edges of the map. I held up a crystal attached to a silver chain. "I found this in Mémère's things. Her family did this kind of thing all the time. I thought... I thought it would be appropriate."

I went into the kitchen and found the sharpest knife there, closing my eyes before I sliced my hand open.

"What the hell are you doing?" Nathan demanded, following the scent of blood.

I dabbed the end of the crystal in my blood. "I'm not sure, but she said the power was my blood. Can't hurt to try. It's kind of a sacrifice. In fact, letting all of these people see this side of me is a massive sacrifice. It's got to work."

"Be careful," he urged, and I followed him back to the others, who all looked a little nervous.

"What do you want us to do?" Nathan asked, speaking calmly even though his heart thudded so loud, I could hear it plainly.

"Hold hands, pretty much. In a circle. Two people's hands on each of my shoulders, so we're all connected. Think of Perdita. Think of her happy and well, but picture her face. Close your eyes and try to see her. Let go of the embarrassment and fear and *see* her."

They all gathered around me as I held the chain in my hand. I swallowed hard and closed my eyes. Two hands on my shoulders,

Nathan and Joey, and the circle was complete. We were ready, but I shook inside in the hope it would work and the fear that it wouldn't.

I chanted under my breath, reciting something I had written based on incantations I had found online and in books. It was less of a spell and more an invocation of power, calling power to me in the hope I could use it. I wasn't confident, but a shudder ran through me, and I realised vibrations from everyone else were rushing through my own body. That was real. So far so good.

With Perdita's bracelet around my wrist, I swung the chain gently, still muttering. Ripples of life and love ran under my skin, foreign sensations from other people, and my strength grew, swallowing up the energy until the power swelled.

"Where is Perdita?" I whispered, confident that it was enough, that I could do this. Although the candles flickered, nothing appeared to happen, and my arm began to shake. "Damn it," I hissed, throwing down the chain. "Where *is* she?"

A gust of wind blew upward from our feet, and the crystal shifted abruptly on the map, dragging the chain along with it. Tammie screamed, and everyone else stepped back abruptly, but I cried out with happiness, keeping my feet rooted to the spot. We were finally getting somewhere.

"Don't panic!" I shouted, but I had trouble hearing my own voice. The wind kept up, whipping my hair off my face, but the candles remained lit, and I felt fear, real fear, coming from everyone in the group. "Everyone get back together, quickly."

They all joined their hands again, but it wasn't until I was linked to everyone through the hands on my shoulders that I felt the power. The real power inside me. Kali's power. The power of my blood. It rolled and boiled, ready for the taking, ready to be used.

"Wicklow," I muttered, glancing at where the crystal had come to rest. I slipped the largest map onto the floor, a map of Leinster, and arranged the crystal and candles around it.

"Where is she?" My voice was deeper than usual. The words came from deep in my soul, yet outside of me. My veins burned with power, and I swallowed down the triumphant voice that said I could do anything, *anything*, with this kind of juice. If I thought the omega power was addictive, it was nothing compared to this.

But the gypsy guide had warned me about selfishness. I wasn't going to ruin this for anything. I would learn my lessons this time.

I heard a voice whisper something about my eyes being silver, but I ignored it and focused on finding Perdita. I sensed her out there, felt her bracelet pulse, and I knew we would find her.

The crystal moved.

Wicklow again.

"Hold on," I shouted. "I need to find a better map. A better…" I brushed through the maps I opened, desperately trying to find one suitable for our purpose. I slammed it onto the table and threw the crystal down as if it burned, forgetting about the candles this time.

"Where is Perdita Rivers?" I demanded, and a chill made the hairs on the back of my neck stand up straight. Wolf was well and truly in the back of her cage, but something else was coming to the surface, some part of me long hidden. I would always be two halves, and I would always fight the temptations that came with my gifted power.

I would give up all of it if I could find Perdita. Every bit. It was the only thing I could think of that might make up for the way I had acted. My eyes felt as though they boiled in their sockets, my heart as though it would burst in my chest.

"Where. Is. Perdita?" I called out again, and both Joey and Nathan shrank back at the sound of my voice. "Don't let go," I demanded, and they gripped my shoulders harder as if they couldn't refuse my command.

The crystal moved again, and the candles extinguished themselves. The breeze died, and the burning in my eyes cooled. I breathed deeply, trying to centre myself, find my footing, but all I was aware of was the pure ecstasy of the power I held in my hands.

"Holy crap," I whispered, seeing the terrified faces around me. "That felt amazing!"

I wanted to do more, to test myself, stretch this newfound power, but I shook myself out of that frame of mind. We weren't finished yet. I peered at the map. "It's in the middle of the mountains, the middle of nowhere. How do we even get there?"

Stephen pushed me out of the way, the quickest to recover. His reaction to everything had surprised me. He wanted his daughter back—he didn't care what he had to believe to do it. "Look, the quickest way will be through Newtownmountkennedy. We can drive along this road, and eventually..." He glanced up at Nathan. "You'll be able to cut through here. It'll be a long run."

"Quickest one of my life," Nathan promised.

"Ryan can track her from this," I whispered.

"What the hell is going on?" Tammie said. "What just happened?"

"Oh, I've no idea, love, but let them go," Perdita's gran said impatiently. "Hurry now. Hurry." She ushered Nathan, Stephen, and me through the door, but Joey called my name, and I hesitated.

"I don't want to know," he said firmly.

I nodded my understanding.

We headed back home with news. I prayed I had done the right thing. Prayed I wasn't too late.

Perdita

I sat next to the door and waited for it to open, more nauseated with every tremble of my body. When Martha came in and saw me there, she kicked me aside, but I didn't make a sound. I glanced at the girls, who stared at each other in silence.

"Why are you doing this to me?" I asked Martha loudly. "I saw you before, giving Vin ideas. What's your problem?"

Martha flew across the room and grabbed my throat. "What's my problem?" she hissed, leaning over me as her nails lengthened. "Lia Evans is my problem. I've been under her shadow my entire life. His wolf doesn't recognise me as mate. Recognises her, doesn't it? Couldn't have a child, so she went and had two healthy wolf boys. He's sent the strong wolves, the ones who could rival him one day, after her family, and when it all goes wrong, when somebody dies, he kills our wolves without hesitation. Sent my nephew after *her* daughter-in-law. Tore out his throat in front of everyone to prove a point when she died. He's dragged us from forgotten hole to forgotten hole, each one worse than the last, all in an attempt to soothe his rotten soul. All for *her*. That one ruined my pack, ruined all of us, and I'm going to destroy everything she's ever done. That includes ripping apart your lover boy."

I choked out a sound, barely able to breathe. Her nails dug deeper into my skin, her fingers putting more pressure on my throat, and I struggled to grip the sharp-edged rock I had hidden in my shoe the last time we had been taken outside to pee. I had bruised the sole of my foot, but I had gotten away with it, and that rock was my only hope.

In an instant it was gone, falling away from the tips of my useless fingers. An odd sound rang in my ears, and the hands on my neck loosened. Martha collapsed on top of me, and I pushed her away in disgust.

"Thought it looked like you needed a hand," Rachel said, panting heavily, the bloody rock still clutched in her fingers.

"I told you to run," I scolded as she let the rock fall. "Come on, before she wakes up."

We ran to the door, but a werewolf stood in our way.

"Micah," Rachel said softly, pleadingly.

He stared back at her for too many heartbeats. "Let's go," he said. "This way. Come on."

I ran after them, unable to believe our luck. He led us behind the shed and made us crouch as he checked for guards, but everyone was too busy getting ready to even think about us. We were Martha's responsibility. She should have been able to handle a few human girls.

We ran and were soon covered by trees. Not long after, we heard a howl, and Micah looked over his shoulder in concern. "They've noticed," he said, and he hesitated.

"Run, you idiot!" I cried out, but I tripped and tumbled down a hill, thorny plants and bushes scratching at my skin as I fell.

The others came scrambling down after me, but when I tried to put weight on my stupid ankle, I collapsed to the ground.

I shook my head, trying not to cry with fear and frustration. "Go," I urged. "I can't move. Go and run for help. Try to find someone. Quickly! Get out of here and don't come back!"

"We can't leave her," Meg protested.

But Micah grabbed her arm and pushed her on. "She's right. We can get help." He nodded at me, and they ran.

I was left to crawl along the forest floor, afraid to stop for too long. I heard wolves running in the distance, and I froze, waiting for them to find me. They ran past, probably on the trail of the others. I hoped Micah could get them away. I hoped…

Two figures burst through the trees, and my heart leapt into my chest until I recognised their faces.

"Ryan!" I cried. "The girls, they're with another wolf. He's helping them, so don't kill him." I pointed in the way they had gone. "Quickly, you can catch up to them. But hurry because the others are after them."

He ripped his clothes apart and shifted into wolf form. He let loose an angry howl and raced away.

Nathan knelt before me, his face a mixture of a million emotions. He ran his hands frantically down my arms as if trying to fix me somehow.

"You're late again," I teased in hopes of calming his obvious distress.

He held my hands. "It's the very last time, I swear."

There was another howl in the distance, and his grip tightened.

"We need to get you out of here," he said. "There's a car waiting for you."

"I seriously do not have a problem with that, but I kinda need a hand. I twisted my ankle or something."

He nodded, and I put my arms around his shoulders to help myself up, but he pressed his face against my neck, holding me so tightly I could barely breathe.

"Hey," I said. "It's okay. I'm fine, Nathan."

"I love you, Perdita. Don't… don't do this to me again, please."

A weird rush of warmth ran through my body, but I pushed him away. "Really, Nathan? Now? Now's the time to say that?"

He saw my grin and spluttered out a laugh. "Sorry, I'm just… sorry. We have to hurry, I know."

"Help me up, please."

He lifted me to my feet easily, supporting me when I couldn't stand by myself. I pulled myself closer to him, fully aware of how badly I stank, but not really caring anymore. I held on to him, gazing into his brown eyes, seeing his worry and concern.

"Nathan, I love you, too. But they're after us, so let's get out of here."

He grinned and stood there staring at me with a massive smile on his face until I elbowed him.

"Sorry," he said, still grinning. "I'm just glad you're okay. Put your arm around my shoulders. Try not to put too much weight on your foot."

"How did you find us?" I asked as we half-hopped back the way he had come.

"Amelia. Magic. Ryan tracked you to Vin's camp, but I caught your scent going in the other direction so we followed it. We thought we were going to have to break you out. Never really thought you'd have already escaped."

"Got bored."

He laughed again, lifting me in his arms. It was all very damsel in distress, and I put up a little fuss.

"Get over it," he said. "This will go quicker if you aren't limping. We just need you to get to the jeep, and then your dad will drive you to safety."

"Wait, what? Dad's here?"

"A lot's changed," he said.

I clung to him, praying he wouldn't fall, but we made better time with him doing the running, despite how heavy his breathing had become.

"Someone's behind us," he said after a minute. "Try to look less vulnerable."

I made a face.

"Also, I'm going to get naked now. Try not to get too excited."

I grinned despite the breathtaking fear. It was just him and a limping me. How could we do this?

He shifted and howled, readying himself for battle, and I inched away. I heard the wolf before I saw her, but I knew it was Martha. She would never let me go, and I recognised the same evil gaze in her eyes. She was the one pulling Vin's strings. She was worse than he was.

Martha rushed at me, jaws moving soundlessly, and Nathan took his chance to attack. She never reached me, and I couldn't help giving her a smug smile as he dragged her back with vicious tugs. I managed to get a solid kick at her head with my good foot as payback for all of the times she had hit me, for all of the times she had egged Vin on and made everything worse.

They fought hard, but he gained ground on her easily. His control was stronger than his anger, and a bitter rage was all Martha had. Beaten, she limped away, and he let her. I was proud of him for staying calm, no matter what she deserved.

But a naked figure strolled through the woods, laughing. "There you are, Martha. Did you really think I would let you away with it all?" He kicked her foot, then glanced at Nathan with surprise. "Are you actually trying to show her mercy, boy?" he asked, and he stomped on her back as he sauntered by. The bones cracked noisily, and she lay whimpering.

Lay dying.

"So this is your boy," Vin said to me. "He would have given you a healthy strapping wolf to mother if he had lived long enough. Keep your eyes open, my dear. I want you to see the end. All of us will see the end today."

Nathan growled ferociously, keeping himself between Vin and me. He ran at Vin, but the older wolf had phased and leapt out of the way before Nathan reached him.

Vin glanced at me, his tongue hanging out as if he were laughing. I backed away farther, unable to watch the madness in his eyes. Nathan would have to kill him. This wolf wanted to die. Deep down, he was eager to meet death. Until that happened, he would keep killing, leaving a trail of destruction in his path.

They fought, rolling around, snapping and attacking with deadly seriousness. It was intense, the scariest battle yet, but Nathan kept his cool long enough to draw first blood.

My heart thudded in my chest so loudly that I never heard the second wolf approach.

Jakob Evans knocked his own grandson out of the way in his attempt to get to Vin. Nathan snarled, but he backed away.

Nathan came over to sit with me as Jakob and Vin tried to destroy each other. They fought for Lia, fought for everyone who had died, and when Vin ran off on three legs, Jakob followed without so much as a glance at us.

I ran my hands along Nathan's fur, checking frantically, but he was okay. At least on the surface. The same couldn't be said for Martha. We stayed there, not knowing what to do, until Jeremy came along two minutes later and put her out of her misery. At least, I thought he was being merciful.

Nathan turned his back and shifted again. He was shaking, covered in dried blood, and I could hear in his voice that he was upset.

"Opa's gone after Vin," was all he said to Jeremy, who then sped off after his grandfather. To help him or stop him, I had no idea.

Nathan helped me limp away because I refused to let him carry me after fighting.

"I'll leave you with your dad," he said. "Get home, listen to whatever your dad says to tell the police, and I'll be with you as soon as I can."

"You're going back?"

He shrugged. "I have to, Perdita. This isn't over."

"That was…"

"I know." He kissed my cheek and rested his forehead against mine, yet another shudder running through him. "I know, but it's all happening in the other direction. I'll be back."

"Swear."

He smiled. "I swear to you, I will come back."

"She told me that he killed the ones who hurt your parents," I said softly. "She made it sound like he murdered anyone who hurt Lia in some way."

He nodded. "But the others let it happen. Enabled Vin. They have blood on their hands, too."

"Don't hurt them. Most of them are human, and they're all terrified. It's not their fault." I hesitated. "Except there's a skinhead called Dar who I wouldn't mind having terrified into submission."

He tensed and grunted noncommittally, but when I looked at his eyes, they were the same beautiful brown I knew and loved.

"My point is that the strongest wolves are all gone now. You won't have to fight to the death. There are too many humans, too many people forced to be there. I know it's hard to see them as anything other than the enemy, but if you stay calm, you'll see what I mean."

He laughed softly. "Stay calm? This is what I'm always going to be, Perdita. The anger is part of the package. There are some parts of me that I can't change, no matter how much I want to."

"I know," I whispered, holding on to him tighter. "I can handle it. I get it, but I also know you're a better wolf than Vin."

His pain showed in his eyes. He kissed me, and we kept going in silence.

We found Dad quickly, and when he saw me hobbling, he hurried over to us, despite limping himself. "What happened?"

"I'm fine. I fell over like a child is all," I said. "Dad... I mean..."

"Don't worry about anything right now," he said. "Nathan, the other kids are in the jeep. Ryan and your sister went back in."

Nathan nodded. "Get them all out of here. We'll find our own way home."

"Good luck," Dad said, shaking Nathan's hand. "And thank you."

Nathan grabbed my hand and squeezed, making sure I was looking at him. "I love you," he said in a firm voice, more for Dad's benefit than mine, and then he was gone.

"I didn't hear that," Dad said.

"Dad, about everything…"

"I love you, Perdy, and you're safe. That's all that matters." He hugged me. "They've told me everything. I'm so sorry you've had to deal with all of this on your own."

Tears came to my eyes. He didn't hate me. He knew, and he didn't hate me. The relief made me stumble, but Dad caught me.

"Let's get you home," he said, his voice hoarse with emotion.

I climbed into the jeep with Dad's help, but I winced constantly at the pain in my ankle. Inside, Meg squealed when she caught sight of me, but Micah was pale.

"Dad scared him," Rachel said, and she gave me a real smile for the first time.

"I can imagine," I said. "Don't worry, Micah. If he didn't bite you, you're probably okay."

Meg giggled and reached forward to squeeze my shoulder, as excited to be free as I was. But it wasn't over yet. We still needed our werewolves to get home.

Dad drove us back to our house. He strapped up my ankle before leaving messages for somebody to call off some search party. He evaded our questions until we had all cleaned up and eaten. We were to tell the police we knew nothing, that we had been dumped on the road, found a phone, and rang my dad to come get us. He hadn't been able to wait for police help.

He left the others in the living room while he waited in the hallway for the police to arrive. I followed, leaning against the wall to limp after him.

"This is going to be bad, right?" I said.

"Probably, but we have you back. That's all that matters."

"I'm sorry, Daddy," I whispered.

He glanced at me and shook his head. "I can't believe you've been going through all of this." He moved to hug me, holding me tight.

"You don't blame me?"

"You? No, not you. I could happily blame it all on your boyfriend's family, but I suppose I can't even do that now that they've brought you back to me."

Tears brimmed in my eyes. "I can't believe you know everything now. That you believed it all. That you don't hate me. I was so afraid this would be too much to deal with."

"You're my daughter. It doesn't matter what happens. Nothing can change the fact I love you. I'm responsible for you, and I wish I had been there for you. I wish I had known the truth all along. Maybe everything would have been different."

"I didn't mean to hurt him, Dad. I swear I didn't mean to. I was just trying to stop him from killing another one of Nathan's grandparents. Lia was already dead, and Jakob was dying. He wanted to kill me and Amelia. He was…"

"I know," he said. "They told me. You must have been terrified." The blackness in his eyes shone through, that lingering trace of werewolf that sent his emotions into overload.

"I wanted to tell, but they wouldn't let me. They said nobody would believe me. There wasn't even a body. I didn't know what to do, and I've been so… I haven't been able to stop thinking about it. I can't get it out of my head."

"That's normal, but I'm going to help you get through it. We can get through anything as a family, right?"

I nodded, the sense of relief dizzying. Since Dad knew, somehow I felt sure I would be okay. "Think Nathan will be safe out there?"

He sighed. "I think he's very determined to get back to you, whether I like it or not. He'll be fine."

We stood there for a while, and at least one part of my life felt healed.

"Prepare yourselves," he warned the others as the police finally arrived at the house, but I could never prepare myself for the sheer number of questions they had.

"And they just left you there?" one garda asked with disbelief. "Mr. Rivers, you didn't call us? You let them wash away possible *evidence?*"

Dad got some lectures about that, but by the end, everyone seemed relieved that it was all over. When Gran returned, I saw wariness in her eyes, and I wondered what had been going on while I was gone.

"Are you okay?" she asked, looking me over. "I'm so... this has been a nightmare."

"I'm fine," I said. "Just glad to be home."

For a second, she stared at me, but then she hugged me as hard as Dad had.

But I kept thinking of Nathan, back with the other wolves, and wondered if it was all just beginning.

Nathan

I raced back through the trees, part of me automatically relaxing since I knew Perdita was safe, part of me still anxious because my family was likely fighting without me.

Finding Perdita had been easy once we headed in the right direction. Ryan had been close enough to track where they were hiding out, thanks to my sister. Before we arrived, I had caught Perdita's scent and followed it in a panic. The other scents were Ryan's daughters and a werewolf who helped them. I knew that now, but at the time, I had assumed Perdita was being moved to a new hiding place. I couldn't believe she had escaped, and seeing her injured had made wolf roar in my head, but she seemed fine, and her dad had her heading back to safety.

Unsure of what was happening, I sped up when I heard a familiar howl. Rushing through the undergrowth, I caught sounds on the wind. My stomach turned as I realised the fight wasn't over. The werewolves were defending their territory, but at least we had what we wanted.

I came upon the camp, ready for war, and I saw... mostly

ordinary people. I understood then what Perdita had meant. Werewolves circled Byron and Jeremy, but there weren't as many as I feared. Ryan and Amelia were there, too. I joined them, darting after the circling wolves in a bid to even the score.

I smelled Perdita on a dark brown werewolf, and he was the one I attacked first. He was larger than Jeremy, and I didn't care that he would probably destroy me—he had touched Perdita. Maybe he had been the wolf who clutched her throat. Maybe he was the Dar she had mentioned. He had to pay the price.

He was so startled by my attack that I drew the first blood, my teeth tearing his shoulder open, revealing raw flesh. He recovered quickly, jumping for my throat after finding space between us to retreat a little. A wolf like him did better when able to use his strength, but I was fast enough to get out of his way, snapping at his flank as he struggled to turn in time. I was on him before he could find me again, on his back, my teeth sinking into his skin with a ripping sound that was extremely satisfying.

I shook him as hard as I could, and he attempted to roll me off, but I clung to him, tasting his blood, feeling him weaken. Finally, he gave up, showing me his throat in a bid for mercy. I let go at his submission and sniffed at him, growling. I touched his throat with my teeth, pulling back before I broke the skin. I kept my eyes on him, and he looked away. Just the way he was supposed to. I began to understand why Jeremy was so addicted to the power that came from dominating another wolf.

A yelp caught my attention. I glanced around. Byron stood over three wolves, snarling an alpha warning. Even *I* wanted to sit down and shut up at the sight of him.

Jeremy pinned a wolf down by the throat, while Amelia sat still, staring at two werewolves who lay at her feet, her teeth only slightly bared. She turned her head, and I realised there was blood on her mouth and blood matting the fur on the throat of the largest wolf. She had been fighting. My heart sped up at the idea of my little sister fighting a werewolf that size, but it had obviously turned out okay in the end.

Ryan was having trouble. The werewolves apparently saw him as a traitor, and a number of them circled him, trying to get their taste of his blood.

I growled harshly at the wolf before me, then raced over to help Ryan. He barked at me, and we both attacked at the same time. The werewolves hadn't even noticed me, so intent were they on hurting Ryan. One by one, we pinned the wolves. One by one, they succumbed. Some refused to give up until Byron appeared, dominating them completely.

We didn't have to kill to win. That wasn't the way. Too many of the wolves were low-ranking and too cowed to battle us. There weren't enough dominant wolves. They couldn't win alone, and their pack was too disjointed to work together.

An hour later, Byron stood in front of a crowd of people, wearing only a pair of trousers that were far too long for him. Many of the people were humans of a variety of ages. They mostly seemed terrified. Some were angry because they had watched us keep their loved ones pinned to the ground. But even so, they had provided us with ill-fitting clothes so we could speak to them.

Vin and Opa were still missing, and Jeremy headed out to search for them. Ryan helped Byron figure out who he could trust, who was bloodthirsty, and who had been pressured into running with Vin. Amelia flitted through the werewolves, subtly calming anyone who needed it. Eventually, they noticed, and word quickly spread via rumours.

Ryan pulled me aside. "Any sign of that wolf? Malachai?"

I shook my head. "Vin probably dealt with him already."

He nodded, unsatisfied, but I had probably spoken the truth. Ryan returned to Byron's side, thankfully leaving me be. I had my own wolf to search for.

I scanned the crowd, looking for a skinhead. The one I spotted was large, and his eyes kept turning black when he gazed upon my family. I had fought him already. He was covered in blood. But it was his human side that Perdita knew.

"You Dar?" I asked, closing in on him.

He glared at me, but he didn't make a move, didn't utter a word.

"That's Darius," an old woman said. "One of Vin's favourites."

"You put your hands on her, didn't you?" I whispered, my entire body shaking. "You hurt her."

He showed me his teeth in an aggressive grin, and I punched him in the face, unable to stop myself.

"Enough," Byron said, hauling me off Darius.

I couldn't even remember jumping on him. "I owed him one from Perdita," I said, but my spine stopped twitching as Darius cowered on the ground, blood spurting from his nose. The old woman who had named him nodded at me, a small smile curving her lips. Apparently, Darius had only been popular with Vin.

"Leave him," Byron said, laying an arm around my shoulder to gently guide me away. "He'll be punished the right way." Byron had been hurt, a horrible seeping wound on his chest.

"You need to get that looked at," I muttered under my breath.

"After," he said. "After we sort out what we're going to do here."

"How many of us are you going to slaughter?" one man called out.

Byron smiled, and I saw the man gulp down whatever else he was going to say.

"How many of my family have been slaughtered?" Byron asked in a pleasant voice. "How many of our loved ones have been hunted down like animals? Explain to me why I *shouldn't* tear all of you apart."

Everyone fell silent.

"I'll explain then, shall I?" Byron continued. "Because it doesn't have to be this way. It's time to cut the feral wolf act before it gets you into any more trouble. You can't live like this. Half of you look starved. It's more than time to get back to the real world."

"That's what some of us want," a young woman said, hiding behind her hair when the people around her gave her vicious looks.

"Some of us didn't choose to be here."

Jeremy made his way through the crowd of people. "I found Vin's body. It was pretty bad. No sign of Opa, though."

"They murdered the alpha," someone shouted.

Byron sighed. "This is going to take a while."

"Shut up for a second," Ryan ordered the werewolves. "What did Vin do for you? You're running around, moving from one hovel to another, and for what? So he can pick you off one by one like he did Willow? It doesn't have to be like this."

"Just leave us be," an old man said. "Vin's gone. Leave the rest of us alone."

"I can't trust you," Byron said. "My family isn't safe unless one of us is your alpha."

More angry words followed.

"I'll stay with them," Jeremy said. "If anyone wants a challenge, here I stand."

A couple of men stood up, but Jeremy stared them down, and none of them took the next step.

Amelia moved forward. "The curses are over. The men who started this war aren't here right now. There's no reason we have to be enemies." She stared at the crowd of unhappy people at the front, and her eyes narrowed, her voice turning colder. "Besides, you all know we would win. Most of you could never face my uncle in a challenge, never mind actually beat him. We're outnumbered, and yet it's you sitting on the ground, waiting to see what we'll do with you."

That silenced the complainers for a while. They glanced around nervously, all knowing my sister spoke the truth.

"She's an omega," Ryan called out, sounding calmer. "Most of you know what that means. An end to the madness, to the hate, to the anger. I know some of you, know that you didn't want to walk this path, but you had no choice. Now you do. So do I. I've chosen to be a part of *this* pack. A strong pack. One with an omega. One with balance. One with healthy werewolf children. One that doesn't promote murder or encourage our sons to kill each other to get ahead."

He moved to stand behind Byron's left shoulder, and whispers ran through the crowd. I moved to Byron's right, nodding at Jeremy as he stood shoulder to shoulder with me. Amelia leaned against Ryan, showing how he wasn't an outsider to us.

An old man moved through the crowd, pushing his way to the front. "I want to go home. I'm old. I'm tired. I've had enough of travelling around. I want to die in peace in the place I was born. Will you force me to stay?"

Byron shook his head. "I can't make anyone join us, and I don't want to. But I can help anyone who needs it. Come to me when you're ready." He held up his hand. "But know this. If anyone attacks my family the way Vin did, there will be repercussions. A challenge is fair. Attacking humans can never be."

A young woman joined the older man, linking his arm. "Thank you," she said, her eyes full of tears.

It wasn't that easy, and it didn't end there, but when some of the crowd asked for permission to leave or set up their own packs in their homelands, Byron let most of them. But not the wolves who had taken Perdita or come to our home to attack us. Not the ones who would hunt us down still. For them, he had other plans.

Perdy
August

I awoke abruptly, sitting up straight in my bed. A trickle of sweat ran down my back as I remembered my dream, but that wasn't what had disturbed my slumber. My phone vibrated under my pillow, and I saw a call from Nathan. My stomach flipped over as I answered, hearing his voice again.

"Come outside for five minutes," he said before hanging up.

I threw on jeans and a shirt and limped downstairs as quietly as possible. I opened the front door slowly, grinning when I saw him waiting outside.

He lifted me into a hug, nuzzling my neck. "I'm sorry I haven't been able to come over. It's crazy back home."

"I know." I kissed him, wishing the moment would never end. But I didn't have to think like that anymore. We had plenty of time. "It's been crazy here, too. We see either a solicitor or a barrister or a liaison officer or a garda pretty much every day now. It's driving me mad. Can't wait for it all to be over."

"They have to do things the right way as much as possible. I have to get back in a few minutes, but I *needed* to see you tonight."

"You okay?"

"More than okay. I think it's all over, Perdita. The worst parts anyway. There are so many people out there who don't know where to go from here, and a ridiculous amount of them needed passports and documentation, but I think the problems are going to leave us alone now. A lot of them are happy to be on our side, some others don't want to be involved in any big pack, and the ones who took you and Ryan's girls are going to see jail time."

"What? What happened?"

"Byron's made them confess."

"Are you serious? He's been here this week getting his stitches redone by Dad, and he never said a word."

"He wanted to be sure first. Dar and the others all turned themselves in. You, Rachel, and Meg probably won't have to testify against them. It's finally working out."

I let out a breath I hadn't realised I'd been holding. "That's such a relief. Tell Byron thanks for me."

"He knows. You don't have to say it. It's the least he could do after everything that happened. I'm so sorry about it all, Perdita."

I wrapped my arms around him. "It wasn't your fault."

"Tell that to Rachel and Meg's mother. She's pissed at Ryan, at all of us. She's demanding he bring the girls back to her as soon as possible."

"I hope I get to see them before they go. What about Micah?"

"Byron's sending him with Ryan and the girls because he practically wets himself whenever he looks at me or Jeremy."

"Bullies," I whispered. "He's harmless."

"But he was with Vin. It's hard to forget that when I look at him."

"He helped us escape. Besides, it's over now, right?"

"I know. I'm still… I wish you hadn't gone through any of it in the first place. I feel like we made everything worse than it had to be."

I held his gaze steadily. "I don't blame anyone but Vin and his mate." I made a face. "And maybe your grandfather, too. Any sign of him yet?"

His face fell. "Amelia reckons he isn't coming back. I don't know. He seemed like he didn't care about the family anymore."

"He lost his mate. He didn't have the capacity to care about anything but revenge."

He kissed me softly. "Which is why I can't let anything happen to you."

"Self-preservation, huh? That's your best reason?"

"Shut up and kiss me, woman."

"Bossy werewolf." But I kissed him anyway.

***

Amelia made a face as Nathan propped a cushion under my ankle. Since his family's werewolf problems had calmed down and he had more time for me, he had been going out of his way to make up for letting me get kidnapped by werewolves, despite the fact it hadn't been his fault.

"Any news yet?" I asked as he sat next to me.

"Nope. No sign of Opa. No sign of any werewolves trying to pay us back for anything. It's been calm."

"Except for Jeremy," Amelia added as she rummaged in her bag. "He's itching to leave with the others."

"I can't believe Byron's letting him go," I said.

"He's a big boy," Dad butted in. "It's better for the pack here if he isn't around. Too many males. Never a good idea."

I bit my lip to stop from laughing. Dad insisted on speaking about werewolves as if he had known about them his entire life. Gran, on the other hand, was pretending none of the last few weeks had ever happened. When she heard Amelia was coming over to heal Dad, she made an excuse to leave, quick smart. She told me she wasn't comfortable with Amelia's lifestyle choices, which made me laugh. A lot.

When we were alone, Gran kept telling me how scared she had been, and we spent as much time together as possible. A direct contrast to Meredith, who had gotten halfway to our home before turning back and deciding she couldn't deal. I didn't blame her. Loving somebody was terrifying. I was just glad to be braver than she was.

"Here," Joey said, handing yet another bunch of pages to Amelia. "I printed this lot out last night."

"Oh, cool, omega stuff? He's so useful." She winked at me. "I may have to keep him around."

"Keep it up, and I'll stop helping," he retorted, but he was grinning. "And Perdy, Mrs. Reed wants you to know she's forgiven you for not showing up for the rest of your work experience."

"She knows I was kidnapped, right?" I asked, bemused.

"Leave her alone. She sent you chocolates, didn't she?"

I burst out laughing. "She kept all of the coffee creams from boxes you gave her and put them in an old box to give me because she doesn't like them. Not quite the same thing."

He smiled. "She made an effort, though."

"Anyone hear from Ryan yet?" I asked hopefully.

Nathan shook his head. "Probably won't arrive for another half-hour or so. Then he has to deal with his ex and try to explain Micah."

"I hope he comes back," Amelia said wistfully. "Ryan, I mean. He's part of the family now. Byron will totally miss him. They had a bit of a bromance going on there."

I grinned. "Feels like everything's going to work out."

Amelia's face fell. "Except for Opa. I think… I think he's gone away to die. I mean, everything he was living for is done. Mémère is gone. He got his revenge."

"That doesn't mean he's going to die," Nathan insisted.

"I see what she means, though," I said. "Vin was well and truly ready to die. Your grandfather could easily have ended up as mad as him. It's like Vin was a couple of years down the same track Jakob was on. It's weird how that works. The madness, I mean."

Amelia nodded. "I think maybe the pack and mates are a huge part of the whole. Hopefully, the madness won't be as bad now the curse is gone. And now there's a bit of balance, thanks to *moi*."

"Yeah, you man-wolves really need to stop relying on women to make you happy," I teased.

Nathan glared at me. "Don't make me take away your cushion."

Dad tutted. "Can we get back to me now? I have a date tomorrow. I want to be at my best." He grinned at the look on my face. "Yes, we're still talking even after she witnessed Amelia's *display*. Yes, I begged for forgiveness. No, she hasn't given it, but I'm going to keep trying. Happy now?"

"A bit, yeah," I said.

"Okay, I'm ready," Amelia said. "Stephen, if you could, like, lie on the floor or something, that would be great."

Nathan, Joey, and Amelia moved junk out of the way and helped Dad lie down.

"This better work," he said as Cú licked his cheek.

"I'm going to lay crystals all around you, okay? On your forehead, over your heart, on your wrists, and on your solar plexus. Now I want you to put a drop of the paste I'll be using later on the tip of your tongue. Don't swallow it, just hold it there."

"What is it?" Dad asked.

"Just a salve I made from wolfsbane."

He jerked up his head. "This better not be poisonous."

"I'm... relatively sure it isn't going to poison you."

"Amelia!"

She held up her hands. "Well, I haven't done this before, you know. I know it will feel uncomfortable, and you might puke, but at best, you'll sweat it out of you. Don't worry so much. The wolfsbane is just to make doubly sure."

Nathan began to undo the buttons on his shirt.

"Not in front of my daughter!" Dad bellowed.

Nathan widened his eyes at me, and I tried not to giggle. He left the room, and a couple of minutes later, returned as a werewolf. Joey covered his eyes, unable to deal with looking at a werewolf. We hadn't given him many details, but we weren't exactly careful about keeping secrets around him either.

Cú yawned, but when Nathan opened his jaws too close to Dad, the dog growled until I laid my hand on his collar.

"It's okay, Cú," I whispered. "This is what we want."

"Try not to struggle," Amelia said in a soft voice to Dad. "We don't want to provoke him, okay?"

Dad clenched his lips together tightly, making faces at the taste of the putrid-looking gunk Amelia had made him put in his mouth.

Nathan glanced at me once, but I refused to look away, and he sank his fangs into Dad's forearm. Dad's face reddened, but he didn't cry out or try to move.

"That's enough," Amelia said, pushing Nathan's head away. "Go do whatever you have to do."

Nathan ran back upstairs. Amelia smoothed some salve over the rather nasty-looking wound on Dad's arm. Since her grandfather had disappeared, there had been nobody to tell us what to do, so Amelia had come up with a ritual based on further research with Joey and her own instincts. She had been relying on those a lot since she was able to find me.

Dad's face paled, and he began to tremble, sweat slicking his forehead.

"Is he okay?" I asked.

"He's fine. His body is purging the werewolf juice for good, I think."

Dad rolled over suddenly and puked on the floor. Black puke.

"Yeah," Amelia said, studying the vomit closely. "I definitely think he's going to be okay."

Dad puked for the rest of the day, but he claimed to be feeling better, so we let him relax in bed, but still kept an eye on him.

"I should get on," Joey said. "As interesting as this has been, I have plans. Oh, happy birthday, cousin. Sorry it sucked."

Nathan's hand tightened around mine.

"It's not over yet," I said.

"Well, if you two are going to keep making eyes, I'm going to see Connor," Amelia announced. "Don't forget to check on Stephen. If he gets sicker or seems… weird, give me a call."

When she left, I cosied up to Nathan. "I think this might be the first time we've been alone in forever."

He kissed my forehead. "And you're so badly injured that I'm afraid to touch you."

"Cuts and bruises never killed a soul," I whispered, and he leaned down to meet my lips.

A bang from upstairs had us jumping apart.

"Ah, but fathers have," Nathan said with a grin. "I'll go see if he's okay."

I rolled my eyes. At this rate, we would never be alone for longer than five minutes.

***

By the time Amelia's sixteenth birthday rolled around, Dad was much better. His recovery seemed almost miraculous, according to the hospital. He still had time off, but he would eventually go back to work, and he was working on things with Erin.

Byron, his date Monica—the lovely brunette who had organised Lia's memorial service—Nathan, Amelia, Joey, Dad, Erin, and I all got together for Amelia's birthday dinner. We raised a toast to those who weren't there: Jakob and Lia, Nathan's parents and Byron's deceased wife, Jeremy, who had moved on with the new pack, and Ryan, who was still spending time with his daughters in Scotland. We even raised a silent glass to Willow, who had died because she helped us.

It was our way of putting it all in the past. The horrific things that had happened. The fighting, the danger. It was all over.

Nathan squeezed my leg under the table. Not everything was over. Some things were just beginning.

Perdita
Four years later

I closed the hall door behind me as gently as possible, but a giggle let me know it wasn't necessary. I ditched my stuff and ran into the living room to untangle my ten-month-old brother from a grey, wirehaired, half-grown wolfhound pup.

I waved at my stepmother as I pretended to scold the dog. "Setanta, no eating the baby."

Erin laughed. "I think it's the other way around. Poor Setanta's full of baby slobber."

"Oh, no, Robbie." I held my brother up over my head, enjoying the way his stomach tightened as he held up his legs with another gleeful giggle. I loved making him laugh. "No chewing on the puppy."

Chubby hands grabbed my hair, pulling me closer for an extremely wet, open-mouthed kiss.

"Lovely," Erin said with a snort of laughter as I wiped baby drool from my face.

Robert let go and reached down for Setanta. I was not as much fun as the dog.

"You'll be the death of me," I said as he made a good effort to somersault out of my arms. I let Robert down and moved out of Setanta's way. "You can't chew my shoes while I'm wearing them," I scolded, but I scratched behind his ears.

The lanky pup had been a gift from Byron Evans. To grow up as Robert's protector, he had said.

"You look wiped," I told Erin. "No nap again?"

She nodded. "No nap and the dog decided to climb into the high chair for scraps while Robbie's dinner was still cooling. It's been a long day." But she was the happiest I had ever seen her.

"Want us to take Robbie to Gran's tonight while you rest? You could follow on tomorrow; give you and Dad the night off."

"And get in the way of the big lover's reunion?"

I grinned. "It's only been five days."

She made a face. "I've seen the way you say hello to him. No way am I getting in the middle of that."

The door slammed, and Dad ran in, still sweating from his run. "Hello, my beautiful family," he sang, and Robbie immediately crawled in his direction. Whatever Dad's concerns had been, Robbie was his shadow.

"Perdy, do you want dinner before you leave?" Erin asked, getting to her feet to kiss Dad on the cheek.

"Nothing for me. Worked through lunch, yet somehow managed to consume enough food to feed a large family. We haven't exactly gotten the whole ordering for a group thing on point yet."

"Worked through again?" Dad asked. "Still busy at college?"

"Yeah, we're working flat-out for the exhibition. Getting nervous now. It's been insane all month, really. I haven't had an evening to myself."

"I'm glad you're taking a break for this," Erin said, taking Robbie from Dad.

"Couldn't miss Amelia's birthday. It's been so long since I've seen her. I can't wait. She's going to freak when she sees how big

Rob's getting." I rubbed at the paint on my hands, wondering if I had time for a shower.

"Did Meredith say if she was going to be around?" Erin asked.

"She can't make it this time." My relationship with my mother hadn't set the world on fire, but she had gotten closer to Gran over the last couple of years, and if it made my grandmother happy, I was fine with that.

"Can't wait to see Ryan's face when his girls arrive," Dad said.

He and Ryan had become close after everything happened. Byron, too. It made it a lot easier for my two worlds to join together. Rachel and Ryan had gone through a couple of tough years as she found it hard to adjust, but a year ago, she had turned wolf for the first time. Her dad was the person she had turned to, and she had been given a natural way to burn off the anger that had been festering inside her.

"I can't wait to see them either," I said. "Even Joey's taking the night off."

"I don't know how you managed that one," Dad said. "Just make sure you remember to spend at least a little time with Ruth this weekend."

"I don't need to be reminded. Besides, with everyone home, there's going to be a lot of werewolf business going on."

Erin's eyes lit up. "Imagine Robbie's face if he caught sight of the entire pack together."

Dad and I exchanged bemused glances. Erin had taken to the werewolf situation like a duck to water. No fear and not all that many questions either. Then again, Dad had handled it well, too. He had thrown himself into my new life as if he were making up for lost time. He had become the unofficial doctor for the pack, the one person who wouldn't ask awkward questions, and he was working toward eventually opening his own practice at home.

"I should get ready. Himself will be here soon. I told him not to come in. We'll never get going if Robbie and Setanta find him."

I ruffled Robbie's dirty-blond hair and ran upstairs to get ready.

Dad had been so supportive of my attendance at the College of Art and Design that he had upped sticks to temporarily move closer to the place. Erin had joined him, and while Gran had been upset, I went back home to be with her, and the other people in my life, every weekend.

I loved the city. I loved college. I even loved my part-time job in a café. But by Friday, I was always dying to go home again.

A car horn beeped outside, and I didn't hesitate for a second. I ran downstairs in my bare feet and flung open the front door. Nathan had me in his arms before I could take two steps outside.

"I could have waited another twenty seconds for you to put some socks or something on," he teased.

I coiled around him, stealing a kiss until we were both breathless.

He sighed. "I've missed you this week."

"I know. Me, too. Sorry I missed your class on Wednesday."

He pretended to frown. "No worries. You just missed out on how to escape from a headlock, that's all. Your loss."

"Oh, shut up and kiss me."

He did, then I pulled away. "I'm not ready yet."

"I only came here to hang out with the kid anyway." But as he let me go, he cupped my cheeks with his hands. "I hate missing you."

I hated it, too. But after school finished, we had both agreed to do whatever made us happy. For me, that meant moving away during the week so I wouldn't spend half my time stuck in traffic on the way to college. For Nathan, that meant staying home to help the pack adjust.

He and Byron had set up a dog training business, and Nathan volunteered at self-defence classes while he waited to be paged for his job as a retained fire fighter. He was always on call, but he was doing things that made him feel like a better person, made him use what he once thought of as a curse to everyone's benefit. All of these things had helped him fit in with the community. The past was long forgotten, and for the most part, his family had grown to be considered a valued part of the community.

"I should get ready. Like now," I said, and he grunted, letting me go. He swatted my backside as I ran.

By the time I was ready to leave, Robbie was screaming with hysterical laughter, and Setanta was on his best behaviour. The single greatest thing about having a werewolf for a boyfriend was how obedient mischievous puppies were around him.

"We should head on," Nathan said, knowing I had entered the room without looking in my direction. "Are we taking the little fella with us?"

"Not unless you mean Setanta," Dad said. "He's still freaking out at the sight of the car."

"I'll get him used to it this weekend. I have a class on Sunday morning. Can I make an example out of him?"

Dad grinned. "Please, do."

"Okay, we should run if we're going to make it to the bakery in time to pick up the cake," I warned Nathan. "I'm staying at his tonight, Dad. See you all later."

Dad ignored my words, somehow thinking only his open reaction would make the fact real, but when I hugged him, he returned the embrace even tighter.

We took Setanta with us, and as we pulled away from Dad and Erin's home, my boyfriend relaxed. "Your dad gave me another lecture."

"What was it this time?"

"No engagement rings for at least a decade. Oh, and Robbie needs to be a teenager before he's an uncle."

I stared at him for all of three seconds before bursting into laughter. "Oh, poor Dad."

"It's not that funny," Nathan said, scowling. "I'm the one who has to sit there nodding and looking serious while Erin makes faces at me."

"Maybe it was lucky we moved out here, then. Limits the

amount of lectures you get."

"Ah, I don't mind. I'll put up with him if it means I get time with you. I've learned the more serious I look, the shorter the lectures are."

Laughing, I thumped his shoulder. "Such a lack of respect for my father. Is Jeremy coming back with Amelia? Last time we spoke, he still wasn't sure."

"Yeah, he's up for it."

"Try not to knock him out this time."

"One time. Two years ago. Get over it." He grinned, but when he next glanced at me, he had sobered. "Byron reached out to that werewolf, you know. Tried to make peace. We're still working on it."

I nodded. "That's great." The fight with Jeremy had been about their time on the mountains in Europe, when Jeremy had tried to attack a werewolf's human mate. Nathan still felt guilt over that, and I knew he needed forgiveness.

He took my hand and squeezed it briefly. "I can't wait until you see Ryan's house. We've almost finished it. He's so excited that his girls have their own place to stay here."

"Oh, and is Micah allowed to stay, too?"

"Only when the girls are in Scotland," he said, laughing. "Our old meeting place is still available. I thought maybe I should start working on it."

I made a face. "You want us to live next door to Byron and Ryan? Awkward."

"I'm just saying it's still an option for us. It's the cheapest, and therefore, quickest option."

"I would never get to college on time."

"Obviously. But it wouldn't be ready for ages, and I could live there in the meantime. You could stay with me for the whole weekend instead of at Ruth's. We could try it out."

His cheeks flushed red, and I could see how serious he was about it. His family had bought up the houses next to them for cheap over the years, hoping to give some of the werewolves a chance to live a normal life in our neighbourhood. It had taken a while for things to settle down, and there were still problems, but life ran smoothly with them more often than not.

There were a lot more werewolves in the area than before, although most people hadn't noticed. There was some surprise, and a fair amount of pride, at the fact lots of "foreigners" suddenly found our hometown irresistible. It had brought a bit of life to the place again.

"Stay with you the entire weekend? And have to get up early on a Sunday?" I asked, making Nathan laugh.

"I would totally bring you breakfast in bed," he said.

"Well, I suppose it couldn't look worse than any of the other times we've been there."

"What? You always told me it looked great."

"I'm a terrific liar. Didn't you know that, Evans?"

"Apparently not, Rivers. But that's okay. I kind of like you anyway."

I smiled. "I kind of like you, too."

***

That evening, the long extended garden behind Nathan's home and all of the adjoining houses had filled with people. I had practically suffocated Amelia with a hug when I saw her looking tanned and gorgeous as usual. She had been travelling around Europe with Jeremy all summer, checking on werewolves, keeping the peace, and trying to learn more about her heritage.

"Well," I said. "how did you get on this time?"

"Great." She flashed a grin. "Met a lot of people, including my spirit guide again."

"The old woman?" I had only heard about her, and I was glad I hadn't met her if she was some kind of ghost.

"Yep. I sort of slipped off the path again, and she veered me back on track. Gotta hand it to her, she knows the right emotional blackmail for the job."

"You'll be great," I whispered, earning myself a hug.

The power that Amelia had inside her took a lot to control, and she sometimes struggled with the sacrifices she had to make.

"Connor not here yet?" she asked, looking around.

"I thought you were done this time."

"I'm back for a week or two. Thought it would be nice to reconnect." She winked at me. "Don't have to be soul mates for that."

"I don't need to know the details," I said. "Stay with any werewolves this time?"

She proceeded to tell me all about her summer adventures, and I listened, enjoying her enthusiasm.

After the Evans family had gotten rid of Vin, many of the families he had tormented refused to fight back. Lots of them were human, forced into travelling around on the whims of crazy werewolves. Some wanted normal lives, but a surprising amount of them wanted to be near Byron, their new alpha.

Jeremy still kept an eye on wandering werewolves, particularly the loners, but Byron had allowed almost everyone to choose what they wanted to do next. Every now and then, a family would turn up, looking to pledge their loyalty to Byron, sometimes seeking a place to stay. Byron never sent anyone away, and he had gotten into a serious amount of debt to find them all places to live.

But then the werewolves and their families had surprised him by doing their best to pay him back. They sent their children to the local schools, worked, helped him with his new business and with restoring the houses on his street. They wanted to please him so badly, it felt a little awkward to be around them at times. There had been some challenges over the years, but Byron had won them all.

Jeremy wasn't happy trying to fit in at home, and he had found a mate amongst the reluctant werewolves who kept trying to hide away from Byron. It was difficult for Byron to see his son distance himself, but maybe one day they would work things out.

Jakob had never returned, and a couple of months after he had left, two urns full of ashes had been sent to the house. Jakob and Lia. There was no explanation, nothing that would help his family understand. The only request was that they remain together.

Byron had buried some of the ashes under the flower patch, making sure he planted violets, and he had sent the rest to the wind, free to disperse. There had been no tears, only relief that Jakob's pain was over and that they finally had a real resting place for Lia.

Joey, Ryan and his girls, and my dad and Erin all arrived before dinner to a lot of hugs and kisses and catching up.

"You look great," I told Joey. "I haven't seen you in forever."

"Not quite that long," he said, grinning. But he had been busy. He had finally allowed himself to listen to the full truth about Nathan's family and how they affected my own family. It had influenced his decisions about his future. He was working toward being in a position to properly test what exactly made up the genetics of a werewolf, amongst other things. He had taken more of an interest than even Dad. Between Amelia seeking the answers through magic, and Joey through science, I knew that some day we would unlock the remaining secrets. "Tammie said to say hello and all that. Dawn and Abbi are visiting her right now, so she's probably suffering through a two-week hangover."

Tammie had gone to Australia on a holiday that had so far lasted almost two years. She and Dawn had slowly become friends again after school. I missed her sometimes, but we all had to spread our wings.

"I saw the last set of photos she uploaded. I hate her. Actually hate her now," I joked. "I hate Amelia too." I pulled her over to us. "Tell him where you've been this summer."

I left them to find Nathan, but Rachel and Meg got in my way, the teenage girls looking impossibly tall and slender. "I'm so glad you're home. Well, you know. Your second home," I said, laughing as Meg had to bend down to plant a kiss on my cheek.

"It's great to be back," Rachel said.

"She just missed Micah," Meg stage-whispered, making sure everyone could hear us, including Ryan, who choked on his drink.

"Dad's are the worst," I said even louder.

Ryan winked at me in reply. He had somehow managed to become an important part of all of our lives, and he had made a special effort to make up for everything he had done in his past. He was always there when we needed someone. The werewolf who had stalked me was long gone. The father in his stead had a special place in my heart.

Later that evening, I finally got a chance to snuggle with Nathan on a swinging seat in the garden, his gift to me on my last birthday. An aging Cú rested at our feet as we watched our friends and families laughing and joking together, completely comfortable around each other. There was no danger in the air, nobody looking over their shoulders.

"Your dad looks so happy," Nathan whispered, kissing my hair.

"He is. So am I."

And I was. Happy and *safe*.

CLAIRE FARRELL is an Irish author who spends her days separating warring toddlers. When all five children are in bed, she overdoses on caffeine in the hope she can stay awake long enough to write some more dark flash fiction, y/a paranormal romance and urban fantasy.

For more information about Claire and her books, visit her:

Facebook: https://www.facebook.com/clairefarrell27
Twitter: https://twitter.com/DoingItWriteNow
Blog: clairefarrellauthor.com/blog
eMail: Claire_farrell@live.ie

Other Titles by Claire Farrell

Verity (Cursed #1)
Clarity (Cursed #2)
Adversity (Cursed #2.5)
Cursed Omnibus (The Complete Series)

Thirst (Ava Delaney #1)
Taunt (Ava Delaney #2)
Tempt (Ava Delaney #3)
Taken (Ava Delaney #4)
Taste (Ava Delaney #5)
Awakening (Ava Delaney Vol. 1; books 1, 2, & 3)

A Little Girl In My Room & Other Stories
Death is a Gift
Stake You
One Night With The Fae
Sixty Seconds & Other Stories

Made in the USA
Lexington, KY
20 April 2015